Sweetest Enemy

by Joanna Czechowska

SILKMILL PRESS

Sweetest Enemy

This novel is the sequel to The Black Madonna of Derby published by Silkmill Press in 2008. The Polish edition, Goodbye Polsko, was published in 2006 by Foran Media.

Published by Silkmill Press

This book is set in 11/11pt Palatino

ISBN 978-0-9558840-3-0

Cover design by Isobel Cianchi

Design for Solidarity Underground by Jan Pienkowski

Printed and bound in Great Britain by CPI Group (UK) Ltd, Croydon, CR0 4YY

Acknowledgments

Many thanks to Anna Kanthak, Tim Cianchi, Keith Braithwaite, Joseph Cianchi, Debi Alper and the members of the East Dulwich Writers' Group for all their help.

This book is dedicated to my grandmothers, Maria and Barbara

– I wish I had known you

Chapter 1

Lenin Shipyard, Gdansk, 1980

It's hard to know when a revolution has actually begun. React too soon and you could end up losing your job, your family, even your life. But go on like nothing has happened and you might lose the initiative, end up on the wrong side of history. Aleksander Lato had joined the new trade union but still wasn't sure if he was doing the right thing. Even the name of the union, 'Solidarity', sounded like just another arm-lock in the guise of friendship.

Had things been like this during the Russian Revolution, he wondered. When had people realised that they no longer needed to obey orders, to turn up for work, to carry on going to school? At what point during the French Revolution had the servants realised it was not necessary to bow anymore?

Aleksander checked his watch – nearly 10am. The sun was beating down on the concrete walkways, steam rose from the puddles of an early morning shower. The smell of hot engine oil filled the air, the cranes with their dangling chains were moving huge steel girders across the skyline. Aleks had been told an English journalist wanted to interview some of the shipyard workers and he had been called upon to act as interpreter. Over the past few weeks, Aleks had found his command of English to be increasingly in demand. The union had organised quite a sophisticated press and PR machine to communicate with the outside world, and to do that they had to speak English.

Aleks hurried over to the administration office passing
gangs of chatting workers. Some devout men were kneeling
on the ground among the discarded cigarette ends,
threading through their rosary beads. The loudspeaker
system was blaring out the morning mass to its captive
congregation. Aleks dodged round them and into the
payroll office. He felt a foreboding in the air, twin feelings of
fear and euphoria.

Pausing at the filthy window in the cracked and peeling
office door, Aleks peered in and could just about make out a
man standing in the middle of the room. He was sandy-
haired, aged around 30. A heavy, black camera was hanging
from his neck. Aleks quietly put his head round the door for
a better look. The man was wearing blue jeans, a black
blazer and green T-shirt. The lapel of his jacket was covered
in badges. Everything about his attire and his casual, almost
arrogant attitude proclaimed that this man was from the
West. Aleks watched him gesticulate slightly with his hand,
as if rehearsing a speech.

Pushing open the stiff door further, he approached with
his hand outstretched, his heavy work boots stamping on
the wooden floor.

'I'm Aleksander Lato, I'm happy to meet you,' he said.
The English words sounded strange in his mouth and, as
always, he was worried his accent was too strong, that he
wouldn't be understood.

The man turned quickly in surprise, composed himself
and fixed a charming smile on his face. 'Hello,' he replied,
coming forward to shake hands. He stared in a direct
manner, without fear. His eyes were bright blue.

'Nice to meet you. I'm from *The Observer* newspaper in
London.' He pulled out a press card so quickly Aleks didn't
get the chance to see the name. 'Thanks for agreeing to meet
me. I hope it won't get you into any kind of trouble.' There
was that warm, reassuring smile again.

Aleks nodded. 'I think it is all right' But he glanced
uneasily over his shoulder. 'Let's sit' He pointed to two
chairs and a little table. Aleks could see the young man was
looking him over, checking out his appearance. As he'd
been sleeping on the floor at the shipyard for the past two

days, he was aware that he looked somewhat dishevelled and probably smelled pretty bad. No doubt it made him look older than his 55 years.

The journalist sat down and took out a small Sony tape recorder and put it on the table between them. Aleks hadn't seen such a compact little device before.

'Is it ok to use this thing? I don't do shorthand – I'm actually a photographer but my fellow wordsmith wasn't granted a visa.'

'Sorry?' asked Aleks, frowning.

'I'll just record the interviews and then take some pictures. Is that all right?'

'Yes, I think so,' said Aleks with a shake of the head, indicating it might not be.

The man pressed some buttons on the little machine, bending forward to check how it worked. It was hard to see in the gloom. Aleks shifted in his seat, uncomfortably aware of the stink of stale cigarettes and body odour. He looked at the notice board behind the man's head, covered in leaflets, all with that now familiar red heading in the bold font: *Solidarnosc.* Next to the notice board hung an old picture of Lenin.

'I shouldn't really be working as I'm just on a tourist visa,' the man said, looking down at the machine and continuing pressing buttons as the tape rewound. 'I'm staying at the Hotel Morski.'

'I'm surprised you managed to get through the gates here – we are in a sit-in occupation. We are continuing to work but no longer taking orders from management.'

'They let me in when I showed them my press badge'. The man ran his fingers through his hair. 'I need to find out what's going on – not much news is reaching the outside world. Shit, I'm not sure if this thing is working.'

'The authorities have issued a news blackout. What information has reached England?'

'Nothing much yet. Word is filtering through but I don't think many journalists have been allowed in. Actually, I've haven't seen any other English people here.' He paused and looked out of the window as the loudspeaker system, having finished broadcasting the church service, was now blaring out *Yellow Submarine*. He looked back at Aleks and pulled a quizzical face.

'A favourite song with the workers,' Aleks smiled.

The man shrugged. 'Mm. I've never been to Poland before. In fact, I never really heard of Gdansk before a couple of weeks ago. Well, I suppose I'd heard it called Danzig – from school history lessons.'

'Yes, sometimes it's a German city, sometimes Polish. Borders change.'

'It's funny - I come from an island so we're not used to movable borders.'

He paused and smiled again then his gaze lowered to Aleks's dark blue donkey jacket, patched with leather at the elbows, and old checked shirt. Some chanting was audible from outside.

'Ah, now I think the tape's working. Fingers crossed. Let's start. It seems to me the economy is obviously in trouble. Earlier I had lunch in an outdoor café. It was in that beautiful long street with the gate and river at the end. They showed me a menu so I ordered pierogi and the waiter said they didn't have that. So I ordered fish and they didn't have that so I chose lamb and they didn't have that. So I asked the waiter what they did have and he said – hunter's stew. I had hunter's stew. Why do they bother printing menus?'

'Just for the tourists,' said Aleks. 'We like to pretend there is some choice. The authorities keeping putting up prices and cutting rations. As you can see, communism doesn't work, especially here in Poland. Even Stalin said forcing communism on the Poles was like putting a saddle on a cow - it doesn't fit.'

The man raised his eyebrows and then pulled out a packet of cigarettes, Players No 6. He offered one to Aleks and lit both with his lighter. He blew smoke into the air and continued. 'Well, let me ask *you* a few questions first before we get to the strike leaders. What do you do?'

'I'm a welder. We're still working but getting no pay at the moment.'

'I see. And how are the workers living?'

'*Solidarnosc* has been given donations from Trade Unionists in the USA, France, Germany – although not from

Great Britain, I notice. Actually, I've been ordered to sort out the money that's coming in.'

'I've heard about this Solidarity union,' the man said leaning forward. 'I think the unions in Britain are rather slow in recognising it. I understand it is the first free trade union in the Eastern bloc. If you join, are you punished?'

'This is what I am thinking myself,' Aleks said. 'I don't know. Maybe it is a risk but maybe more of a risk of not joining if things change. The secret police are watching all the time of course.'

Outside, some men were singing along with the loudspeaker, in heavily accented English. The man smiled at him, his eyes a little narrower.

'Your English is good - where did you learn it?'

'In 1970, I make friends with a young fellow called Bronek. He was born in London to Polish parents. He came to Warsaw to find his parents' culture and he was giving English lessons to make money. He lived above my flat so I am his first student.'

'Well, he did an excellent job.' The man leaned back. 'I keep hearing about this man Walesa – how do you pronounce the name? What's his job here?'

Aleks looked at the man, wondering how much to tell. Could he be trusted? Was it dangerous to talk? Actually, having a contact in London would be useful. He might need to get out of the country in a hurry one day. Perhaps it would be wise to give the man some information for his article – he might then feel obliged to give something back in return.

'You say it Va-wen-sa. He doesn't work here any more, he was fired a while ago but he just jumped over the wall and started organising everyone. He led shipyard strikes back in 1970 as well. I don't really know him – he is always rushing around, very busy.'

'Do you think he is the man who will instigate change or is he just following what has already started? You know like that man in the French revolution who said, 'There go the people. I am their leader, I must follow them!'

Aleks smiled. 'Who knows?' He leaned forward with a whisper deciding to trust the man with his innermost thoughts. 'Walesa can hardly string two grammatical words together in my opinion. He's passionate but...' He leaned back again.

'Maybe there will be a big civil war here. Perhaps like in Spain in 1936 and all the famous intellectuals from around Europe will come and fight.'

'To have a civil war you have to have two sides of the population against each other,' said Aleks. 'Here all the people think the same, it's just the small number of communists in the government who think otherwise.'

The man shrugged. 'Yes, I'm not sure the Spanish civil war analogy holds up. Who has the gravitas of George Orwell these days? Would Harold Pinter lay down his life for the shipyard?' He laughed.

'Sorry, I don't know...' Aleks felt the conversation was slipping away from him.

'Nothing. Walesa isn't an educated man, is he? You seem well educated.'

'Well, that's why they put me in charge of the finances, sorting out the donations.' Aleks fingered the bank notes in his pocket, hoping no one would notice his latest haul. It was amazing that people from abroad were actually sending in cash: dollars, Franks, Marks. Aleks noticed the man's eyes drift away from him and fix on the cranes out of the window. He was losing his interest – accounts didn't inspire anyone. Aleks had to regain the initiative – the man would be a useful ally.

'Actually I'm really an artist.'

The man looked back at Aleks, his blue eyes questioning.

'I'm graduate of film school in Lodz, I was student with... Roman Polanski. I'm also sculptor but much of my art was confiscated. I also made a film the authorities didn't like. I put my sculpting talents to use by becoming a welder – it's a safer occupation.'

'Really? That's interesting. So your art has landed you in trouble.'

'Yes, I was in prison for two years. The secret police watch me. I had a wife and son so I had to give up art and take an ordinary job.'

'How these tyrants stifle expression, creativity. I'm really sorry. Look, may I take a picture of you for my newspaper? Let's go outside, I want to get some of that magnificent, huge machinery in the background – it'll look good. Don't worry, the picture will only be published in England. Oh, and here is my card – perhaps I can be of help to you at some point – as one artist to another.'

Aleksander looked at the card. It read The Observer, Roger Elliott, Photographer

Roger stood up. 'I'd like a picture of you in front of that ship's hull, by those huge chains. After that, you can introduce me to this Walesa fellow.'

He headed for the door leaving his English cigarettes on the table. Aleks popped them into his pocket.

Chapter 2

Derby, December 1980

'Whenever you put on the news this days, it's about Poland. I can't believe it. Strikes, free speech, trade unions – they'll be putting the crown back on the Polish Eagle and restoring the monarchy next,' remarked Helena glancing at the screen.

Wanda nodded and watched her mother sit down on the sofa, take off her shoes and rub her feet. Helena leaned back against the neatly plumped cushions, stretched her long legs in front of her and sighed. Even when she's flopped on the sofa, mum manages to look elegant, Wanda thought.

The small sitting room at 16 Porton Crescent felt cosy, deliciously warm. The orange glow from the gas fire was heaven on cold feet. Hot air rose from the vents causing one of the Christmas cards on the mantelpiece above to flutter down onto the rug below. There was a comforting tapping noise from the slim white radiators as the recently installed central heating geared up for the evening. Three photographs adorned the mantelpiece: a young, smiling, dark-haired girl holding a piece of paper that was fluttering in the breeze; an older woman of similar beauty who was wearing the clothing of a century earlier, and a couple arm-in-arm wearing the utility dress of the 1940s.

Three-year-old Anna ran up to her grandmother with her latest work of art.

'Babcia, look I drew you and mummy and daddy and granddad.' Helena sat forward again. 'And I wrote my name, Anna Lato, see?'

'*Kochana*, it's beautiful and you can write so beautifully. Is that me wearing a bright green dress? Lovely. Can you draw a picture of our house too?'

The child wandered back to the table clutching her crayons. Wanda handed her mother a cup of lemon tea. 'Pawel's mother blamed 'reactionary elements' for the strikes in her last letter,' she said.

Helena laughed. 'Thank you, darling. Yes, we all know where Irena's allegiance is, always with the communist state. If she's not careful, things will move along and she could end up on the wrong side.'

The TV was showing a man with a large moustache making a speech to assembled crowds of workers. Helena stared at the screen. 'This Walesa has won them the right to have a free trade union. That's incredible. I hope they know what they're doing. Remember what happened in Hungary and Czechoslovakia when they tried to break free of the Soviets.' She pursed her lips in anxiety.

'Pawel thinks the strikers will be crushed, sent to prison, tortured. He thinks they have no hope,' said Wanda.

'I'm not sure – it will be difficult but it seems something has started that can't easily be un-started.'

Wanda looked at the scenes of crowds pushing flowers through locked factory gates to outstretched hands inside. Always flowers. They must have lots of flower shops in Poland, she thought. She looked back at her mother whose head was resting against the sofa, eyes closed. Her mother's brown hair now had a good deal of grey in it.

'How did your talk go today?'

'Good,' said Helena opening her eyes. 'The Mental Health Foundation are part funding my PhD. Dr Cope seemed very interested in my proposed thesis on schizophrenia.'

'I hope you told them you got a first class degree when you were over 50. They should be impressed with you. I'm impressed with you.'

Helena smiled. 'Are Tadek and Pawel working late tonight?'

'No, they should be back soon.' She checked her watch: 5.30. 'I'd better finish cooking. I've been making shepherd's pie and chicken roasts too often lately so we're having pierogi tonight. Traditional food. Did you hear that, Anna? Mummy's making your favourite – pierogi.'

'Yummy, yum yum,' said the little girl not looking up from her colouring book.

'It will be good to have some real food – I endured leathery beef, mashed potato and peas in the college canteen today, disgusting. *Kochana*, come and tell Babcia about what you did at nursery today,' said Helena. Anna ran over and clambered onto her grandmother's lap.

Wanda walked into the kitchen. As she reached up to take the red and blue flour tin off the top shelf, a sudden flashback stopped her, a memory, in vivid, blurred colours like an old super 8 film. Her grandmother, tall and stiff in a green and black patterned dress, had once stood on this spot and asked eight-year-old Wanda to pass her that same tin. Wanda had been standing on a high kitchen stool. As she had pulled the container from the shelf, it had slipped from her fingers and landed on the floor. The lid had pinged off and a puff of white flour had spread out onto the blue and white linoleum. Her grandmother had tutted and muttered something crossly under her breath as she'd bent down to clear up the mess. Five-year-old Zosia, her pale beauty a constant taunt, had smiled a knowing smile.

Wanda closed her eyes for a second, wiping away the memory of the dead. Then she turned to stare out into the darkened garden. Frost was starting to form on the panes. They would be holding the usual Christmas dance at the Polish Club next Saturday but her brother, Janek, was having his firm's dinner on the same night and she knew she'd be expected to attend that.

Wanda flicked through the unopened batch of Christmas cards on the kitchen table - no word from Poland. She thought about the letter she'd sent. Was it a mistake? Her stomach did little turns – churning up and grinding. What would Pawel say? Would he be angry? She should have told him… On the other hand, she most probably wouldn't receive any reply.

She opened the kitchen drawer and moved aside the mats and napkins. Beneath them was a copy of *The Observer* magazine from two months earlier. The front cover showed a man standing in front of the huge chains mooring the ships in the Gdansk yards. The photo was grey and threatening, full of raw energy. Wanda had seen the same picture reproduced elsewhere: on political placards, posters, the television news – even on T-shirts. The photograph was becoming the symbol of Solidarity – the man representing Poland and the ship behind, the Soviet machine. Someone on the radio had remarked that it looked like the famous 19th century photograph of Brunel, standing near one of his ships. What really interested Wanda, though, was the strong resemblance the man in the picture bore to someone she knew very well. She'd looked at the small credit at the side of the picture and raised an eyebrow at the photographer's name, Roger Elliott. Then with a magnifying glass, she'd looked at the man's lapel to see his name badge. It was tiny but she could only just make it out: A. Lato.

Wanda covered up the magazine and shut the drawer with a snap. She got back to making the meat filled, dough parcels for the evening meal. Half an hour later, she heard the clattering of tools in the sitting room indicating her father and husband had arrived home. She turned and smilingly held up floury hands as Pawel trudged into the kitchen.

'Hello, good day at work?' she said.

Pawel didn't reply but set about removing his paint-spattered overalls. Then he went to the sink and began to scrub fiercely at his hands with a nailbrush. Wanda's smile vanished and she studied him nervously. His blonde hair flopped over his eyes, smears of white paint streaking across his prominent cheekbones. The other day, her friend Pam had casually remarked that Pawel looked like the actor Michael York. Wanda had secretly glowed with pleasure at that thought. She looked towards the sitting room where she could hear her father talking to her mother while Anna interrupted asking him to admire her drawing.

Pawel dried his hands on the tea towel instead of the hand towel and Wanda resisted the urge to tell him off. He went through to the sitting room and she followed, taking the food dishes to the dining table. Tadek was asking his wife how her talk had gone. Wanda looked at Pawel. He still had not spoken. She felt a little spike of fear, her hands were clammy as she served the food. The meal was punctuated by Anna's excited comments about Father Christmas, about her presents and her stocking. In the middle of the chatter, Pawel banged his fist hard on the table making the crockery leap. They all jumped, Wanda dropping her knife onto her plate with a loud noise. Pawel growled at his daughter, 'You think it's all about you, don't you?'

There was a shocked silence and tears sprang into the little girl's eyes.

'Pawel, Christmas is for children and since she is the only child here, it obviously is all about her. What's the matter with you?' said Wanda.

'I can't stand this prattle. Endless chatter and this shit...' He threw his spoon down in his soup.

'Pawel,' Wanda admonished, indicating Anna with a sharp nod of her head.

'Stop fucking telling me what to do.' Pawel leapt up, grabbed his jacket from the back of the chair and went out, slamming the door. They heard the van starting up and the squeal of tyres as he drove off at speed. There was silence. Wanda looked at her parents in distress.

'Did something happen at work today, Dad?' she asked trembling.

Helena pursed her lips and said nothing. Tadek raised his eyebrows and sighed. 'He cut his hand with a screwdriver while he was trying to open a paint tin and let off a tirade of abuse. He seems – I don't know – rather stressed.'

Wanda turned to Anna who was crying, tears falling onto her dress. 'Come on, sweetheart, let's go up for your bath. Daddy hurt his hand at work, that's why he's cross. Up we go.' She held her hand out to Anna and the child clutched it, sniffing. Half way up the stairs, she sent the little girl ahead to the bathroom and asked her to get her towel and bath toys ready. Wanda then crept back down to the foot of the stairs.

'What's wrong with him, do you know?' she heard her mother saying.

'When he was having his outburst today, he said something about 'my pointless, petty life.'

Wanda brought her hand to mouth and closed her eyes as the tears caught on her eyelashes and began to fall down her face.

'Huh, who does he think he is? He's only been in this country five minutes and he thinks he has the right to complain. Does he know what we went through back in Poland and how hard it was starting off here?' asked Helena.

'Maybe something has happened. I don't know. I wish he and Wanda could afford their own home, it can't be easy living with us.'

'It may not be easy but – young people today don't know how good life is. When we came after the war we knew no one here to help us.'

'I think he finds it difficult being a father. He doesn't know how to be patient, how to engage.'

Helena then mumbled something Wanda couldn't quite hear. Pawel's father had abandoned him when he was a child and Wanda felt more and more this was having an impact on his relationships now. This is why she had written that letter. She wanted to help.

'He's a lazy, spoilt boy, in my opinion,' said Helena. 'He was doted on by two women all his life, his mother and auntie Mira. He always wants more, is never satisfied. He's very lazy, isn't he?'

'He's not a great worker, it's true. But I try to teach him all I know. He thinks he should be doing more high up work, I think.'

'I hope he doesn't follow his own father's example and suddenly disappear,' said Helena.

Wanda wiped away her tears, turned and made her way up to the bathroom.

She went to bed early that night and heard Pawel return in the early hours. Had he been drinking again? It was something he'd only started doing lately and he didn't handle alcohol well. Wanda got out of bed, stood at the top of the stairs and called to him but there was no reply. He probably wouldn't even come up to bed but sleep fully clothed on the sofa.

Wanda slept badly, a nervous knot in her stomach. She woke next morning and instinctively put out her hand to the other pillow. It was cool, empty. The sheet was wrapped tightly round her legs and the blanket had fallen off. She could hear Anna chatting to her grandmother in the other bedroom. A thin, grey light peeped through the curtains. Wanda heaved her heavy body out of bed and pulled on her blue, fluffy dressing gown. She went downstairs and peered into the sitting room. Pawel was lying on the sofa, fully clothed with one leg on the floor. He was asleep and snoring.

She went into the kitchen, put the kettle on the hob and lit a match. The gas ring burst into blue life. She switched on the radio.

'...and for the rest of the morning we will be playing the music of John Lennon,' said the DJ on Radio Derby.

The slow strains of *Imagine* began.

Wanda frowned. Frantically, she fiddled with the dial and switched to BBC Radio 4. Brian Redhead was saying, '....shot outside his apartment building by an unknown assailant and died later in hospital. We'll go to our correspondent Tom Brook in New York where vast crowds are already gathering.'

Wanda put her hand to her mouth. She stood still for a moment as the steam from the whistling kettle began to fill the room. She didn't switch it off. The windows began to run with condensation, water pooling on the tiled sill.

As the horror of what she'd just heard began to sink in, she shouted out loud, 'I can't believe it, why, why, why?' Sobbing, she pulled an oven glove to her cheek for comfort.

Pawel stirred on the sofa and sat up, his hair in an untidy spike. He rose and stumbled over to his wife in the kitchen. 'I'm sorry – I went out for a drink,' he said, trying to hug her to him. 'I met someone in a bar. I'm sorry, I didn't mean to shout, to be cruel, it gets too much. I'm sorry – I'm not myself these days'

'There was absolutely no reason for that,' Wanda sobbed trying to push him away.

'I know. I'm just a malcontent, my mother always used to say so. It won't happen again, I promise you. I am not my father.'

'Why do that? What's the point? It will never be the same again. It's over.'

She pushed him away as he tried to hug her to him.

'No, no, it isn't over, I'll change, I promise,' he pleaded.

Wanda stared at her husband, 'It's got nothing to do with you,' she shouted.

Chapter 3

John Allsop glanced up at the huge portrait on the hotel wall. It showed an overweight, middle-aged man in a white wig, blue tailcoat and white breeches sitting open-legged on an ornate chair and pointing at some mechanical device on the table beside him. His smug expression and rich clothing indicated he was a man of considerable wealth. In the far background, the painter had depicted the source of the man's wealth; black smoke billowing from his numerous textile mills set amidst the Derbyshire hills. The little bronze plaque fastened to the bottom edge of the frame read: Obadiah Stepp, 1780.

John smiled. He imagined the day when he would have a portrait of himself painted for posterity. What a blessing he didn't have such a ridiculous name. As a child, though, he had been a little embarrassed by his birth name, Janek Baran but, oddly, he occasionally missed it these days. It had been politic to take his wife's surname when they had married, but it did mean he sounded stunningly dull.

John shrugged and turned his attention back to the menu in his hand.

THE STEPP HOUSE HOTEL

Pottage of foie gras

or

Smoked Scottish salmon, brown bread

Lamb cutlet, dauphinoise potatoes

or

Green salad with artichoke hearts

Rice pudding

or

chocolate mouse

Coffee

'Derek,' called John,' This nouvelle cuisine thing, it doesn't look like much food – I think people are going to be hungry, don't you?'

Company accountant Derek Hoar was also holding a copy of the menu and frowning. He walked over. 'Well, I hear it's all the rage down in London,' he replied, 'and this is a prestigious place so hopefully they know what they're doing.'

John nodded, unconvinced.

'A style of food with no actual food – what a brilliant marketing idea,' John murmured. 'How can we translate that to the print business?'

Derek came up closer. 'I suppose we just have to trust them. Reg always insisted we have our Christmas party here. We generally leave the food arrangements to them. One year we did use the Irongate Grill but Reg said it wasn't posh enough. The Grill's idea of nouvelle cuisine would be to have the custard *underneath* the jam roly-poly.'

John nodded and smiled. His father-in-law, company boss Reg Allsop, had always personally involved himself with the preparations for the Allsop's Printers Christmas party and he made sure everyone who was anyone in Derby was invited: the Mayor and his wife, local councillors, businessmen from Rolls-Royce, Derby County footballers and any available actors or media types. Brian Clough had got spectacularly drunk at the 1974 party and at another Alan Bates had made a wonderful speech detailing his early life in Allestree.

Reg always made sure his small, family print company punched above its weight in terms of hospitality and entertaining. John remembered him saying, 'Never underestimate the importance of entertaining, networking, gifts and favours – it oils the wheels, my lad. I'm optimistic this year. I never thought I'd say this about a woman, but Mrs Thatcher is going to do the right thing by this country, you mark my words.' Unfortunately, Reg never had the chance to mark his own words as he had a heart attack on the golf course only a week later. Stone dead at 52.

That meant John, at only 22, was in charge of the whole shooting match. His wife Maxine, and mother-in-law, Lily, were also on the board of directors but they were still busy with their grief and looking after two-year-old Clarke and baby Amber to worry about the running of the firm.

John, resplendent in his dinner jacket and black tie, put the menu on the bar with a sigh, pulled down his cuffs and stood ready to greet the 65 guests, slightly down in number from the previous year. The tables were set with white plates, four selections of cutlery each side, three sizes of wine glass, a little gift near each nametag. A display of pink and white helium-filled balloons decorated each table. A fire blazed in the grate, the string quartet was tuning up in the corner and a huge Christmas tree dominated the room.

In view of the firm's recent loss, John had brought a formal portrait of Reg, his well-oiled comb-over, tiny bristling moustache and large facial wart in plain view, and placed it in a prominent position on the wall behind the head table. It was a timely reminder to everyone that the former boss had now passed on and there was a new kid in town.

John looked at Derek, who seemed to be clearing out his ear with one finger. Derek was aged around 40, probably more, with light ginger, sparse hair, ugly spectacles and rather prominent teeth. He'd worked at Allsop's for 20 years, Reg's right hand man. John knew he had to keep an eye on him.

'I just heard from the office that Maxine rang,' said Derek examining the wax in his fingernail. 'She said she is feeling too unwell to attend the party and Mrs Allsop senior will stay at home to keep her company. She asked that you give their apologies in your speech.'

'Yes, well, I was expecting that. It's only a week since her father's funeral so it's not surprising they don't feel like coming to a party. It's all very bad timing.' John looked round the room, silently counting the number of tables.

'No, well I'm sure Mr Allsop senior was looking forward to attending the party but death can be very inconvenient.'

John looked back at him sharply. "Naturally, we are all grieving for Reg but it was his wish, his express wish, that this party should go ahead. He made so many of the preparations himself and I don't want to let him down.'

'Of course not. Mr Allsop's mantra was that the show must go on and he thought this party was essential to business.'

John looked at the door expectantly as it opened. It was only his parents coming in with Wanda and Pawel. He fixed a welcoming smile on his face.

'Merry Christmas, lovely to see you. Hello, Pawel – I've never seen you in such a smart suit.' John kissed his mother. 'Hello, Mum.'

'Do I get a seat at the top table now that I'm the boss's sister, eh Janek?' said Wanda kissing her brother on the cheek.

John winced and looked at her. Did she have to be so crass, especially as Reg had only just died? And what on earth was she wearing? An orange, sequinned dress two sizes too small and a black shawl she had obviously crocheted herself.

'Well, as Maxine and her mother aren't coming perhaps … but maybe mum and dad should really sit there,' he said. 'Look, you're sitting here just next to the top table. I'll even sit with you for a while – how's that?' John hoped that would placate Wanda. When she was in this mood, she could be quite an embarrassment, with her loud voice and clumsy gestures. He would talk to her and keep her calm until other people arrived.

'You'll slum it with us, will you?' said Wanda loudly with a laugh. John looked hopefully towards the door to see who else was arriving. It was Derek's wife Pam. She sauntered in, looking around to see who she knew. Wanda spotted her. 'Derek, your lovely wife is here,' she shouted. 'Pam, you're sitting next to me and Pawel. I like your frock. Where did you get it?'

John frowned. Did she have to shout across the room like that? What was the matter with her?

As Pam walked towards Wanda, John had a good look at her - beautiful, restrained and hard as nails. She was wearing a fitted, dark green dress with a black necklace and dangly earrings. John viewed her with a mixture of lust and mistrust. She paused next to her husband - Beauty and the Beast.

'I really need a drink. Bring on the champers, Janek,' called Wanda. She slipped off her black shawl and fanned herself with the menu.

'What's the matter with you?' drawled Pam. 'A hard day slaving over a hot stove?'

The waiter filled the glasses with champagne and Wanda took a large gulp. 'I don't know, I'm just… It's so sad about John Lennon, isn't it? If only he'd stayed here where he was safe. I wish they'd succeeded in deporting him, he'd be alive now.'

John saw Pam pull a face and shrug her shoulders. Hard bitch, he thought.

'You were always a Paul fan at school, weren't you?' said Pam. 'I saw Lennon once, actually I saw all four of them.'

'Did you? Where?' asked Wanda, her face lighting up with interest.

"I had a Saturday job waitressing at the Upper Deck café in the bus station. They came in and ordered fish, chips and tea. Must have been 1963. I was a Stones fan, though, so it was wasted on me.'

'Why on earth do you get so upset about a man you didn't even know, Wanda' said Pawel. 'People get killed all the time. Probably other people were killed in New York on that same night. You don't see me weeping and wailing about it because I didn't know them.

Wanda's face fell. They are ganging up on her, thought John.

'Have you never had a hero, Pawel?' said John.

'You should never make a person into a hero,' said Pawel with a shrug. 'You'll only be disappointed.'

'But I did know John - in my heart,' said Wanda sadly.

'Rubbish! You are not grieving for him, you are sorry for yourself, for your lost youth. By the way, you look very beautiful, Pam. That colour suits you so well,' said Pawel.

'Why, Pawel what a gentleman you are. Derek, you would never say anything so gallant.' Pam took a sip of her champagne and her eyes sparkled over the rim of her glass.

'Of course you look lovely, Pam. I said so before we came out,' said Derek pushing up his glasses.

'But it sounds so much better with Pawel's sexy accent,' murmured Pam into her champagne.

John got up. He needed to get away from this tight-knit, oppressive group. He had to meet the movers and shakers. The room was filling up and there was the general hum of conversation in the air. The leader of the council Robert Bookbinder, the mayor, the editor of the Derby Evening Telegraph were all there. They'd go anywhere for free drinks and canapés.

'I'd better go and mingle with the guests,' said John. 'I have to make a speech later!'

As he walked away, he saw Pawel smiling broadly at Pam.

Chapter 4

Helena sat in her study and quietly placed her hands, palms down, on the desk in front of her. She looked at her fingers, the short broken nails, the veins on the back of her hand. The skin had become wrinkled, dotted here and there with brown liver spots. When had that happened? She noted, without emotion, that they were her mother's hands. This room had once been her mother Barbara's bedroom – the crucifix and icon of the Black Madonna still hung from the wall. A photograph of Barbara with her brother Witold still had pride of place on the little shelf above the old Victorian fireplace.

Sighing, Helena turned her attention to the battered green folder sitting on the corner of her desk. She opened it and read, for the umpteenth time, the considered thoughts of Dr Nathan Weinberg.

Could schizophrenia be a collection of disparate illnesses rather than one condition? Maybe it is caused by poor maternal nutrition, inadequate mothering, or damage to the brain during birth? Or perhaps it is a hereditary condition, a reaction to stress or a chemical imbalance in the brain? I intend to make a thorough study of this phenomenon and hopefully come to a useful conclusion that may alleviate the awful plight of those suffering. This is my life's work.
N. Weinberg, 1920

The uneven blue letters had been committed to paper using an old Smith-Corona style typewriter. In places, the paper had been pierced by the keys striking it a little too violently. Written in old-style Polish, the bit of paper was stuck to the inside cover of the file. It was Helena's habit, from time to time, to take the bulging folder from her drawer to once again rifle through its contents. It contained scores of documents: research papers, letters, photographs, an address book, newspaper clippings and business cards. Some papers were stuck together with rusted paper clips, others were carbon copies and almost illegible. Helena persevered, reading each scrap of paper. It would take a while to make sense of it all.

From family folklore, Helena knew that Nathan Weinberg had been Jewish, an ear, nose and throat doctor who had married her father's sister Maria – an aristocratic Polish woman. That, she assumed, must have caused some conflict with his family and hers but she didn't know the details. They had no children. When the Germans invaded he was taken away and died in Auschwitz, so she heard. Everything else she knew about him came from this precious folder, a random selection of documents, the detritus of everyday life. He was an enigma, a life cut short like so many others but this life came with a file full of cryptic clues.

There were papers containing important case study interviews as well as mundane notes such as shopping lists. Some scraps of paper just had a telephone number or a hastily scribbled name - a long-forgotten aide memoir to a half-remembered acquaintance. There were some pencil drawings signed by her aunt, theatre notices and restaurant bills.

Helena had spent many hours examining each document, every scrap of paper. She was Sherlock Holmes looking for clues, Champollion deciphering the Rossetta stone. She had only been given a fragment of information but she had to break the code of this man's life.

The photographs were fascinating but, maddeningly, none had any information written on the back: no name, no date. There was a collection of pictures in a white envelope which Helena guessed were all taken around the same date, probably in the 1920s. One was apparently taken in Nathan's surgery as a stethoscope and blood pressure monitor were just visible on the table in the background.

Nathan himself stood in the foreground, a youngish man with thick, wavy black hair, full lips and bright eyes. Another picture showed him with his wife Maria. He was seated and dressed formally in a black suit and stiff white shirt. A small black and white terrier dog was perched proudly on his lap, looking straight at the camera, its tongue lolling from the side of its mouth. Maria, wearing a shapeless dress and pull down hat which obscured much of her face, was standing behind her husband, her hand on his shoulder, looking down affectionately at his curly hair. Another picture showed a youthful Nathan holding a violin.

On its own at the back of the folder, Helena found a group shot taken outdoors in the sunshine in front of some large, metal gates. Nathan and Maria, looking middle aged by now, were posing with another couple of a similar age. The woman was smiling and shielding her eyes from the sun, a young boy was peeping out from behind her skirts. The man was holding what looked very much like a small monkey in his arms. He held it gently like a baby. An odd pet! The clothes and style of the photographic print made Helena think it dated from the 1930s.

But it was perhaps the earliest picture that fascinated her most. It was a formal study of a very young Nathan alone, sitting on a chair, holding a book. The background had been whitened out and he was staring away from the camera. His hair was a rich dark colour, his stiff collar looked uncomfortable and his pince nez gave him an intellectual air. Possibly he had just graduated from medical school, but he looked lonely, distant. The photographer's name in gold, curly lettering was etched into the bottom of the frame – *R. Ritkowski, Warszawa*.

Helena gently traced her fingers over this last image of her uncle. *What happened to you? How did you die?*

Having spent a good deal of time during her psychology degree and the research she was conducting now, analysing people's motives, Helena found herself wondering why she was obsessed with trying to get close to this long-dead man. After all, he was no blood relation. Was it just a way of getting close to her own father – a man she'd never known, a shadowy figure, filled with inner demons?

The weight of her father's mental illness bore down heavily on her and it was a burden she carried alone. She didn't want to discuss her fears, this was her private cross to bear. There seemed to be no evidence of it reappearing in subsequent generations but still... To give herself some comfort, Helena re-read one of the early interviews Nathan conducted with her father. The date at the top said 1920, a time before her parents married. Helena knew it was earlier than any of the other interviews included in the file. It could possibly have been the one that sparked Nathan's interest in the whole subject of schizophrenia.

Warsaw, March 1920

NW: Your sister Maria tells me you have been having problems for about eight years with sleeping, with your nerves, with repetitive thoughts. Why do you think this has come about?

JP: I think it stems mainly from the insomnia. When you can't sleep it's like a kind of torture, isn't it? Probably the thoughts and nervous feelings are a result of lack of sleep. [He laughs]

NW: There seems to be more to it than that. She told me you said you heard voices.

JP: I do sometimes but I realise they are only in my head. Other people can't hear them so I know it must be just me. Sometimes I can conjure up my nursemaid's voice, it comforts me.

NW: Yes, Maria tells me your nursemaid died about five years ago. That must have been traumatic for you.

JP: Nanny Antonia, that's what Maria and I called her, was like a mother to us. We don't have a close relationship with our real mother – or father for that matter. Nanny Antonia was with me since I was a baby, she was my wet nurse as well.

NW: What happened when she died?

JP: They did not let us go to the funeral. Antonia was buried in her home village far away and mother said it would be a peasant funeral and it would be beneath us to go. I thought to myself, 'You considered it acceptable for this woman to feed me, hold me, care for me but I can't go to her funeral because she was beneath us socially'.

NW: You must have felt grief stricken.

JP: I had this terrible dream that she was not dead but they had buried her by mistake and she was crying and screaming in her coffin under the ground. In my mind she called, 'Janek, save me, save me.' I just couldn't get that image out of my head.

NW: You were away at military school then, weren't you?

[He pauses for a long time and stares out of the window]

JP: I hated living there. It was cold, dark and brutal. I'm not a soldier. I wanted to be a poet but my father said no son of his would write flowery language as if he were a homosexual.

NW: So these problems with not sleeping and hearing voices and the need to perform small tasks over and over again started at this time.

JP: I think so. I was 16 and was challenged to a duel by one of the students who was considered a great soldier and leader. He was older than me. They thought he would be a fine general one day. By sheer good luck, or bad luck, I killed him. No one could believe that I was the victor.

NW: What was the duel about?

JP: I was in...

The page was ripped from this point, the rest missing. Helena found this unbearably frustrating. The other case notes, where her father illness had progressed to such a stage of insanity, she found too distressing, heartbreaking. This one, however, she read and re-read as her father appeared to be a caring man suffering grief and loss, a poet, a gentleman in the true meaning of the word. Sadly, there was only one example of his poetry, the last poem he ever wrote...

Helena sat tapping her pen on the folder. Her father had suffered two traumatic incidents – the death of his nurse and the duel. Was trauma at a young age a trigger for schizophrenia as Nathan postulated?

The door of her study opened and Helena quickly shut the folder, as if she harboured a guilty secret. It was Tadek.

'Wanda made chocolate cake and she thought you'd like a piece while it's warm,' he said. He put a cup of tea and a plate on the desk and sat down in the armchair.

'Thank you,' said Helena. 'I thought I could smell something lovely cooking.'

'How are you getting on with your work?' Tadek asked, picking up one of the old photographs Helena had placed at the corner of the desk. 'Who is this?'

'It's my uncle Nathan. It's from auntie Maria's old folder, you know the one Pawel brought over when he first arrived.'

Tadek sat looking at the picture.

'Are you searching for something specific?' he asked.

Helena looked out of the window, twisting her wedding ring round and round on her finger. That was a loaded question. 'I don't know,' she said quietly. 'Maybe I'm trying to get rid of the feeling that I have been punished for my life, but I don't know what I did wrong.'

Tadek looked at her in surprise. He hadn't realised he was asking anything of great significance. 'You did nothing wrong,' he said.

'My father suffered from schizophrenia and Nathan was trying to help him. At least, I imagine he was trying to help. It was in the early days of psychoanalysis.'

Tadek sat forward, a worried expression on his face. 'But your mother always said…' He paused. 'When did you find this out? How do you know? You never told me.'

'It's all here in the documents. I've known for two or three years now. I didn't want to burden anyone else with it.'

'I'm not anyone else – you should have told me. What have you done with this information?'

Helena looked round at her husband. 'Why? Does this change anything? Are you worried there is madness in my family?'

'No, no, of course not, but we should share our worries. So he didn't die of war wounds?'

'He killed himself with an overdose of morphine. The morphine was prescribed by Dr Nathan Weinberg and my father took too much, probably aided by my mother.'

'Aided? What do you mean?'

'My father had turned violent. It's all here in the notes. He almost threw me off the third floor balcony when I was a baby.'

'He what? Holy Mother of God,' said Tadek. 'Why was none of this…'

Without warning, Helena started to sob and covered her face with her hands. Tadek jumped up and put his arms round her, burying his face in her hair.

Chapter 5

Warsaw, March 1981

Walking into the cobbled city square of the Stare Miasto, Aleks Lato found himself going through a list of doubts in his mind.

a. Would he still recognise Irena after all these years?

b. Was he making a huge mistake in arranging to meet her and dragging up old memories and quarrels?

c. Had he done the right thing in leaving Gdansk and pitching up in Warsaw again?

He was down to his final cigarette, he'd eaten his last meal the previous day and he must have left one glove on the train so his left hand was starting to go numb. It felt a bit depressing to be back. The capital city was where many things in his life had started to go wrong and there were plenty of people here he wished to avoid. On the other hand, Gdansk was also proving unwelcome. His habit of gently trying to feather his own nest always seemed, unfairly, to rebound on him. His dealings with some unsavoury characters many years ago meant he sometimes received threatening phone calls. During the last one, an anonymous voice had breathed down the phone, 'You will die, you will die, you will die.' Aleks had replied in the same deep monotone, 'So will you, so will you, so will you,' before slamming down the receiver. He wanted to make light of it but it was the final straw.

It wasn't just the past that was pestering him, the present was a problem too. The ridiculous price increases meant he was having trouble surviving on his wages, especially after the hardship caused by the strike. Food was getting so scarce people were even sleeping on the pavements so as not to lose their place in the queue outside the bread shops. Sometimes they paid a child to keep their place in the line for them. It was a ridiculous waste of time and money. This nonsense couldn't go on.

Also there was the small matter of the missing donation money…

Aleks looked around at the pastel coloured gables, horse-drawn tourist carriages and ice-cream sellers – the acceptable face of the capital. He spotted Irena before she saw him. She was sitting in the window seat of a cafe, just another middle-aged, invisible woman, wisps of greying hair falling round her face, her eyes fixed on her coffee cup.

He had phoned her a few days previously, out of the blue. He noticed her voice trembled when she realised who was speaking. He told her there was a risk the telephone system from Gdansk could be cut any day. She said the whole strike thing was ridiculous and must be caused by provocation from reactionary elements.

Aleks looked at her face, slightly distorted through the café window. Her jawline was sagging, time is cruel, but there was still a vestige of that 21-year-old beauty he'd first met in 1946. That wretched life amid the ruins when Warsaw had smelled so awful as it emerged from the detritus of a devastating war: concrete dust, decayed bodies under rubble, charred timber, the stink of sewage. The day they had first met, Aleks had been filthy, hungry and thirsty. He'd only walked into a meeting of the Communist League in the basement of a bombed building because a sign outside on the street said 'Free Soup'.

Going down the steps into a bleak little room, Aleks had seen a man standing on a makeshift stage, giving an impassioned, cliché-ridden speech about comrades in arms, socialism and the glorious revolution. Aleks had looked around among the foul-smelling old men and black-swathed women to see where the soup was. That's when Irena had turned round to look at him and he'd even momentarily forgotten his hunger. Among the thin, drab, miserable population she had looked radiant as if delighted to see him. He later found out it was because she glowed with passion for Comrade Stalin but by then it was too late - he'd fallen madly in love with her. His own sudden conversion to the Lenin/Stalin love-in was only tactical. It got him the girl. Irena was beautiful, intelligent, serious, sober and industrious. She had absolutely no sense of humour.

Irena had been training to become a doctor, in her spare time she ran a soup kitchen and helped with the reconstruction of the old town. She didn't smoke, drink alcohol or eat and sleep much either. Aleks did all these things to excess. They were married two years later. For their honeymoon, Irena insisted they go to Moscow and visit the mausoleum where Lenin lay in state. They stood for two hours in the freezing cold to see a corpse that looked like a wax doll.

Back in Warsaw they lived in a little flat with Irena's widowed mother Mira and then Pawel had been born. The government was encouraging women to have children, to replenish the devastated population. Irena specialised in paediatrics, caring for other people's sick children and left little Pawel in the care of her mother. Despite working with children all day, she seemed to have little idea how to play with them. For Pawel's fourth birthday, Irena bought him a copy of the *Communist Manifesto*. She'd stared as Aleks had cried with laughter

Thirty years later, Irena's tired face stared sadly from the café window. Aleks stood up straight, fixed on a smile and walked through the café door, tinkling the bell. He plonked his newspaper down on the table in front of her. She stared up at him with frightened eyes.

'Irenka,' he said pulling the cigarette out of his mouth. 'Still wearing that old brown coat – I'd know it anywhere.'

Her face relaxed. 'Well, there's nothing wrong with it – waste not, want not,' she said, pulling it round her shoulders. 'I can't afford to buy new coats all the time and anyway, there is no necessity.'

Aleks smiled. She always mistook his banter for aggression. Within a minute they had fallen back into the pattern of petty rowing which had characterised their relationship for more than 30 years. Aleks sat down on the chair opposite.

'Still working at the hospital?' he asked. At the next table, some American tourists were laughing and talking loudly.

'Yes, of course, what else would I be doing?' she said briskly, looking away.

'Are you making any decent money yet?'

I'm head of the paediatrics department, if you want to know - first woman to head that particular section. I was awarded the Red Banner of Labour. Anyway, it's not about the money – it's about the principle.'

'Principles are fine things – so I'm told. But where's the money? That's the point. You work all those hours for a pittance and they give you a little tin medal and you say, "Thank you sir, thank you, madam," and bow your head. Jesus, do you realise you're the last person in this pathetic country who actually still believes in all that shit?'

Irena put her purse in her handbag, buttoned up her coat and started to rise. 'I knew this would happen. Why am I here? You are just a boorish, stupid...'

Aleks leaned over and pulled her hand, 'I'm sorry, Irenka, really I'm sorry. You know what a prick I am. Sit down. What I really wanted to talk about was our son.'

Irena paused, looked at Aleks and sat down again. 'You never bothered about Pawel before. For years I cared for him on my own. Why are you concerned now?' She opened a little packet of brown sugar and poured it into her cold coffee. The waitress approached.

'Coffee, black,' said Aleks and the woman walked away without a word.

'We are grandparents, I know that,' Aleks continued.

'Who told you?'

'I have my spies.' He laughed. 'Pawel's in England, isn't he?'

'Yes, he went there in '75 and married – to my cousin Helena's daughter, Wanda.'

'Yes, Wanda – I know all about Wanda.'

'Do you? Have you been in contact with Pawel?'

'No, with Wanda. She wrote to me a few months ago.'

'She wrote to you! Why? How did she find you? What did she write to you about?'

Aleks searched in his jacket pocket, his cigarette clamped between his lips, smoke swirling toward the blackened ceiling. He placed an envelope on the table in front of Irena.

It was addressed to Aleksander Lato, Lenin Shipyard, Gdansk, Poland.

Irena picked it up and pulled out the letter.

16 Porton Crescent
Derby

November 6 1980

Dear Pan Lato

You do not know me but my name is Wanda Lato nee Baran and I am married to your son, Pawel. I saw your picture in The Observer magazine and worked out you must be Pawel's father (at least I hope you are). We live in Derby, a town in England. I was born here (my mother is cousin to your former wife, Irena). Pawel came to visit in 1975 and never returned to Poland because we fell in love and married.

You will be pleased to learn you have a beautiful little granddaughter, Anna, who is so lovely and intelligent.

We have never met and you must have had your reasons for leaving Pawel when he was a child but I hope you have always thought about him and feel some duty towards him. I'm writing to you because he needs your help. I think he really suffers from not having had a father figure in his life.

Perhaps we can talk. I know it may be difficult by letter but can you ring me? Please call during the day when my husband and parents are not in as I didn't tell anyone I had written to you.

With regards,

Wanda Lato
(If I have the wrong person, I will feel very foolish so please discard the letter)

Irena handed the letter back. 'I would ring her but she forgot to put her phone number on the letter. I assume you have it,' said Aleks.

Irena looked worried. 'I wonder what the problem is with my boy. Wanda never said anything to me about it. I had a letter from her last week and it was full of news about little Anna and her school. Oh, it's all your fault, you selfish....'

'Look, it's a bit late for that now. I told you – I'm just not husband material. That's obvious. But listen, give me Wanda's number and I will see if I can help. I'm hoping to get to London before long – I have some contacts there now. I am an artist remember. I thought I'd get the art community to back me up. I think I'll dust down my old sculptures. I left you my masterpiece – Diadem of Sorrow. Do you still have it?'

'Of course I still have it, it's too heavy to get out of the flat,' said Irena. 'I wish you'd take it away. I did think about having it melted down. I could do with a new sauce pan.'

'A joke! That's not bad for you, Irenka!' said Aleks, smirking.

The American tourists got up to leave with much noise and commotion. The door tinkled as they left and the café was plunged into silence.

'I've also got a box of those weird films you used to make as a student. Glad to hear you actually have a proper job doing honest toil at the shipyard. I hated all that Theatre of the Absurd stuff.' Irena shrugged and looked away. A horse and carriage clip-clopped past the window.

'That's because you have no soul, all you think about is bandages, medicines and clean sheets. I was at the Lodz film school with Roman Polanski.'

'What do you mean with Polanski – you left before he came. Anyway, you were only there a year. You never stick at anything.'

The waitress appeared with the coffee and put it on the table. As soon as her back was turned, Aleks took a small hip flask out of his pocket and added a tot of vodka to it.

'Anyway, I need my art back now,' he continued. 'Got to get my artistic credentials sorted out. Stricken poet, film-maker, sculptor forced to work in shipyard – that would go down well in London, don't you think? Can I come round to the flat to check out my work?'

'You know where I live.'

Aleks paused and traced his cigarette round the ashtray. Then he noticed the Americans had left a $10 tip under a coffee cup. He reached over, ostensibly to get the sugar bowl but deftly took the bill and scrunched it into his hand.

'How is Mira?' he asked.

'I can't believe you said that! Mama died in 1974, I told you at the time but you never listen because you don't care about anyone but yourself. Pawel left for England in '75, so I have the flat to myself.'

'Good, that's very good. Not about Mira, I mean, but I'm glad there never was anyone else, Irenka.' Aleks put his hand on hers. She pulled away.

'What's she like, this Wanda?' said Aleks, leaning back.

'Don't rope her into your schemes. She a nice girl – good-hearted girl. I'm worried about this crisis with Pawel.'

'Perhaps I can help – maybe as an example of how not to do things. Watch out Pawel or you will end up like your deadbeat father.'

Irena smiled finally and it lit up her face.

Aleks stared at her. 'Irenka, can you lend me 50 zloty?'

Chapter 6

Wanda was late. She was supposed to be at the Kardomah café at 3pm but she was still hurrying past the Art Gallery in the Strand at 3.20. Her mother was minding Anna but she'd been delayed and Wanda had been forced to wait for her.

She ran down Saddler Gate, past the Old Bell Hotel and the back of Faulds music shop. Wanda had once had four brief and disastrous piano lessons in one of the shop's little back rooms when she was 13. Miss Pullen, the old spinster who gave taught the piano and who always wore a hat indoors, had commented, correctly, that Wanda didn't have a talent for the instrument.

'It's not just piano,' Wanda had replied brightly. 'The list of things I don't have a talent for is quite impressive.'

Miss Pullen had fingered the plastic pearls she always wore around her neck and exclaimed, quite prophetically as it turned out, 'Don't worry dear, they will always need shop girls.'

Wanda rounded the corner into Iron Gate. There was a familiar sight, enough to make her smile. The old Polish Cavalry Man was riding down Irongate as he often did. His horse, General Max, was well groomed, coat shining, tail combed. The Cavalry Man himself wore a brown cap, a tweed jacket and riding trousers. Every day, he rode General Max from Markeaton Park into town – a well-known Derby eccentric and a true gentleman. He doffed his cap to Wanda as he clip-clopped past. '*Dzien dobry,*' he called. Wanda waved a greeting.

She reached the cafe and pushed the glass door open. Searching over the heads of the clientele, she eventually spotted Pam in the corner, checking her make-up in a little compact mirror. Wanda, feeling hot and sweaty, clumsily made her way through the tables and chairs, knocking someone's knife and fork onto the floor as she went. Pam looked up at the resulting clatter.

'Sorry I'm late, Pam,' said Wanda, breathing heavily. 'Mum was delayed and she's looking after Anna. I hope you haven't been waiting long.'

'No, not long,' said Pam with pursed lips. 'I've already ordered. I always have coffee and a doughnut when I come here so that's what I've got for you too – my treat.'

'Well, I'm usually a tea body but it's nice to have coffee for a change,' agreed Wanda. She took off her coat and sat down. She could feel the sweat running down her back. Looking around, she saw the usual selection of old ladies, a few young couples and two mums trying to keep their small children quiet and on their seats.

'I just saw the Cavalry Man and General Max. He's always so well turned out – he took his cap off for me. He's the only man who's ever done that,' said Wanda.

'Oh, yes. I read the Council were trying to stop him riding his horse in the park and in town,' said Pam. 'They said it contravened some stupid law or other. Anyway, everyone protested and told the Council to let him do as he wants – God, he's not hurting anyone, is he?'

'No, he came through the war and everything. I sure he has a heroic story to tell,' said Wanda taking off her cardigan and fanning herself with her hand.

'So, it's nice to see you. How is Anna?' Pam closed her compact with a click and put it in her leather handbag. 'She must be about three now.'

'She's four. She's lovely, obviously,' replied Wanda fiddling with the serviette. 'A real little doll.'

'You're so lucky,' said Pam quietly.

The waitress arrived with tall glasses of milky coffee and two jam doughnuts. Wanda felt her mood lift at the sight of them. The waitress placed them on the table with the bill near Pam.

'You know, I remember years ago going to the Polish club one Sunday with you and we had doughnuts. What are they called in Polish?' asked Pam.

'*Paczki*. Yes, you hated the Kanapki covered in salami and gherkins but you always loved the sweets.'

'Well, I'm a bit more sophisticated these days. I'd probably like them now.'

She took a sip of her coffee. 'So which school will Anna be going to?'

'St Joseph's where I went for primary. Who knows after that.'

'It's all changed now,' said Pam shaking her head. 'Pinecrest is a further education college. St Cecilia's is still going but you won't want Anna to go there.'

'God no, I hated that place. I felt I was left to rot there for not passing the 11+.'

'My parents couldn't believe I had failed it,' said Pam with a harsh laugh. 'Dad was certain I'd pass, him being a teacher. I think he even appealed against it. I didn't care though. I wasn't much interested in academic life. I wanted to be a model. I did some modelling when I was at the art college. The photography department always wanted me to pose for them. I was actually looking at the pictures from those photo-shoots the other day.'

Wanda looked at Pam: at her eyebrows plucked into a perfect arch, her meticulously applied red lipstick and grey eye shadow, her beautifully styled dark red hair. She was wearing immaculate blue jeans and a crisp white blouse. She always looked so elegant, so unhurried. Wanda tried to imagine herself as a version of Pam. Sitting delicately on her seat, legs neatly crossed, nibbling her food instead of wolfing it down. Wouldn't it be wonderful to look like her? On the other hand, though, Pam did have to get into bed with Derek every night.

Wanda stuffed the doughnut into her mouth and took a slurp of coffee. Pam turned the coffee glass round and round in her hands. She seemed lost in thought.

'I was at the doctor this morning, having tests,' said Pam eventually.

'What for?' asked Wanda, her mouth full of doughnut.

'To find out why I can't get pregnant. I haven't taken contraceptives for two years now and – nothing. So far they can't find anything wrong.'

Wanda swallowed her doughnut. She was surprised and flattered that Pam was opening up to her like this. 'Is Derek having tests too?' she said licking the sugar off her fingers.

'No way, I haven't even told him I'm having them. He wouldn't want to talk about it. He'd never go for tests – he'd just say if we don't have children then it wasn't meant to be.'

'But there are things you can do about that these days. Have you heard about test tube babies? I was reading about them in the paper. Why not look into that?'

'That would mean talking to Derek and as I said he wouldn't agree. The thing is, I'm so sick and tired of every dream going wrong for me.'

Wanda paused, a morsel of doughnut halfway to her mouth.

'I wanted to be a model and live in Paris, I wanted to marry a tall, dark handsome stranger,' continued Pam. 'Instead look what happened. None of that came true. Why should I give up on my dream of having a baby?'

'No, well, you shouldn't give up on it. It will probably happen eventually.' Wanda said. 'But then - you do go on fantastic holidays with Derek. You went to Paris last year, didn't you? I suppose you could still be a model. It's harder to do all that when you have a baby.'

'I can't be a model, Derek wouldn't like it. He wouldn't want other men looking at me,' she looked out of the window at the shoppers passing by the window of the cafe. 'Anyway, it's a baby I want.'

Pam slowly and daintily cut her doughnut with a fork and jam oozed out like thick blood onto the plate. Wanda was already wiping the final crumbs of her doughnut from her lips.

'I was sorting out the cupboards at home the other day and found some old photo albums,' said Pam suddenly smiling. 'There were pictures taken at your house in the early 60s. Your grandmother was in one picture – God, I was always so afraid of her. There's another one of you, me and Zosia sitting on the sofa watching television. You are biting your nails with excitement – I wonder what we were watching?'

'Probably *Dr Who*. I used to get so excited I could hardly bear it. Sometimes I even had to go out of the room.'

'My dad was always taking home movies in those days,' said Pam. 'Do you remember? He loved his amateur films. I'm sure he's got some film of us larking around when we were kids. I must get him to look them out one day. It might be nice for your mum to see film of Zosia.'

Wanda smiled but felt unsure if her mother would like it or if the torrent of grief would simply be set off again.

'If there was one person I always envied it was Zosia,' said Pam shaking her head. 'I used to copy the way she did her hair and the clothes she wore. It was so sad, what happened.'

Wanda looked down at her orange jumper and red trousers. Shit - she had put on clashing colours again. Why couldn't she remember to dress in an organised way instead of wearing anything that came to hand? The trousers were too small and were pinching round her hips and she was aware they kept riding down at the back to reveal the top of her bottom. *Somewhere to park your bike, as they used to say at school.*

'Yes, Zosia was lovely all right. I'm sure everyone thought the wrong sister had died,' said Wanda with a small laugh.

'Don't be silly,' said Pam quickly. 'No one thought that. She was pretty but sometimes a little – odd. Do you remember that time a bird flew in the window and got trapped in your kitchen? Zosia went crazy with fear, screaming and crying.'

'Oh yes, I'd forgotten that. It was a sweet little blue tit. It actually managed to shit in the milk jug – direct hit! The bird was terrified too. Daddy calmed it and carefully cupped it in his hand and took it outside.'

'He's a lovely man, your dad. He grew all your vegetables in the garden, didn't he? I remember picking raspberries with you. We held out our skirts and put the raspberries in them. My mum went mad and hit me because my dress was all stained red.'

'Dad still grows food but not so much. He has started making beer at home now,' said Wanda.

'I remember once Zosia saying to him when he came in to the kitchen with muddy hands, 'What a peasant you are!' She was a bit hoity-toity sometimes.' Pam laughed.

'She could be a little bitch, it's true. Funny thing is, you'll think I'm going mad, but I keep seeing her around the house – only in my mind obviously. I remember her standing on the stairs, or at the sink or sitting on the sofa. It's really weird, like a waking dream. Sometimes I call Anna 'Zosia' by mistake. I try not to because there is such pain on my mum's face when I do that.'

'I wonder how different things would have been if she was still here.' Pam finally took a tiny nibble of her doughnut.

Chapter 7

'We've had some big orders cancelled which is worrying. Even The Stepp House Hotel has stopped their order for colour brochures, some loyalty, eh! They wouldn't have done it if Reg had still been alive.' Derek Hoar handed John the year's accounts. On the wood-panelled wall of Allsop's main office hung a portrait of Reg, flanked by portraits of his father, his grandfather and his great grandfather. A decanter full of whisky and four crystal tumblers stood on a silver tray on the sideboard.

'I've made a business plan so we can cut some costs but not make any redundancies,' Derek continued. 'I think that's what Reg would have done.' He took off his glasses and wiped the lenses on a handkerchief.

John flicked through the folder. 'I'll read it at home. I saw in the *Telegraph* today that unemployment has just hit three million,' he said.

'I know and we don't need to contribute to it. You'll find all my ideas documented there. We still have to pay back the loan on those new vans and the two cars, you bought,' said Derek.

John felt the blood rise to his face with annoyance.

'If I have to make redundancies then I will. I do not run a charitable institution, Derek. We have 35 employees – there must be some dead wood there. This business was given to me and I won't let it go under. We can't make the necessary savings by getting cheaper biscuits or switching off the lights more often.' John paused, smiled and tapped Derek on the chest with the folder. 'Don't worry, I wasn't thinking about your job.'

'No – well, that's good.' Derek laughed unconvincingly.

'The main thing is we must keep the print unions out of our business,' said John. 'I've heard rumblings that a couple of our workers are trying to get them in. If they succeed, that's the end of Allsop's. I'll do everything I can to stop that.'

'They are only trying to get the union in because they're worried for their jobs,' said Derek slowly.

John looked at him and narrowed his eyes.

'You are with me in this, aren't you, Derek? I need to have you on board,' he said. 'I need to know I can trust you.'

'Yes, of course. I'm on board, definitely. You can trust me.'

Derek looked away and up at the portrait of Reg. John followed his gaze and pursed his lips.

'I've been reading this new magazine about computers,' John continued. 'I'm looking into investing in new technology. There are modern typesetting machines around now. Do you know about them?'

'No, I don't. I'm a bit behind with the latest ideas.'

'Well I want you to find out about them – cost, efficiency savings, training etc. We must move on,' said John pushing the magazine across the table towards Derek.

'Yes, of course.' Derek picked it up and looked at the back cover.

'Anyway, I'm off.' John held the folder to his chest. 'See you tomorrow, Derek.'

'Actually, John, you couldn't give me a lift home, could you? My car's in the garage – Pam gave me a lift this morning and I rang home for her to collect me but there was no answer.'

'Sure – and you can see my new purchase while we're at it.'

John and Derek walked out to the car park and John pointed out his dark green Jaguar XJ.

They got in and John proudly stroked the beige leather seats. It had that lovely new car smell. He took a tape of Elton John's *Goodbye Yellow Brick Road* out of its cover and popped it in the cassette player. They drove out of the gates, the indicators making a soft ticking noise as they waited to

turn right and John softly sang *Bennie and the Jets* along with
the tape.

'By the way, thanks for giving my dad that decorating
work at your house,' said John as he stopped at the lights on
Osmaston Rd.

'How is his business going? Must be tough in these days
of recession,' said Derek.

John glanced at Derek. He always had the feeling that
Derek didn't think he was up to running things at Allsop's.
Derek had a business degree from Loughborough
University, accountancy qualifications and recently, while
researching his family tree, discovered he was a direct
descendant of Obadiah Stepp's eldest daughter Margaret. A
Derby man for generations. It made John feel like a parvenu,
a cuckoo in the nest.

'It's doing well,' said John stiffly. 'Pawel, my brother-in-
law, works with Dad. The other day he asked me if there
was a job going at Allsop's but I told him we had a
recruitment freeze. He should stick to painting, in my
opinion.'

'He's lucky he has a job. Things are only going to get
worse with this government,' said Derek.

'I think Mrs Thatcher is doing the right thing if not the
popular thing.'

They drove in silence for a while. It would be better to
have someone younger, more dynamic in Derek's job John
thought. But he decided it was too much to consider at the
moment. One battle at a time.

'Your house is at the end of this road, isn't it?'

John watched as Derek got out and walked over to his
house. Pam was standing at the front door wearing a red
jumper and tight blue jeans. She's really tasty, John thought.
She spotted Derek and looked surprised, holding her head
stiffly as her husband kissed her on the cheek. John smiled.
They were an odd couple – Derek would have to be at least
10 years old than her if not more and he wasn't anyone's
idea of a heart-throb. They had no children. What was the
story there, John wondered.

As he drove back down the street, he thought back to his
childhood when Pam Haines, as she then was, used to come

round to see Wanda. Pam always used to complain about the food. His grandmother, who had lovingly made the bigos or whatever they were having, called Pam a peasant when she made a face at the traditional fare. As the insult had been delivered in Polish, Pam had never understood it but John vividly remembered Wanda going bright red and looking furious. Funny thing, he seemed to remember his grandmother saying the words in English – a language she never spoke. He must have translated the words from Polish over time in his head.

John turned the car left into Highfield Road. He saw Pawel heading towards his white van and getting in. John tooted his horn but Pawel seemed preoccupied and didn't see him.

Chapter 8

In that strange twilight period between waking and sleeping, dreams are often particularly vivid. Wanda had nodded off on the sofa in the sitting room while her daughter played on the floor. Wanda was having a familiar dream, a version of which she'd been having for years. Her sister Zosia was standing over her, pointing at some names on a list and shouting that they had got the wrong person, the wrong sister had died. Wanda had to tell them about the mistake, she had to admit Zosia should be alive and Wanda should be dead. Zosia was more useful to the world – the mistake had to be rectified. Wanda awoke with a start, and glanced at her watch – 3.30pm.

Anna was putting on a tea party for her toys. Wanda looked over at her daughter, watching but not seeing. The dreams always had a deep effect on her. She was consumed with thoughts about the fragility of life. Her sister, Zosia, full of vitality, intelligence, beauty had been reduced to dust by a microscopic fragment of botulin bacterium concealed in a piece of rotten meat. John Lennon was destroyed because some lunatic had shot raging metal through his soft, yielding flesh and torn apart his internal organs. No one was safe. Wanda realised her daughter was speaking to her.

'Mummy, I said look at my tea party. Do you like it?'

Wanda sat up and looked at the tartan-clad clown, the white rabbit and Tiny Tears doll sitting in a circle on the carpet. At the head of the group, sitting in prominence on a toy chair, was Lalka. She had long blonde hair, blue eyes and a stupid porcelain face. Lalka had always been a special doll. The floor was good enough for the clown, the rabbit and Tiny Tears but Lalka needed her own chair.

Anna had placed a plastic plate and cup in front of each toy. The red teapot was in the centre of the group with a large plate of coloured bricks as cakes. She carefully poured imaginary tea into the cups and placed the pretend cakes on the plates explaining to the toys that they must eat in a tidy way without making any crumbs.

Lalka, her delicate shoes poking out from under her satin dress, had been a seventh birthday present to Zosia from Babcia. Wanda had never been allowed to touch her. As Wanda watched Anna stroke Lalka's long hair, she could also see Zosia, a little comb in her hand, smooth down the doll's hair. Zosia then looked up at Wanda with her clear green eyes. No, it was Anna looking at her, not Zosia.

Wanda turned away and gazed out of the sitting room window. She groaned in dismay. Her brother's wife Maxine had pulled up in her Austin Princess. The car door opened and Maxine lumbered out. She opened the rear door and three-year-old Clarke barged past her and ran up to the gate, bashing it with his Action Man toy. Maxine reached inside the car, her bottom sticking out towards the house, as she undid Amber's car seat.

Wanda rose and slowly went to open the front door.

'Maxine, what a lovely surprise. It's nice when people can be spontaneous like this, isn't it?' She painted a smile on her face as Maxine walked up to the door, holding Amber in one arm and her bag in the other.

'Oh, yes – that's what I think. Clarke, wait a minute before you rush in. How are you, Wanda? Can you hold Amber a minute?'

Maxine plonked her daughter in Wanda's arms. Amber was a lumpen child with an odd-shaped head. The huge strawberry birthmark on her cheek seemed to be glowing pink. Her nappy obviously needed changing and her nose wanted wiping.

Maxine searched in her bag as they walked into the sitting room. 'I brought you some chocolate Hobnobs to have with our tea. Clarke don't kick Anna's tea party. Look, you dropped your Action Man.'

Anna had retreated to the corner of the room, clutching Lalka to her chest. Clarke stamped on the teacups and kicked over the other toys. 'Kill the dolls, kill the dolls,' he shouted.

'Clarke, come on, here's your Coke – let's find a cup for you.'

'Maxine, I think Amber needs changing,' said Wanda pulling a face.

'She smells of pooh, she smells of pooh, she's smells of shitty, shitty, shitty, shitty, pooh,' sang Clarke.

'You get the kettle on, I'll change her nappy and Clarke can play with Anna,' said Maxine.

She disappeared to the bathroom with Amber. Wanda put Lalka on a high shelf and took Anna's hand to lead her to the kitchen so she wouldn't be left alone with Clarke. When Maxine eventually joined her in the kitchen, the tea was in the pot and the biscuits on the plate.

'That's better,' said Maxine. 'Clarke, play nicely. He's so excited about being here.'

Maxine opened the fridge and got the milk out. She sniffed it.

'I think the milk might be on the turn. There's nothing worse than off milk, is there?' she said brightly.

'Oh, I don't know – rectal cancer might be a bit of a downer,' mumbled Wanda.

'Do you want a biscuit, Clarke? Come here darling,' called Maxine. 'Don't push Amber over – just leave her be.'

They went into the sitting room, Wanda carrying the tray of drinks, and sat down on the sofa. Wanda always struggled for something to speak to her sister-in-law about. Maxine dismissed much conversation with a 'that will work itself out' manner. Anna clambered onto Wanda's knee and lay against her bosom, playing with her necklace.

Clutching as straws, Wanda asked, 'Is Amber sleeping through the night yet?' She wasn't remotely interested in the answer.

'No, she's up every three hours. John said we should let her cry but I can't do that. He sleeps in the spare room when he's had enough.'

'How is my little brother?' inquired Wanda smiling. 'Coping with the world of printing? I saw one of Allsop's new vans in town the other day. I was curious about the letters PMS on the side.'

'Yes, it stands for Printing Made Simple'

So not premenstrual syndrome, thought Wanda.

'Was that Janek's idea?' she said out loud.

'Yes, and he designed the new logo. John is doing so well at the firm – daddy always said he would.'

Wanda shifted Anna a little on her knee, she was getting heavy. She looked down at Amber who was on the flooring sucking a biscuit. Bits of soggy mess fell on her pink gingham dress. Clarke had disappeared upstairs – Wanda couldn't bear to think what he was doing. She looked back at Maxine who was dunking her biscuit in her tea.

'Well, the brat has always been ambitious,' said Wanda eventually. She'd got the impression from Pam that Derek was not too enamoured of the way Janek was running things.

'I always wondered,' said Maxine with a harsh little laugh, 'do you call John 'brat' because he was spoilt as a child?'

'Well, yes, I suppose so. Zosia called him that first – it's a word play as brat is also brother in Polish.' She paused. 'We thought it was funny at the time.'

Maxine stared at her. 'It's strange, you know John never talks about Zosia. When I first met him, she'd only died a few years earlier and I didn't like to pry too much. Now if I mention her he just says, "She's dead, that's the end of it." Did he get on with her?'

Wanda tried to remember how Zosia had treated Janek, indeed how she'd treated everyone in the family. The swish of her plaits, the way she turned up her nose, her precise little fingers. She seemed to treat everyone in the family, apart from Babcia, with equal disdain.

'I don't know really as I was working in London for much of the time they were little,' said Wanda. 'I suppose people often don't get on with their siblings at that stage. I'm sure they would have done later – if she'd lived.' She shrugged. 'I don't why he doesn't talk about her but he was terrified by her death – well, we all were. It was too much, we couldn't handle it. She was only 18.'

'And she was so lovely,' said Maxine looking at a picture of Zosia on the mantelpiece. It had been taken when Zosia was 16. Her long dark hair was hanging down over her slim-fitting lilac top. She was smiling, holding a copy of her O level results.

'So beautiful and your mum says she was so clever with such high expectations,' continued Maxine brightly. 'Funny isn't it? She was nothing like you.'

'None taken,' murmured Wanda into her cup.

'You'd never have known you two were even sisters. Clarke, what are you doing?' she called, as they heard a crash from upstairs. She made no effort to get up and see what he'd broken.

Wanda looked down at her tea. 'No, Zosia and I had nothing in common, absolutely nothing. I sometimes felt she wasn't really my sister.' Wanda looked round the room. And yet, she thought, I keeping imagining her around the house. Perhaps I'm going mad?

'I was always desperate for a sister – or a brother,' said Maxine. 'Anyone. At least you still have John. But anyway we are so blessed to have children of our own. I was at John's office the other day and Pam came in to see Derek. Poor soul has no children. She may have a lovely waist, immaculate hair and a manicure but it doesn't compensate for a baby, does it?'

Wanda shrugged her shoulders and didn't answer.

'She's always... well a little rude to John, a bit, I don't know.. Do you like her?'

An old memory came into Wanda's mind as she considered the question. It was one morning at school assembly when they were all lined up waiting for the headmistress to come in. Pam had turned around and suddenly started shrieking with laughter and pointing at Wanda's feet. Wanda had looked down and saw she was wearing one black, lace-up school shoe and one silver party shoe. Everyone else starting laughing too. The heat of humiliation had risen to her cheeks. This, though, had been as nothing compared to the shame of that evening when she'd been wearing white trousers to the school disco and her period had suddenly started....

Wanda looked back at Maxine. 'I like Pam but most people find her... a bit hard, caustic. She was known as Vinegar Tits at school.'

The phone rang and they both jumped. Wanda got up to answer it. There was a crackling sound on the other end and an exaggerated delay.

'I want to speak to Wanda Lato,' said a muffled, distant voice in Polish.

'Yes, speaking.'

'Good afternoon, this is Aleksander Lato, Pawel's father.'

Wanda stood stock-still, unable to speak for a moment. There was more interference on the line.

'Am I speaking to the right person?' said the voice.

'Yes, you are. Sorry, I'm a little surprised. So you got my letter. Where are you speaking from – Gdansk?'

Wanda noticed Maxine look over with a cross expression. She hated to hear Polish, to be reminded of her husband's non-British origins.

'No, I'm in Warsaw actually. It was difficult making this phone call. I went to see Irena to get your phone number.'

Wanda could hardly take it in. Pawel's father was actually speaking to her. Her letter had got through, it was the right person. A small thrill went through her body.

'Oh God, so you're with Irena – that's good, good,' Wanda couldn't conceal her astonishment. 'How long is it since you last saw her?'

'A long time! We had some catching up to do. I also decided to reclaim my art work and start sculpting again.'

'Sculpting? I didn't know you were an artist – I thought you were a – well – a docker or something.'

Aleks laughed. 'Have you told Pawel you contacted me?'

'No, sorry, he doesn't know. I never found the moment to tell him.'

'So, what do you want me to do? Listen, I'm hoping to get to London. I have a contact there. If I can make it, I'll phone you again. Hopefully I can see Pawel. I did send him a few cards and presents over the years. I thought about him, of course. I saw some pictures of him, you and Anna at Irena's yesterday.'

'Will you be allowed to come to this country? Is there anything I can do to help?' asked Wanda.

'Yes, actually there is. Could you send me a letter of invitation? It must state your relationship to me, where you live and that you will support me. Don't worry, I won't turn up there unannounced – it's just something I'll need for the Embassy here. Write copies in English and Polish. They want to know I won't be a burden to them.'

Wanda tried desperately to make notes on the little pad of paper that was always kept next to the phone. Holding the pencil in her left hand she made some illegible scrawls.

'I can do that. Shall I send it to Irena's flat? Is it ok to put your name on the envelope?'

'That would be excellent. Thank you, dear Wanda. Also perhaps you would be able to put some English money in with the letter – just to help with my application. A little hard currency here and there makes life easier in Poland. Let's just hope no one steals it, eh?'

'Yes, of course, I can do that.'

There was a silence as Wanda wondered what Aleks looked like, how similar he was to Pawel. His voice, it seemed familiar somehow.

'I will be in touch again – when I get to London…'

'Good luck with that, good luck.' She put the phone down.

'Who was that?' asked Maxine.

Wanda paused.

'Just my dad,' she said.

Chapter 9

Derwentside was a five-bedroom, detached mock Tudor mansion with a black and white façade and fake Elizabethan windows. The gravel drive was lined with rhododendron bushes; purple clematis wound its way round the porch over the front door. Reg Allsop had had the original Victorian house pulled down and designed the current residence himself in 1953. As a local councillor, he had no problem getting planning permission. Reg had installed a huge snooker table in the basement, with a drinks bar and darts board. He loved to have colleagues over for an evening of games. 'Good way to forge partnerships,' he'd told his son-in-law.

As John drove up and parked the car in the adjoining garage, he took a deep breath, anticipating the usual uproar at home. No doubt Clarke would be demanding ice cream while bashing baby Amber on the head with a toy brick. She in turn would be purple in the face and screaming. John's mother-in-law Lily would be trying to watch *Coronation Street* and turning the volume louder and louder as the noise levels increased. In the midst of this turmoil, a relaxed and oblivious Maxine was often to be found fixing curtains on the kitchen window or stencilling a flower motif above the dado rail.

Maxine subscribed to countless magazines called *Stitching, Rag-Rolling, Easy Stencils* or *Make Your Own Cuddly Toys*. The dining table was always covered in patterns, scissors, glitter, glue, little paint pots and bits of felt. Every evening she sat watching telly knitting outfits for the children or huge jumpers for John.

However, when John got to his front door this time, all was strangely silent. He wiped his feet thoroughly on the mat and went into the sitting room. Lily was asleep, open mouthed in her armchair by the fire. The television was showing an old episode of *Inspector Morse*. John walked to the kitchen, opened the fridge and took out a bottle of white wine. He poured himself a large glass then noticed a piece of paper on the kitchen table propped up against a book called *Prince Charles and Lady Diana Spencer: A Royal Wedding*. The note read:

Gone to see Wanda. Clarke wants to play with Anna. Hugs and kisses, Maxi x

John heart sank a little. He could picture Wanda's stony face as Maxine talked about her mothers' group, their new lounge carpet, and plans for a Royal Wedding street party. Maxine was always keen for the cousins to play together. John had tactfully tried to point out that Anna and Clarke were two very different personalities but Maxine hadn't taken the hint. John sighed. Well, at least he was off the hook for while and he could enjoy the house in peace. He went up to the bedroom to change.

The pink bed quilt was covered with scores of tiny cushions on which Maxine had embroidered the words *Home Sweet Home*. Her cuddly toys were arranged along the headboard and the quilted pig that contained her nightie and dressing gown was placed on her pillow.

John pulled off his tie and jacket and found a jumper in his drawer. He put on his fluffy brown slippers, a Christmas present from Maxine, and walked into the en suite bathroom. The walls had been painted red with thin white veins meant to resemble marble but instead they looked like slabs of raw meat. There were matching basins with gold taps, the spout in the shape of a swan. John reasoned it was Maxine's father's money, so she could have her rag-rolled doors, raw meat walls and gold swan taps. Since having children, she'd shown no interest in the business.

As he walked back downstairs, a voice croaked from below,

'Is that you, John, love? Maxine's at your sister's. She'll be back before 8 because it's the *Kenny Everett Show* tonight. Actually no, is it Tuesday today? Maybe it's *Brideshead Resisted*? I can't remember.'

'Hello Lily,' said John. 'Have you had your tea?'

'Maxine left a fish pie for us – I can put it in the oven if you like. Shall I get you an orange squash, love?'

'I'm on the wine already, Lily. Actually maybe I'll have a gin and tonic. Heavy day at the office. Times are hard.'

Lily pulled her beige cardigan tightly round herself. 'Ah, don't fret, love. Reg always used to say, 'Early to bed, early to rise, work hard and advertise'. Have you heard that? Follow that and you can't go far wrong. Reg was always quoting little antidotes like that. ' Lily wandered towards the kitchen.

John smiled. 'I thought it was, 'Early to bed, early to rise, work hard, inherit a fortune."

'Well, you did, love, didn't you?' said Lily looking back at him.

John absentmindedly walked to the sideboard and poured a double gin with a splash of tonic. He sat down in front of the television, brooding. He'd seen this episode of *Morse* before – it was the vicar who'd done it. John turned his G&T round and round in his hands. What if people found out he didn't know what he was doing? The important thing was not to let people know he was out of his depth. He mustn't lose their respect. He'd overheard Derek on the phone to Pam saying, 'What does he know about anything – he's only 12.' John could only assume the remark had been directed at him. So that was how he was viewed – a boy in a man's job.

He looked up at the clock on the mantelpiece. A picture of Maxine in her pink and gold wedding dress took pride of place. A portrait photo of the children, dressed in their best clothes and embracing each other was next to it. How on earth did the photographer get Clarke to hug his sister, John wondered.

He looked at the Waterford Crystal glass he was drinking from. People would blame him if the firm went bust – a company that had been trading for 150 years. He was only a son-in-law and not a true-born son. John couldn't face the thought of that – he must do everything possible to save the firm, sack people, use cheaper paper, borrow to get more modern machinery – anything.

Chapter 10

The house at 16 Porton Crescent was silent and Helena felt a little thrill of pleasure at being alone. She crept upstairs to her study and quietly closed the door behind her. She had furnished the little room with a large desk, swivel chair, anglepoise lamp, plenty of book shelves and a small typewriter. The old bed, wardrobe and chest of drawers had been removed. It was a proper academic study. Helena sat down and tied her long hair up in a knot on top of her head with both hands. She took up the letter and began reading. It was handwritten in blue ink with a fountain pen on azure notepaper.

Warsaw, 18 March 1930

Dearest Nathan and Maria

We are hoping you can come to dinner this Saturday. Of course, we would love you to bring Feddi as well. We think he will enjoy meeting our latest guest! You'll never guess who that is. Bring your violin.

Much love and felicitations, Jan and Antonina

Helena smiled. How sweet - the ordinary business of social activity went on as normal. This little note, a dinner invitation was tucked inside the flap of an old address book. The slim, leather-bound book, provided further clues. Under the Z section, Helena found Zabinski, J&A with an address and telephone number in Ratuszowa Street. Could this be Jan and Antonina? Who was Feddi? She found nothing under F in the address book but she didn't know his surname.

Under the P section, her own mother Mrs Poniatowska (Barbara) was listed. Also her grandparents – Jerzy and Jadwiga Poniatowski residing in – she couldn't read the street name. Under W there was only one Weinberg listed – Miss Weinberg (Sissy). Where were the rest of Nathan's family?

There were several contacts with addresses in Paris (Dr Claude Jobert, rue Victor Hugo, Mme Terese Herbelin, rue Bertin) two in Berlin (seemingly fellow doctors) and one in Madrid. Had Nathan lived in Paris? A page of lined paper torn out of a book had a note in Nathan's handwriting written in French.

Other addresses appeared to be tradesmen (L. Turek, 'good cleaner', S Gonek, chimneysweep).

Helena was slowly putting the jigsaw together, the minutiae of his life, piece by piece, but she had discovered nothing new.

Almost reluctantly, she went back to her PhD thesis. Her chosen subject was Interviewing Techniques in the Study of Schizophrenia. She noticed there was a high proportion of Polish immigrants among the patients with schizophrenia and it seemed to her the trauma of the war had exacerbated this problem. She'd spoken to 15 inmates in mental hospitals in Derby, Nottingham, Birmingham and Manchester but she was drawn particularly to one elderly man named Lukasz Politowski residing in the Kingsley Hospital in Derby. His sister Teresa visited him every week. Helena had seen Teresa at church and occasionally in the Polish club in the old days but she didn't know her well. Her brother had wild grey hair, staring eyes and exaggerated almost comical way of speaking. He would say something ridiculous, after which Helena would struggle not to laugh, and then follow it with something that sounded almost lucid, even profound. She switched on her tape recorder and began listening to her last interview.

There was a crackling sound before the talking began. Her own familiar voice started after a brief moments then the deep, halting tones of her patient.

Helena Baran speaking to Lukasz Politowski, aged 68, on 22 August 1981 at Kingsley Hospital, Derby

HB: Do you remember the time before you went into the sanitorium in Krakow – before the war?

LP: Sometimes I remember, sometimes not. I was at home with my father and his wife. My mother was drowned – they took away all the pictures of her, they burnt all her clothes. I had her pillowcase to sleep with. It had her initials embroidered on. She, that woman, tugged it from my hands to put on the fire. I tried to pull it back but she was too strong.

HB: Was that your father's second wife?

LP: She was a witch not a woman. I know she could fly and she made potions in the kitchen.

HB: She wouldn't let you keep the pillowcase?

LP: I loved it because it still smelled of my mother. I never washed it. That witch said it was a dirty filthy thing but it wasn't. The pillowcase had magic power and the witch was afraid of it.

HB: What happened after that?

LP: I used to go to her wardrobe and make a tiny rip in her clothes. For months, years I made little cuts in her dresses and blouses.

HB: Did she find out it was you?

LP: She hit my sister with the hairbrush, hard across the face. She thought Teresa was ripping her clothes. Teresa was denying it and the woman was hitting her and pulling her hair and dragging her to my father's study.

HB: Did you own up to it?

LP: I had this strange impression suddenly – when they were screaming and struggling. I thought I was outside my body – I had the idea that my body was an automaton and I was controlling it from somewhere else. I could watch myself.

HB: What did you watch yourself do?

LP: I came up behind the witch with a heavy vase and hit her on the head – very hard. She fell down screaming and my father ran out of his study. There was blood everywhere. Father pushed me and kicked me.

HB: What happened next?

LP: They put me in this place with white walls and long corridors. It was in the country. There were people there who could tie you to the bed and put electricity in your head.

HB: Did that help? Did you feel better?

LP: It hurt. Everything hurt.

HB: Do you remember the German soldiers coming? They took everyone in the sanitorium to Auschwitz didn't they?

LP: I decided to make my automaton normal – I could control it so it said the things they wanted to hear. I could make it act like them.

HB: So what happened?

LP: There was a man there and he said I could look after his suits and put them out on his bed. His wife was there and the children. They let me polish his shoes, iron his shirts, run his bath. I could make the automaton do all these things. But if I showed the automaton's true face – I would be put in the oven like the others.

HB: Did you live in their house?

LP: I had a little room at the top. On the wall was a picture of a scene in the country – a winding path, a little stream, sheep, and a shepherd learning against the tree. I used to imagine I could go down that little path.

HB: Were there any doctors in the camp? Did they ever come to the house – perhaps when the children were sick? Did you meet a man called Dr Weinberg? Here is his picture.

(There is a long pause in the interview)

LP: There was an orchestra. They played every morning. She loved the music – the lady did. She said it made the world better.

HB: So you were protected from what went on in the camp. Did you know what was happening in there?

LP: When you are mad, no one expects you to know anything.

Chapter 11

Warsaw, 1981

Aleksander woke up confused, in a strange bed. He couldn't think for a while where he was – then realised there was a warm, soft body next to him. He was with Irena, in Irena's flat, in Irena's bed. She was curled up asleep next to him. Their dinner and long, emotional conversation of the night before came back to him with a jolt. Before he could think too clearly, she woke too.

'Good morning, husband,' she said softly. Husband - a shocking word but technically true. Throughout the long years of privations, back-breaking work, and struggle, Irena and Aleksander were still, in fact, married. They had never got round to getting a divorce.

Last night they had touched on all the raw subjects: why had he left (he'd felt trapped, unable to accept the responsibility); why had he made so little effort to keep in touch, almost never sending Pawel presents (he thought a clean break was better so as not to upset the boy); had he had other women (yes, but Irena was the only one he'd married, the only one he had a child with, the only he had properly loved); what had happened to the other women (he'd left them as well).

Astonishingly, Irena had seemed happy with those answers and they'd ended up in bed.

'Shall I get you some breakfast, darling?' Irena said. Aleks nodded, terrified that Irena sounded like a woman in love again. She smiled at him, pulled on her dressing gown and went to the kitchen.

He sat up against the headboard, lit a cigarette and looked round the drab little room. How depressing. It hadn't changed much in two decades. There was a picture of Mira, his formidable mother-in-law, next to the bed alongside a photo of her husband Witold, a war hero whom Aleks had never known. There was also a picture of Irena taken just after the war, wearing her Young Communist uniform.

Aleks looked at the other objects in the room: a little brown wardrobe, dressing table, rug and chest of drawers - all so familiar. The threadbare, brown curtains were the same ones that had hung there since the war. The only change was the new television and a radio in the kitchen. This was how Irena thought people should live.

Irena came back into the bedroom with a tray of crusty bread rolls, cold ham, radishes, sliced cheese, tea and stewed fruit. Food was in short supply again, the queues outside the shops were ridiculous, but Irena had managed to conjure up a little feast on a tray.

'They said on the radio that the government was talking to Solidarity again. What do you think will happen? The government won't give in, will they?' said Irena.

'No, the Soviets won't let them give too much. If they do, all the other little satellite states will be wanting it as well.' He sat up, broke open a bread roll and began buttering it.

'I'm scared they will send the tanks in.'

'If it came to that, surely our soldiers will defend Poland against the Russians. Just like they always did!' said Aleks giving her a sideways glance.

Irena chewed her bottom lip looking thoroughly confused and miserable.

Aleks sat up straight, put the tray on the side table, suddenly animated. 'Listen, Irena, let's get out! It's all crumbling here. You know that one day we'll turn on the radio or TV and all they'll be broadcasting is bloody Chopin all day - then we'll know we're fucked'.

'Get out where?'

'Out of the country. Go to England. We can be near Pawel and our granddaughter. What do you think? It's a fantastic idea. What do you say?' Aleks was smiling broadly.

Irena frowned. 'What about my job? The hospital depends on me. I can't just leave.'

'They'll get someone else. I just left the shipyard, walked out - so what? No one is indispensable. They always think they are – but it's never true. The hospital will manage. What do you say? Let's go!'

Let her say yes, for once in her life let her be adventurous, spontaneous, rebellious. He stared hopefully into her eyes.

'But things are getting so difficult now for the children in the hospital,' said Irena slowly. 'As a result of sanctions by the capitalists, there's a shortage of supplies. We have to keep re-using needles, masks, washing bandages – I have to help with that. They need my expertise.'

'You could retrain in London.'

'I can't speak English – don't be ridiculous. What work could I do? Be a cleaner, sew trousers like my cousin used to do, wash dishes. No, at least here I have some dignity.' Irena's voice rose to a pitch and she turned and sat with her back to him. 'It's cowardly to leave our country when we're needed.'

'Listen, my father always said you should look after number one. You don't need to hurt others but you should always make sure you're all right. He used to make illegal vodka. It meant we had enough money so we could all eat. You make your own luck in this world.'

'Vodka! What good is that to anyone? I see so many children brought in the hospital because their parents are addicted to vodka. They are mentally impaired, or malnourished, beaten or hurt in accidents because their parents are too drunk to care. You think your father never hurt anyone? How many people did his illegal vodka kill, eh?'

Aleks sat looking at Irena's turned back and then leaned forward towards her.

'You're lonely here on your own, aren't you?' he said rubbing her shoulder.

'Yes, but…. I can't go to a foreign country. I'm too old.'

'You're 55 – that's not old for God's sake. Didn't your aunt Barbara go to England when she was much older than you? Give it a try. I have contacts, they will help. Who knows what the Soviets will do. We may all be killed here. Think of Pawel, think of little Anna.'

Irena turned to look at him. 'Do you still want me?'

Aleks smiled and held out his arms to her. She put her head on his shoulder.

'Irenka, you were always too good for me – too clever, too beautiful, too idealistic, too honest but yes I still want you. Come on, let's go. It will be our new adventure.' He looked over her head thinking how this might work.

Chapter 12

The family were downstairs watching something funny on television. Helena could hear Wanda roaring with laughter from below. She had spent two hours working on her thesis but her little treat was to look once at the green folder. More scraps of paper:

I just want to let you know, Pan Doctor, that my sinus problem has cleared up.

Pan Doctor, can you give me more of the painkillers I had before.

Here is a little basket of fruit to thank you for your care.

Obviously Dr Weinberg was well regarded.

But it wasn't all work. There were business cards from restaurants:

Imperial Crown,
Fine French Cuisine,
Senatorska St, Warsaw 7

Blikle Café, Nowy Swiat, Warsaw 10
'Where the Artists Eat'

Plus theatre playbills: a revue show at the Morskie Oko and a production of Hamlet at the Narodowy. There was a bill for 50 zloty from the vet (perhaps for the little terrier pictured on Nathan's lap). Two ticket stubs from Warsaw zoo and a leaflet announcing the birth of a rare Indian elephant there were also in the pile. Looking at the small print on the bottom of the leaflet, Helena saw the names Jan and Antonina Zabinksi. Wonderful, Helena thought, she had made a connection. The friends who invited Nathan and Maria to dinner were the directors of the zoo!

Helena remembered going to Warsaw zoo herself as a child and having a ride on an elephant. She had been only five but the excitement of sitting with several other small children on seats strapped to the sides of an enormous creature was a feeling that had always stayed with her.

Other notes in the green folder included numerous shopping lists written in Nathan's small neat hand. He had a habit of underlining certain words: *bread, cheese, newspaper, oil of camphor, bone from the butcher, matches,* salt. Another bit of paper, also written in his hand, read *Show me a sane person and I will cure him for you.'* He was familiar with the writings of Jung.

There were several notes written by his wife Maria. She had huge, illegible handwriting that seemed to consist of a series of 'Es'. On a card decorated with a pressed poppy she had written, *To my beloved Nathan, true to the end.* Maria was also quite a good amateur artist and she'd drawn a few sketches. Two were of Nathan, one of an unknown woman and one of the little dog. Helena then noticed some wording on the medal hanging from the dog's collar. Fetching her magnifying glass, she peered at the drawing. It read 'Feddi.' So, he was the dog! The people at the zoo wanted them to bring their dog to dinner! Helena smiled. She assumed the other guest they mentioned must have been an animal. She felt pleased with herself at making another small breakthrough. This was exciting.

Helena tried to remember who had told her that Nathan had died in Auschwitz – probably her mother. She had not taken much interest at the time as she didn't remember ever meeting him. Had Nathan first been imprisoned in the Warsaw Ghetto? Helena remembered the decrees going round just before the round up of the Jews about a year after the invasion but somehow she hadn't given it too much thought. It felt embarrassing to say so now but she and her mother were too concerned with their own lives. It's easy to be noble with the distance of time and space, but when you're in the midst of it, all you can think about is your own survival and the survival of those you love.

Helena wondered if there were any records kept at Auschwitz that might give a clue as to how Nathan ended his life. Would his name be on a list somewhere along with countless others, would there be any information about how he lived, how he died? What had happened between those happy days of 1920s Warsaw -- of theatre-going, having dinner with friends and treating his patients -- to the world as they knew it ending?

Helena knew Lukasz's sister Teresa had visited Auschwitz just after it was liberated. She might have ideas about how to obtain information on her uncle's death. She telephoned and arranged to pay her a visit.

A few days later, Helena found herself in Teresa's small, Victorian house in Otter Street. The sitting room was filled with photos, ornaments and mementoes. There were pictures of young men in Polish uniform with the traditional square hats, women smiling into the sun as they brought in the harvest, recent colour pictures of laughing babies, little girls in school uniform.

Teresa came in with a tray laden with cheesecake and lemon tea. She set the tray down on the coffee table and took a seat in the armchair. She handed Helena a plate and napkin and offered some poppy-seed cake.

'It's so good of you to take the time to talk to me, Pani Teresa,' said Helena. 'Let me tell you a little of what I'm doing.'

Teresa began pouring the tea. Helena began to speak. She told her about her father's illness, her uncle and his work and how she was trying to find out information. She talked more about her PhD thesis. Helena looked down at the piece of cake resting on the plate on her lap. She collected her thoughts carefully. Then looked back at Theresa and continued.

'My uncle was writing a book called *The Fragmented Mind*. I intend to write a book, with the same title, containing his studies and mine in relation to my PhD thesis. I wonder if you could give me any information about the death camp which might help in my search for him.' Helena paused again, to take a sip of her tea.

Teresa pressed the lemon against the side of her tea cup to extract the juice. She sat in thought for a moment. 'Ever since I witnessed the liberation of Auschwitz, I felt I owed it to the sad people I saw there to tell their story,' said Teresa. 'I went inside to look for my brother but I was so horrified by what I saw, I could never forget it. Millions of Polish Jews and many Polish Catholics were murdered in the camps. How can we ever forget?'

'How did your brother survive?'

'When Lukasz first lost his mind, my father placed him in an asylum near Krakow. He had attacked my step-mother and injured her quite badly. She and my father wanted him out of the way so he was locked away indefinitely. He was 19 when the Nazis invaded and they emptied out the asylum and took all the inmates to Auschwitz. We didn't know what the place was at first. There was a little town there called Oswiecim which had no bad connotations at all before the war. Nowadays just the name Auschwitz inspires such fear. At first, we assumed it was some kind of work camp.'

'You lived quite near - you must have seen train-loads of people arriving and never coming out,' said Helena.

'Yes, we did but that was later. At first we weren't sure.'

'Then you realised what was going on.'

'Yes. We could see the chimneys and smell the smoke. As to your question about how Lukasz survived, I don't know but he did. He was a mad man in a world that had gone totally mad. Perhaps he was the sane one.'

'I believe a shock or trauma can bring on schizophrenia - you never know, perhaps it works in reverse,' said Helena.

'Lukasz was given the job of personal servant to Rudolf Hoess who was the camp commandant. He had to polish his shoes, lay out his clothes – things like that. It's incredible but he actually didn't have too bad a time.'

'It's so hard to imagine that life went on there in some kind of twisted normality.' Helena saw tears in Teresa's eyes.

'Apparently there was a place they called 'Canada' which is where they put all the things the poor people who arrived brought in,' Theresa continued. 'Lukasz was allowed to sort through the stuff and take anything useful.'

'Really? I suppose it operated like a small town with its own gruesome rules. How long was your brother there?'

'All through the war. It's easy for us to be sanctimonious but we never know what we'd do to survive if we were in that position. I don't know exactly what he did as he won't or can't say.'

''My uncle was sent to Auschwitz,' said Helena. 'I presume he was in the Warsaw Ghetto initially, but I'm just guessing.'

Helena felt she was rambling, stupidly trying to find one man in a sea of hopeless humanity. She had absolutely nothing to go on. This was a pointless task.

'You can get the death certificates for certain people, you know,' said Therea. 'Maybe as a doctor he had a special position so there might be some paper work. Are you sure he was sent to Auschwitz? Most of the Warsaw Jews were sent to Treblinka.'

'That's what I heard but I don't know.'

'The Germans kept plenty of documentation so there might be a record of what happened to him. You'd have to go to Poland to find out.'

Helena realised she should talk about Teresa and her experiences otherwise she would appear to be only wrapped up in herself.

'Where did you spend the war, Pani Teresa?'

'I was in Krakow working as a cook in a hotel where German soldiers stayed. At the end of the war, the Russians liberated the camp and I went to find my brother. He was the only family I had left by that time. I couldn't believe it when he was still alive and he didn't look too bad.'

'Do you know anything about the doctors in the camp?'

'There was even an infirmary. Some people survived there. But if your uncle had survived he would have gone back to his wife, wouldn't he?'

'Yes, he would. I just want to know what happened...'

You could find out more if you went there. They have kept it exactly as it was as a museum and a permanent reminder.'

'I don't think I can bear to go,' said Helena.

Chapter 13

Anna Zosia Lato was five years old and it was her first day at school. Wanda had decided to send her daughter to St Joseph's primary school although it was a decision she had agonised over. Should she put her daughter through the same regime to which she had been subjected? She'd been to look at a private school and it seemed like heaven – until she was told the fees. Pawel said gruffly there was no way they could afford it and Anna could go to the local school like everyone else. After all, he said, it hadn't done Wanda any harm, had it?

Wanda had considered that statement. The school hadn't done her any harm. Is that the best that could be said for it? It was true the place was different than it had been in the 1950s – less austere, less strict, much kinder and gentler. In the end she knew she would follow the time-honoured tradition.

Anna had been going to a little playgroup and seemed happy there. What was more, and Wanda hugged this little secret to herself like a forbidden fruit, Anna seemed to be as bright as a button. The child could read at the age of three, she spoke two languages – fluent Polish and English - and she seemed to have a flair for maths. Can you say a five-year-old is good at maths? Anna seemed to be. She always asked what the change was at the shops when Wanda handed over a pound note.

Wanda looked at her daughter dressed in her new blazer, freshly pressed red-checked school dress and her black school shoes. She finished tying Anna's dark hair in two long plaits,

'My blazer has red ribbon all round the edge,' said Anna, fingering the lapels.

'It was the same when I was at school,' replied Wanda. 'And when the cold weather comes you'll wear a dark blue tunic with a white shirt, navy blue cardigan and red tie. You look lovely, Anna. Let me take a picture of you.'

Wanda picked up her little camera and Anna stood straight, arms by her side in a stiff pose. She blinked as the flash went off.

'There, beautiful. Just a minute, before we go I'll show you something.'

Wanda hurried to the bookcase and took out a green photo album. She bent down, opened the book in front of her daughter and pointed to one of the pictures.

'This is me when I was eight and your auntie Zosia when she was the same age as you. It was her first day at school as well.'

'She has brown hair like me but you have yellow hair.'

'Yes, you are very like her. How proud she would be to see you today. Zosia always worked hard, she always paid attention in class and she always got top marks. I want you to be just like auntie Zosia and copy her example. Can you do that, poppet?'

'Yes, mummy.' The little girl nodded with a serious expression.

'Good,' said Wanda, kissing her daughter. 'Best foot forward.'

Holding hands, they walked the well-worn path from Porton Crescent to St Joseph's Primary. Every paving stone, every building, every railing and stretch of water held memories and significance for Wanda. They passed Babcock's Mill, where generations of workers, including her own mother, had spent years hunched over machines. A hundred years previously, little children had spent 14 hours a day crawling around on the floor, picking up pieces of cotton for little pay. It was the slavery on which the industrial revolution had been built. Men had heaved sacks of cotton from the barges on the canal, women had worked at looms and sewing machines. All that work, all that suffering, shouting and crying – now it lay silent.

Wanda looked up at the massive mill chimney. It used to be warm, the heat of power and industry. As children, she and her school friends used to put one hand on the red bricks then look upwards at the top of the tower. An optical illusion gave the odd sensation that the chimney was falling down on the top of them. Wanda could still remember the dizzy feeling, the tingle at the back of the legs.

The tower was now cold and dead. According to the large hoarding, the site was being converted into 'Luxury Apartments'. The canal, still and stagnant with high brick edges, slicked its way past the mill. A duck with five babies in tow made its way through the water down to the town centre.

Wanda glanced across the road. Monks, the little shop where they used to buy their sweets, was now an architect's office. Next to it was a modern block called Derby Design. Once it had been a terraced house where an old woman in slippers and blue housecoat had waited by her front door every morning, watching her grandson head off for school.

There was still a lollypop lady guiding children across the busy road. Wanda thanked her and tugged Anna's hand to do the same. Other children raced and chatted across the road behind them. More were waiting by the school entrance and Wanda recognised a few of the mothers who'd been pupils there too. She smiled and nodded at a few familiar faces.

Wanda and Anna walked through the school door. A picture of the Pope, the Polish Pope, hung on the wall by the reception below a wood and brass crucifix. Wanda glanced in at the gym, refurbished with brand new equipment. The old thick, gurgling radiators had been replaced with slimline white versions and the Lincoln green paint on doors and window frames was now a vibrant red and white.

Some things had not changed, however. Miss Orrell still taught the first class. Wanda led Anna into her old classroom. There were the tiny chairs and tables, the times tables charts on the wall, the play area with the Wendy House, bricks and cuddly toys. The blackboard bore the greeting WELCOME CHILDREN and in front of it stood the teacher - grey hair in a bun, tweed skirt and flat shoes. If you were looking to cast an elderly spinster schoolteacher for a play, you would look no further than this woman.

'She's the same teacher I had,' Wanda whispered to Anna. 'I thought she was 100 back then. But she looks just the same.'

Most of the other children were already seated and their mothers had made their farewells.

'Good morning, Miss Orrell.' Wanda could almost hear herself saying the words in the sing-song voice the class had used when she was five. 'I'm sorry we're a little late.'

'Wanda, so lovely to see you,' said Miss Orrell clasping her hands together. She bent down to Anna's level, smiling.

'And you are…?'

There was a pause. 'I am what?' said Anna eventually.

Wanda pursed her lips to stop from laughing.

'What is your name?'

'Anna.'

'Now then, Anna, let us find you a place to sit - how about here next to Andrew. We'll let Mummy get on with her work – goodbye Mummy - and we will start our school day.'

Wanda nodded and gave her daughter a little wave. She saw tears well up in the little girl's eyes, her cheeks flushed. Wanda knew she had to leave. She felt a parting of sweet sorrow.

As she turned towards the door, Wanda glanced up at the picture of the blue-robed Virgin Mary, hand pointing to her heart pierced by many swords of sorrow. Next to it, hung a picture of the Queen when young, dressed in the same sky blue, a brilliant sash across her breast. As a child, Wanda had often mixed the two women up in her mind.

She walked out of the classroom, leaving Anna for the first time, and closed the door behind her. The familiar smell of the corridor hit her – cooked cabbage from the school canteen sprinkled with the zest of fear. Further down the hall, a little girl was using all her strength to ring the heavy brass bell indicating that classes were beginning. Twenty-five years earlier, Julie Barnes had one day been selected to ring that same bell. She'd declared to Wanda and her other friends that she could do it with just one hand. As she'd left the classroom and gone out in to the corridor, they'd all heard a single clear ring then a discordant thunk as she'd dropped the bell on the concrete floor.

Wanda wandered out through the empty playground past the ash tree they used to play around. She paused, looking up at its huge branches waving in the wind. There was no sound but the swishing leaves. No one was around. Looking down at the base of the tree Wanda saw five-year-old Zosia, her dark hair in long plaits, her red-checked school dress flapping round her bloodied knees, black shoes scuffed. Tears were pouring down her cheeks.

Wanda turned and ran from the school grounds and round the corner. Then she stopped, put her head against the red brick wall of the outside canteen and burst into tears. 'Zosia,' she mumbled to herself, 'Anna…'

After a few seconds, with nobody around, Wanda pulled out a tissue, blew her nose and wiped her eyes. She had promised Pan Batorowicz she would help with packing food and clothing parcels for delivery to needy families in Poland. She headed toward the bus stop on her way to the Polish Club.

As she waited, a car went by with Pam Hoar at the wheel. Wanda half raised her hand in greeting. There seemed to be someone in the passenger seat.

Chapter 14

Warsaw, December 1981

Aleks pulled his suitcase out from under the bed and threw in shirts, trousers, sweaters – any clothes he could find. He put some bread, cheese and an apple in a tin and threw that in to – might be useful, he thought. Now there was a problem. He took a long, hard look at his masterpiece – Diadem of Sorrow. It was large and unfeasibly heavy, made of cast iron with a marble base.

He'd spent six months creating it while he was at the film school. It was intended as a prop but the concept had got a little out of hand. Originally he thought it was to be a cavalry man walking his wounded horse to slaughter – an event he had witnessed during the war. However, something had gone wrong in the casting process and the figures were out of proportion so it looked more like a dog playing with a stick. Still, an artist had to have art.

Aleks carefully wrapped a blanket round the object then half carried, half pushed it out into the corridor and along to the lift. He propped open the lift door with it and returned to the flat for his suitcase. Then he took one last look around the flat and headed back to the lift, pushing his artwork inside.

The trellis-like doors closed and Aleks realised, with a slight pang, he hadn't written a note to Irena. But what could he have written? *Escaped to England without you, will probably never see you again. Regards, your ever-loving husband.* During the six months he'd been living with her, he'd tried to persuade her to come with him but it was no use. He should have told her he was leaving today but it was better just to go. Less painful for everyone.

Bronek was waiting in the courtyard, stamping his feet and clapping his hands together in the icy cold. He was wearing a Russian-type fur hat and thick boots. Aleks paused and looked back up at the window of the flat. He thought back to the last time he'd run away, the sight of Pawel's small face peering out of the window. The little boy had waved to him. Aleks had waved back and doffed his cap with a cheerful smile on his face. As he'd turned away, he'd felt the tears flow down his face.

'Come on,' Bronek said. 'Get a move on – there isn't much time, there's a rumour they might close the borders.' He opened the boot of the tiny Polski Fiat car.

Aleks threw his case inside then ran back to the lift and came out struggling with the sculpture.

'What the fuck do you have there?' asked Bronek

Aleks heaved it up onto the end of the boot. The car sank down as the sculpture landed in the boot. Bronek pulled back the blanket.

'What the…? What's it supposed to be? Is it an elephant with a huge, well, I don't like to say?'

Aleks shut the boot and opened the passenger seat door.

'It's called Diadem of Sorrow. Let's get going.'

Bronek got into the driver's seat and started the engine.

'God, I hate all that modern art rubbish. 'Diadem of Sorrow.' What on earth does that mean? They're always called things like 'Concept For A Radical future' or 'Where Are My Sandwiches'. That junk will really slow us down. I didn't think we'd be dragging a chunk of iron across Europe.'

Ice was forming on the windscreen and the inside of the car almost felt colder than the outside. As the engine cranked into life, a plume of evil smelling smoke shot out of the exhaust pipe. Bronek manoeuvred the car out of the courtyard and onto the deserted street. An ominous gloom was spreading over the city.

'Right, if we head straight for the border, should be in Berlin in five hours – assuming they let us through. Still, I'm

British and it says in my passport that 'Her Majesty allows me to go anywhere without let or hindrance' apparently.

Aleks picked up Bronek's passport from the open glove compartment. He looked at the black cover with gold embossed emblem.

'Nice design,' he said tracing his finger over the motif. 'What should I do when we get to the border?'

'Have you got your passport?'

'No, never been out of Poland before.'

'Then you'll have to hide in the back seat under a blanket when we go through security.'

'What will happen if we get caught?'

'God knows. Let's just hope a British passport is enough for me and they don't find you. The situation is getting worse and worse. If I don't go now, I'm afraid I never will get out. Who knows what will happen.'

He drove down the deserted streets – it was oddly quiet.

'I have a son in England,' said Aleks. 'And a letter of invitation from my son's wife.'

Bronek frowned, 'You never mentioned him before.'

'No, well I decided family life wasn't my thing and they were better off without me. Anyway, the flat was too small for us all. I just had to get out.'

'Of course it was too small with that bloody 'art' taking up all the room. Last I heard you were in Gdansk. When you phoned me out of the blue I didn't know you had come back here.'

Aleks told him about reuniting briefly with Irena and trying in vain to persuade her to come with him to England. When that failed, he decided his best bet was to contact his old pal and former English teacher Bronek.

Bronek suddenly brought the car to a juddering halt at the crossroads and they looked down the street.

'Oh shit, look, the tanks are out,' Bronek said. 'Jaruzelski has done it, he's finally done it – he's declared war against his own people.'

Aleks looked to see a column of tanks moving down the street towards them, a platoon of soldiers walking alongside. As they watched, a crowd of children ran out of side street towards the soldiers and began pelting them with rotten vegetables. There was a look of absolute bewilderment and hurt on the soldiers' faces and they raised their hands to ward off the old potatoes and stinking cabbage.

'They are getting all the equipment into place. We haven't got long. Let's get out,' said Aleks.

'I have a friend in West Berlin. He will put us up for the night if we can get there,' said Bronek.

'But we won't be able to get through the Polish border let alone through Checkpoint Charlie at the Berlin Wall. What are we going to do?' asked Aleks looking at him.

Bronek frowned and gripped the steering wheel.

'OK, let's think. Maybe our best bet is to head for the Czechoslovak border and then get to Austria. That border won't be so heavily watched. We need to head south. They will watching all the borders to the west.'

Aleks nodded and Bronek turned the car in the other direction and headed south out of the capital gathering speed towards the main road. They drove in silence for a while – the image of the tanks preying on their minds.

'What's London like?' asked Aleks suddenly.

Bronke paused and seemed to be collecting his thoughts.

'Well, it's enormous – I don't know the whole city, most Londoners don't – except taxi drivers maybe. People just know their own corner and the central bits - the West End and City. The important thing is it's big enough to lose yourself in.

'Yes, that's exactly what I want – anonymity. Do you have to queue for food?'

'Of course not! That's just in communist countries. But I heard there are economic problems and very high unemployment in most of the country. Usually, though, you can find work in London.'

'Sounds good, very good. It's a land of opportunity. I should have gone years ago. Why on earth did you leave to come here?'

'I don't know really – searching for something I suppose. Didn't know if I was British or Polish. So I came here to find out. I've been back home for holidays over the years, of course.'

'But you could have gone back permanently any time. Why now?'

'Since Ania died everything has changed. I nursed her for a long time. I don't know what to do with myself. I just want to go home for good.'

'And you chose the middle of a military coup to do it.'

'Timing must be my forte.'

Aleks leaned forward and twiddled the dial back and forth on the radio. Every station was playing Chopin.

They approached the border around 6pm that evening. Pausing in a layby, Aleks got in the back and made himself as inconspicuous as possible in the footwell behind the front seats. Bronek put a blanket over him and the two suitcases on the back seat so they were also resting over Aleks's back.

'Don't cough, sneeze, fart or laugh,' he warned. 'Keep completely still and we just might get away with this.'

Aleks said nothing and waited for the engine to start up again as they queued for the border.

The car stopped and he heard the window being wound down.

'You are British?' said a voice.

'Yes, I am, Sir. I am on my way to Austria before I go London.' Aleks smiled because Bronek was speaking bad, grammatically incorrect Polish with a very strong English accent.

'Why were you in Poland?'

'Visiting the sister of my father and the brother of my mother.'

'You have a Polish name?'

'Yes, Sir. It is the ancestral name of my ancestors.'

Aleks put his fist in his mouth to stop himself laughing. It was not a funny situation but the stress made him want to giggle. He heard the boot being opened.

'What's this thing?'

'It's called The Decadence of Capitalism,' said Bronek. 'Rich men in the West will pay good money for it. I have to meet a dealer in Salzburg. He is interested.'

The guard tutted.

'Better to melt it down and sell that. What rubbish. Go on, go through.'

The car started up again. Aleks popped up from under the blanket.

'Unbelievable!' he said. 'I was nearly wetting myself there. But we made it!'

Chapter 15

Derby, 1982

John raised his eyes to the ceiling as he sat on a kitchen stool listening to his mother-in-law Lily. Company accountant Derek stood nervously by his side. Lily was just back from the hairdresser who had tightly permed her grey hair and sprayed it rock hard with lacquer. Her neck was still bright red from the heat of the dryer. Spotting a smear of jam on the work surface, she was aggressively spraying it with bleach and wiping it off with a cloth.

'I'm glad you're here Derek,' Lily was saying. 'I wanted to tell you Paddy Deakins, who has worked at Allsop's for years – Reg gave him a job when he was 16, was round here to see me. I don't like it, John. People being laid off. Reg wouldn't have done that kind of thing. Paddy was crying and all sorts. Had to bring him in for a cuppa. Asking me to get him his job back. See what I can do, I said. It's not right. It's immortal is what it is, people getting the sack after so many years service. What do you think, Derek?'

'The trouble is, Mrs A, we have to compete and we don't want to start losing money. We have to make efficiencies,' said Derek, rubbing his nose which John took to mean he didn't believe what he was saying. John poured himself another cup of the tea from the large brown pot.

'Reg didn't have to deal with the state of the economy we have now,' said John. 'Also new technology means we don't actually need so many people.'

'What does your Pam think, Derek?' continued Lily. 'Folks losing their only wage and such like.'

'Pam doesn't have too strong an opinion on things that don't involve shoes and handbags,' he commented quietly.

'I hear she's had your house decorated again,' Lily said. 'She only had the place painted two years ago.' She started scrubbing at the sink and taps.

Derek smiled and looked at John. 'John's father and brother-in-law did the work and a good job they made of it.'

John decided to bring the conversation back to the redundancies. 'You see, Lily, that bloke Deakins has been trying to get the print union into our place and if that happens we might as well give up. The union will ruin the business – Reg always managed to keep them out and I will too. Deakins is trouble. I need to invest in new machinery and there is only so much money to go around. Also I want to do something different, something special – I don't want us to spend our time just printing wedding invitations and business cards.'

Lily stopped cleaning and turned round to look at him.

'What are your plans?' asked Derek

'We need to look at things from a different point of view, think a bit bigger. At the moment we print small things – but what if we branch out a bit, do stuff that's not so local, stuff that can go national. And with new technology it's possible now.'

'What stuff?' asked Derek.

'Things with a much bigger print run. I don't know – magazines, books.'

John could see Derek looking at him with an incredulous stare. He thinks I'm delusional or over ambitious or stupid, thought John.

'What, like *Derbyshire Life*?' asked Derek. 'Or local history books? We can't do book binding on our premises – although that can be outsourced.'

'I mean something that would appeal to the masses. Perhaps fiction.'

'What about Samantha Foy's books – she always scribbling away in her lunch hour.' Derek laughed.

John looked at him questioningly. He's making fun of me, thought John, so I'll take him up on what he's says.

'Who's she?' he asked seriously.

'I was just joking actually. Samantha's our proofreader – you know the quiet, tall girl with the long, curly red hair. When she joined Allsop's she thought we were a publisher not a printer. The others tease her because she has this little black notebook she takes with her everywhere and she's always making notes.'

'Is she any good?' asked John.

'I've no idea. She's good at proofreading. The other day, she caught a letter before it was sent out that said, 'We are not prepared to complete your order' instead of 'We are now prepared to complete your order.' That was a close thing, we might have lost that.'

John paused, thinking. Lily was emptying a box of PG Tips into a red tin marked TEA.

'Reg always said it was the little print jobs what people needed – you'll always want an invite or a leaflet or a business card,' said Lily.

'Ask Samantha to bring her work to me. You never know,' he said eventually.

'Unlikely to be any good,' said Derek rubbing the bridge of his nose, which was red and sore from his ill-fitting glasses.

That evening, John settled down in his armchair. It had been Reg's old chair. John rested Reg's Waterford crystal whisky glass on the arm of the chair, turning it round in his hand. He heard the doorbell ring.

'There are no such things as problems, just opportunities,' he murmured to himself. He'd been reading his American self-help books. He even had some on tape to listen to in the car. 'I have to think outside the box. Madness is doing the same thing and expecting different results. We have to innovate, branch out.'

Maxine came in. 'John, Samantha Foy to see you. Says she works at Allsop's – said you asked her to come round.'

'Yes, that's right. Come in, Samantha, sit down.' John half rose from his chair.

Timidly, the girl came towards him. She was tall and very slim with pale, lightly freckled skin, bright blue eyes and an amazing mane of glorious curly red hair. She looked like a work of art, a fragile 19th century sprite from a Dante Gabriel Rossetti painting. She was absolutely stunning. John took her hand – it was limp and slightly damp.

'Can I call you Sam?' he asked, trying to put her at her ease.

'No, it's Samantha actually, Sir.' She had the broadest Derby accent.

'Right, good,' John smiled not sure if she was joking. The accent sat so oddly with the pre-Raphaelite appearance. As if Ophelia had risen from her watery grave, garlands of flowers falling from her hair, water cascading from down her breasts and exclaimed, 'Mek a brew, me tongue feels like Ghandi's flip-flop'

'Sit down, please. Maxine, can we have some coffee?'

He sat back in his armchair and Samantha perched on the sofa opposite.

'I'm told you write books, novels and I asked you to bring me some examples. What are they about?'

Samantha was looking around at the room, the chandelier, the large television, the flame-effect fire with fake pieces of coal. She probably lives in a two-up, two-down in Abbey Street, thought John.

'They are all set in Derbyshire, around Buxton and the Peak District. They are about folk who lived there in the old days.'

Samantha looked down at the Tesco carrier bag on her lap. She flexed her toes in her white, flat shoes. John nodded encouragingly.

'My nan used to tell me all about it, she was a great story teller,' Samantha continued. 'She told me about her nan, and the things she used to get up to and what people did. Ordinary stuff, you know, but also what the high up people got up to. So you know, like all sections of society. I just can't stop thinking about those times, those people. I write about them so much they are as real to me as you.'

John tried to get a glimpse of her figure under her flowery dress and little green cardigan.

'How many books have you written?' he asked.

'Seven – well I've actually written four but I have all seven in my head. They're an ongoing saga and the same families. It's all in here,' she tapped her forehead. 'Their lives, marriages, deaths, love affairs - everything.'

'Do you think I could read one of them?'

Samantha hesitated.

'The purpose of writing is so that people will read what you've written isn't it?' said John. 'They're not private diaries are they? You want to communicate your thoughts to others, don't you?'

'Yes, Sir. But why do you want to read them?'

'Because I'm interested in what my employees do. I'm not making fun of you.'

Samantha reached into the plastic bag and pulled out a manuscript of papers held together with a large, thick rubber band. She stroked the first page lovingly then handed it over to John. He looked at the cover sheet which read, *Buxton Belles by Samantha Foy.*

The title sounded terrible.

'Thanks, Samantha, I'd love to read this.'

Later that night, Maxine was applying thick coats of Nivea cream to her face and putting in her curlers. She reached over to her bedside table and took up her book: *Diana: The Radiant Princess.* John was sitting up in bed reading *Buxton Belles,* laying each page on his knee as he read it.

'*Lord Hargreaves pulled at the stays on her corset, "You are mine,' he cried in a jealous rage'.* Oh God, this is awful.' He collected the pages together and pulled the rubber band back round them. What a shame. For some reason I thought I'd discovered a new Emily Bronte. Perhaps it's all that wonderful hair.'

He put off his bedside lamp and lay down to sleep. 'Lizzie Siddal, she looks like that model Lizzie Siddal. The one who posed as Ophelia for that painter. You know the one. Didn't she catch pneumonia and die?'

'You what?' said Maxine.

'Nothing,' said John.

Chapter 16

Aleks Lato stood on the deck of the P&O Ferries ship *Pride of Dover*, spits of salt spray hitting his face. Lurching up and down on the waves he saw an incredible sight. Sheer cliffs, made of brilliant white rock dropping straight down into the sea were looming before him.

'Here's some coffee,' said Bronek coming up behind him. 'I put in four spoonfuls of sugar as you like it. Why are you standing up here in the wind and rain? Come on down below where it's warm.'

Aleks took a sip of coffee. 'Look at those cliffs – amazing.'

'You've never heard of the White Cliffs of Dover? To English people it means – now we're home. They're made of chalk.' Bronek pulled the hood of his waterproof jacket tighter round his face and warmed his hands on his drink.

'Chalk, eh,' said Aleks, 'Not very durable. That means the country keeps getting smaller and smaller.'

'And there, you can see the bluebirds flying over,' said Bronek laughing.

'Where?' asked Aleks, puzzled.

'It's a song. Actually, there are no bluebirds in England. An American wrote the words during the war and got it wrong. It should be: *There'll be sea gulls over the White Cliffs of Dover*. Come on, we dock in 15 minutes. Let's get back to the car.'

Aleks stood for a moment, staring at the cliffs, jutting down aggressively in to the sea. 'A good defence,' he thought. 'Makes it harder to land, to invade.' He smiled and turned to walk down the metal steps.

They headed down to the carport in the bowels of the ship. The little Polski Fiat was covered in mud and grime after its journey through Czechoslovakia, Austria, West Germany and France. It had done pretty well, considering. They only broke down once on a Sunday morning in Germany near Bamberg. Two young Germans towed the car to their garage and worked on it all day until it was running again. Afterwards, they would take no payment. As they drove away, Bronek commented on their generosity. Aleks just shrugged and said, 'Perhaps they have guilty consciences.'

The cars were unhitched and the ship's massive bow doors creaked opened. Bronek and Aleks waited their turn then drove clanking over the ramp of the ferry and onto British soil.

'I'll go through immigration and you have to say you're applying for political asylum.' Bronek flicked through the *Daily Mail* he had picked up on the ship. 'News of the martial law in Poland is all over the papers. Lots of stories of dissidents being put in prison, people being persecuted. Tell them you're an artist, hit them with the Roman Polanski story. You should be fine. I'll wait for you.'

He handed Aleks a piece of paper.

'Here is my parents' address. You can tell the officers you have contacts here and somewhere to stay. Make sure to tell them you will not be trying to claim any benefits. That should do it.'

'What do you mean?'

'That you won't be expecting them to pay for your food, accommodation and stuff. Tell them the Polish police beat you up and put you in prison. I don't know, play whatever sympathy card you can think of.'

To Aleks's surprise, the immigration officials turned out to be reasonably sympathetic. Aleks smiled politely, used the best English he could muster, told them he had friends he could stay with. They questioned him for an hour, made him a coffee, asked about his job, his family. When he mentioned his son lived in England, they nodded approvingly. One of the officers commented to the other, 'At least this one's white.' He was given papers that he had to present to the High Commission in London in 30 days. He was in, now he could just disappear!

Aleks grabbed his bag and made his way to the waiting room where Bronek was sitting. He made a thumbs-up sign.

'Right, let's see if our little car can get us to London.'

They stopped in the outskirts of the city to buy some cigarettes and chocolate. Aleks followed Bronek into a small shop. The shelves were full of food, magazines, wine, beer, detergent, tins, toilet paper – everything. Aleks stood and looked around in amazement.

'Hello,' said the young man behind the counter. Aleks saw his very first brown face.

'Hi,' said Bronek. He placed a Twix, two packets of Polos and a copy of Private Eye with a picture of Mrs Thatcher on the cover, 'Can I get a packet of Players No 6 for my addicted friend here.'

The man smiled and turned to the shelf behind him.

'Here's your drug of choice.' He spoke perfect English with what Aleks took to be a London accent.

Aleks followed Bronek out of the shop.

'Amazing – there was so much stuff in that little shop, the man was black and he was so friendly.'

'He's Indian, well, Indian descent. People like him own many of the little shops. They're convenient because they're always open and sell everything. These people work really hard and make a ton of money.'

'Is everyone here as friendly as him?'

'Of course not but when people are trying to sell you stuff, they are usually pretty pleasant. Not like Poland where the shops have nothing and the staff are as rude as possible. Welcome to London!'

They drove on towards the Thames and waited at lights to cross Chelsea Bridge.

'You'll fit in here,' said Bronek. 'It's a city of immigrants – always has been. My parents came here in 1946. We lived in 'Little Poland' in West London along with the Italians. Every nationality has their area: the Jews in North London, the Bangladeshis in the East End, Chinese in Soho.'

'And they never fight?' asked Aleks.

Bronek snorted. 'Not often. Black youths rioted in Brixton last year but that was against the police. It happens, but not as much as you might think.'

Aleks looked out of the car window, at the view down the Thames. Tall red buses drove past – they were all driving on the wrong side of the road. It felt calm, secure.

'It's very peaceful here,' said Aleks.

Bronek banged the steering wheel with his hand and said, 'That's what I always say and most Londoners don't believe me. I tell them they should try Poland. Here everything is secure – the result of a thousand years with no invasions, no sudden shocks.'

'No invasion for a thousand years?' echoed Aleks. 'That's incredible. In Poland we seem to get invaded every other Thursday. So there has been peace and harmony for all that time?'

'Well, no, of course not. There was a very nasty civil war a few hundred years ago and we cut the head off *our* king long before the French ever thought of doing it to theirs. But republicanism didn't suit so we brought back the king's son and he carried on with reduced powers. Little by little, democracy came in and autocracy went out. We don't really do sudden revolution.'

'Stability is what I need.'

'I'm feeling a tingle of home coming,' said Bronek, taking a bite of his Twix.

Chapter 17

Wanda looked through the kitchen window at her father digging in his vegetable garden. He didn't do so much work there these days. At one time, most of their vegetables and a good deal of their fruit came from the garden. Wanda could remember the days when the understairs cupboard was filled with sacks of homegrown potatoes, onions, leeks and swedes. There would be jars of preserved fruit from their apple, pear and cherry trees and boxes of eggs from the chickens. Unfortunately, a fox had got into the coop a few years back and left chicken innards all over the garden. That had put an end to that.

These days it was more of a hobby garden and there was more emphasis on flower – particularly climbing roses. Wanda watched Anna dance round her grandfather, no doubt plying him with endless questions about flowers, worms, the sun, the soil, the clouds.

Wanda smiled at them. Tadek had an old shirt on and his sleeves rolled up. He was wearing his work trousers and boots, his bald head reddening in the sun. Wanda thought she should take some sun cream out for him.

Anna was wearing her red summer dress with the white flowers. She sat down on the lawn and began making a daisy chain the way her babcia had taught her. Wanda tried to guess what they were talking about. Probably Anna was asking her grandfather if they could have a pet – a cat, or dog, or parrot or chimpanzee. Wanda looked past them to the top of the garden and drew her breath in sharply – Zosia was standing under the large lime tree. She was wearing her pink summer dress, a white sun hat and her legs were bare. Her hair was loose and waving in the wind. She was holding her box of treasures. She looked about eight years old.

Wanda quickly turned away from the window, shaking her head. Stop it, stop it, for God's sake, stop it! She must stop seeing her sister everywhere. Why did she keep doing it? Wanda rubbed her eyes with her hand but turned with a fixed smiled as she heard her father coming in through the kitchen door carrying a basket full of potatoes.

'It's getting quite hot out there. I think I will finish for today – I feel rather tired,' said Tadek.

'You should take it easy, Dad, there is no need to work on your day off. We can always buy the veg at the market.'

'I have always worked and always will. I can't stop now. Work is prayer, my mother used to say.'

'Was Anna asked for a pet again?'

'Yes, she suggested a panther.'

Wanda laughed. 'I always longed for a dog when we were little.'

'I know but it was too difficult to have a pet then.'

'Remember that time I brought a stray dog home? Zosia screamed with fear. It was such a friendly little thing and so enthusiastic but Zosia was frightened when it jumped up at her.'

Tadek laughed. 'Zosia wasn't an animal person.'

Zosia hated dogs, thought Wanda. She said they were smelly and vicious. She hated dogs because Babcia hated dogs.

'Maybe we should get Anna a pet. It would be company as she doesn't have a brother or sister.'

Wanda fell silent. She felt guilty about bringing up an only child but Pawel had said he didn't want any more children. He said Anna was perfect and another child might not be, so it would be tempting fate to try to replicate her. Tadek was wiping his head and neck with a handkerchief.

'Would you like to try some of my home made beer?' said Tadek, taking off his work boots. He went over the barrel bubbling in the corner of the kitchen. 'I need something to cool me down.'

'I've been waiting to try it,' said Wanda. 'You could make vodka too – only I think that's illegal.'

Tadek laughed. 'I'll stay with beer for now.' He found two glasses and poured some amber, foaming brew from the fermenting barrel. Wanda glanced back outside at Anna. She was happily playing on the swing, singing a song as she flew higher and higher, back and forth.

Wanda and Tadek went into the sitting room and Wanda put on the lunchtime news. As often these days, it was detailing current events in Poland. Tadek settled in his armchair with his feet on the little footstool. He tutted.

'Things are not good over there. Food prices are high, there are curfews, no jobs – this martial law must be terrible for people.'

Wanda nodded.

'Your mother sent a parcel with some food and clothes to Irena – she thought she might need help,' he continued. 'Have you heard from her lately? How is she coping?'

'She said she is well but Pawel says the letters are censored she can't tell the truth. He is worried about her. I was helping pack parcels for Poland the other day and Pan Batorowicz is driving a van to Poland to deliver them.'

They paused and watched Walesa speaking to a crowd in Gdansk. It was old film as he was now in prison, having been arrested by the authorities.

Tadek looked at Wanda. 'I was sorting out my tools in the understairs cupboard and I found something you might recognise.' He went over the sideboard and opened a cupboard. He took out a box, a Polish wooden carved box and handed it to Wanda. 'Do you remember this?'

Wanda smiled. 'Yes, of course. Zosia's box of treasures. She'd never let me touch it.'

Wanda took the box and turned the tiny key to open the lid. There lay an old penny with the head of Queen Victoria, shards of blue and white pottery, some smooth pebbles, a piece of sealing wax, an amber necklace and an ornate cross threaded through with a length of black velvet. There was a folded piece of paper. Wanda opened it and read the childish writing:

Zosia's Box

Keep out (Wanda and Brat). My property

Wanda closed the lid and turned the key. 'Daddy, Anna's teacher said she should be put in the gifted and talented programme. She said Anna could get a scholarship to a private school.'

'That's wonderful – she is such an intelligent girl.'

Wanda looked at the television screen. Riot police were turning the water cannon on protesters in the streets of Warsaw. A young woman was thrown hard against the wall of a building by the force of the jet. Tadek shook his head sadly.

'Daddy, I didn't tell anyone but I contacted Pawel's father. I found out he was working at the Gdansk shipyard. I sent him a letter and he phoned me.'

Tadek looked at her in astonishment.

'Really – I'm amazed. I thought no one in the family had heard from him for years. What did Pawel say?'

'I haven't told him. The thing is, Aleks – that's his father – said he was trying to come to England. He might be here already for all I know.'

''Why didn't you tell Pawel?'

'I was worried he might be angry. He has never been very complimentary about his father. He always said he wanted nothing to do with him but I think it would be good for him to have things out with his dad.'

Tadek nodded and said nothing.

'Pawel told me he remembers his father playing a trick on him,' she continued. 'He was about four at the time. His father said, 'Get under the table and I bet you will come out by the time I count to three.' Pawel said he shouted, 'No, I won't' and he crawled under the table. He heard his father say loudly, 'One, two' then returned to reading the newspaper. After what seemed like ages, Pawel got out from under the table thinking his father had gone away. His father then turned to look at him and said, 'Three'.

Tadek smiled. 'When a boy has so few memories of his father, it's not much to model himself as a dad. You need to be patient with him, Wanda.'

'Pawel told me the other main memory he has of his father was when he left. Aleksander was down in the courtyard below, wearing a cap and carrying a guitar. He looked up and smiled up at Pawel, who was waiting at the window. He took off his hat and waved it. Then he disappeared. For years afterwards, Pawel said he used to look out of the window and see men in the street below. He would choose one and pretend that man was about to come in and announce he was his father.'

'Poor little boy. Yes, I agree it would be good for Pawel to see his father. Let's see if the man actually turns up.'

Tadek got up and patted Wanda's hand.

'If you don't mind, I think I'll go and have a lie down. The good news, though, is that I've managed to get some work at the new Canal Apartments.'

Wanda looked down at Zosia's precious box of treasures in her lap. She took out the old penny and felt the weight of it in her hand. The very last person Zosia had seen in the seconds before she died had been Pawel. Wanda's husband had held her sister in his arms and heard her last words – words spoken in English, a language he didn't understand at the time. Wanda had tried to get him to recall what she'd said but it was no use. Her words were gone forever. Pawel had told Wanda how Zosia had vomited black bile all over her nightdress while in her death throes. It was shocking, disgusting.

Wanda knew it still troubled him, he had nightmares about it and cried out in his sleep. Other times he whispered Zosia's name gently in his sleep. Wanda guessed he was dreaming that Zosia was still alive. And she felt frightened – she was terrified that her husband didn't love her. He loved a dead girl more.

Chapter 18

'The Shipyard Worker', Press Photograph of the Year, 1981.

Aleks leaned closer to examine the framed picture that hung in pride of place on Roger Elliott's kitchen wall then stepped back to admire it. That day in 1980 he had been wearing his rough work clothes, holding his welder's mask by his side, standing in front of the hulk of the ship. It was a powerful, brooding, magnificent picture. He had felt no significance at all at the time, but somehow Roger had managed to capture so much meaning and import.

Aleks had seen it reproduced numerous times in magazines and newspapers. It had even been used as the poster for a documentary on Solidarity and had been plastered on walls around London. He was famous, if anonymously so. He greatly enjoyed that notion. On a practical level, it had made Roger well disposed towards him – even to the extent of letting him live in the top floor flat of his Camden Town house.

'Fantastic picture,' said Aleks. 'I never tire of looking at it. There I am, the symbol of the noble Polish worker. Some of my friends would find that a little ironic.'

Bronek came up and stood behind him. 'I can't think of any one less suited to that role,' he said.

'It doesn't matter, I can make anyone look exactly as I want them to look,' said Roger from his seat at the kitchen table. 'My camera lies for me every time.'

Aleks turned to look at him. 'Well you've done it to perfection this time.'

Roger shrugged. 'Anyway, shall we get this meeting started?'

'Pompous fool', thought Aleks. He reluctantly took his seat at the table and glanced through the partially open window. It was a Thursday evening and the traffic on Camden High St could be dimly heard through the open window. Every so often there was the roar of a car as it came racing down Arlington Road. It was a lovely day and they had to sit discussing worthy subjects such as trade unions and workers' rights. It was all just grandstanding and Aleks hated it. Bronek sat down next to him, taking a drink from his coffee cup.

Aleks leaned back on his chair. It creaked under his weight. Someone had put a huge vase on the table filled with irises, lilies and small carnations. That would be Eunice, Roger's on-and-off girlfriend, thought Aleks. No one else would think about flowers.

Roger looking round the large pine table. 'Come and sit down Eunice – the cakes can wait,' he said.

'Just a minute,' said Eunice licking her fingers. 'No one can get through a political meeting without a flapjack.'

Roger picked up his notes and rapped them on the table as he waited for her to take her seat next to Bronek. 'He really thinks he's important and the four of us matter,' thought Aleks.

'So - we were all at the meeting in Conway Hall,' said Roger, 'I want to know your thoughts on the Polish Solidarity Campaign. Are we getting anywhere with this? Should I press for more support from the National Union of Journalists?'

'I'd like to propose we move in another direction,' said Bronek raising his hand slightly. 'I attended a Solidarity With Solidarity meeting last week. I've been covering it for the BBC World Service. Solidarity With Solidarity seem rather more moderate than the PSC'.

'You're working at the Beeb are you?' asked Roger stroking his chin with a smile on his face. 'And why do you prefer the SWS? Are you a Tory voter?'

Aleks looked at Bronek who shook his head with annoyance. 'I want to tell the truth, simple as that. The BBC must be impartial at all times. Do you know why so many people in Poland listen to the BBC as opposed to the Voice of America? Because they believe it tells them the truth. That is all I'm getting at. Also I think plenty of Stalinists have infiltrated the PSC.'

'Infiltrated? What do you mean? Don't these people have a right to join?' asked Roger, still smiling.

Aleks wondered if Roger was pushing all the right buttons to get Bronek wound up on purpose.

'Listen, unlike you I lived and breathed communism for 25 years and up close and personal and it isn't pretty,' Bronek shook his finger at Roger. 'You – they - don't know the reality of it! I just liked the SWS meeting, it was reasoned, logical. There were plenty of young, second generation Poles like me and moderate Labour supporters. The PSC have got their knickers in a twist because their brains tell them they must support the communist authorities at all costs but their hearts tell them they have to support ordinary people wanting a free trade union. They don't know what to do.'

'What do you think, Aleks?' asked Roger.

Aleksander paused as if he were in profound thought. He wasn't. In fact, he found this analysis of where on the line of political extremism everyone was positioned tedious. But he didn't want to seem like the odd one out, the political pygmy. He had to say something to show an interest.

'I know the real communism too. I also know people want to be free, to choose what they really want.' Was this true? Plenty of people love to be told what to do, not to have to think or make decisions for themselves, not to have any responsibility. Communism was like prison – you are given shelter, food and warmth but not freedom. Some people love prison.

'So you agree with Bronek, do you?' asked Eunice offering the flapjacks round. 'I just made these, they're still warm. Anyone want one?' Aleks looked at her dark, pretty eyes and shiny hair. Her figure was excellent although personally he liked women with a little more meat on their bones. Political discussion bored him – food and women on the other hand…

'What I don't understand,' said Bronek, 'is what connection you two have with Poland anyway?' He looked at Roger and Eunice and shook his head at the proffered cake. 'I mean, tell me, why do you really care? I just think the Polish Solidarity Campaign is too left wing. The Solidarity With Solidarity people are more moderate and they support the real Solidarity. As I said, those hardliners who support the Polish Solidarity Campaign are so accustomed to propping up the communist authorities they are not actually supporting the common people any more. It's like *Animal Farm*.'

'It's actually more like *Life of Brian*,' said Eunice, pressing her finger on the table to pick up the crumbs of oats. 'The Judean Popular Front, the Popular Front for Judea.'

'When I was photographing the shipyard strikes in 1980,' said Roger, 'and I saw Walesa kneeling down in the dirt with his rosary thing. I looked at him and thought, isn't he just in thrall to the Catholic Church instead of the communist party? It's pretty similar.'

'You may have won the News Picture of the Year award or whatever but it doesn't meant you know anything about Poland and Poles,' shouted Bronek. 'This is just an intellectual exercise for you. You have no vested interest in it. You don't have to queue all night to buy tea, you don't have to live in a flat with five other people - you live in this fucking mansion.' He gestured to the high-ceilinged, Georgian room. 'You don't have censorship, people reading your letters, turning off the heating in April whatever the weather. It's just …'

'All right, Bron, keep your hair on,' said Aleks. 'Roger has a point about Walesa. They used to say he was a double agent.'

'Don't be ridiculous,' said Bronek his wide face red with anger. 'He's an honest man fighting for the freedom of his people. You lefties are trying to say Solidarity is just a Catholic, CIA, Tory plot aimed at the Soviets whereas in fact it's a real, grass roots movement. I've heard talk Walesa may be awarded the Nobel Peace Prize for Christ's sake.'

'Well even that war monger Henry Kissinger got one – it don't mean a thing,' said Roger.

'We are sitting here in comfortable London house debating a movement we have no control over,' said Eunice.

'We can send food parcels and money but our influence is negligible.'

'What if Solidarity could bring down the whole Soviet empire? What if that happened, eh?' said Bronek. He sat back in his chair with a satisfied smile on his face.

'That will never happen – not in our lifetime,' said Aleks. 'What is more likely is that the Soviets will lose patience and crush them utterly.'

'I don't know. I think the whole Soviet thing is a house of cards – it could fall,' said Bronek. 'If the Russians invaded, the Polish army would fight them, they would never attack their own people.'

'Wishful thinking on your part,' said Roger. 'Anyway, if communism did fall that would give America a free hand in the world and we don't want that.'

'The thing is,' said Aleks 'I'm not so interested in politics. I want to make my sculptures in peace.'

'You told me the authorities were stopping you practising your art so politics affects you as it affects everyone,' said Roger. 'I'm afraid you can't opt out.'

Bronek laughed. 'Aleks, I've known you for over 10 years and I only found out about your 'art' when we were trying to get through the border,' said Bronek. 'I thought you were more interested in....women, money and most of all, yourself.'

'You don't know much about me then, do you? I laboured in an iron foundry for eight months to produce that sculpture,' said Aleks.

Eunice smiled at him.

'Diadem of Sorrow – pound for pound the heaviest work of art in London for its size,' she said. 'Just getting it in the basement here was difficult. It must have been a struggle to get it across Europe. I like it though – it has style.'

'Roger, would you really be happy if the authorities came and forcibly filled this house with another five families and left you just two rooms on the top floor?' asked Bronek. 'Hand on heart, would you be happy with that? Politics is just a game for you. It isn't real.' He leaned back in his chair. 'Is there any more vodka? I want to get drunk.'

There was a silence – deep and heavy – filling the room. No one spoke. Outside in the street a workman shouted something unintelligible to his colleague in a deep, gruff voice.

'I'll be down in a minute, Mother,' said Aleks.

Eunice burst out laughing, Bronek smiled and Roger raised his eyes to the ceiling.

Aleks shook his head, got up and went through to the sitting room, leaving the arguing behind. He sat on the sofa and took out the letter. He wanted to read it through once more. He'd decided to pen a short message to his son. It was difficult. How do you restart a conversation after 25 years – especially when the last time you saw your correspondent he was four years old. He decided to keep it really concise.

6 Arlington Rd
London NW1

Dear Pawel,
This may come as a shock to you but I am in London and I would very much like us to meet again. It's all very difficult I know and feelings run deep. For my part, I want to hug you and for you, well you would probably like to punch me in the face. It would be good for both of us. So let's do it! I'm staying with a friend in London. Do you fancy coming down here?

With love
Your father, Aleksander Lato.

Chapter 19

'How long are you going to London for?' asked Wanda standing in the bedroom doorway.

Pawel had his back to her, hastily stuffing clothes inside a suitcase open on the bed. He was wearing a new pair of jeans and a shirt she hadn't seen before. His hands were scrubbed free of paint and he smelled of aftershave.

'I'm not sure – a few days probably.'

'Are you leaving me?' She pulled at the buttons on her maroon cardigan.

'For a few days, yes. As I said, I'm going to London. Don't be so melodramatic.'

'Who are you going to see, why is this a secret?'

'It's someone I used to know in Poland. No one you know – and yes it is a man before you accuse me of seeing another woman.'

'I didn't accuse you of that. Where will you be staying? Will you give me a telephone number.'

'I'll phone when I get there, ok? I'll be staying in Camden Town – you wouldn't know the place.'

'I do know it – I lived in London for five years.'

Pawel brushed past her with his suitcase banging into her shoulder and headed down the stairs.

'There is a parents' evening at Anna's school tomorrow night. Will you be back for that?' called Wanda.

'Probably not. I'm sure she's doing very well so we don't need to worry. I'll phone you when I get there.'

The front door slammed and Wanda heard the van start up and drive down the road. Maybe Pawel's father had contacted him – that must be the explanation. Maybe this was all good, maybe a meeting with his father was just what Pawel needed. It could be a hopeful sign.

The next evening, Wanda went along to her daughter's school. She was looking forward to it. Any opportunity to talk about Anna was always a blessing. She sat down with Miss Kay, the second year teacher.

'I just want to tell you, Mrs Lato, that it is a privilege to have Anna in my class. Her reading is fluent, her writing exceptional and her conduct outstanding. She is seven years old but she writes like an 11-year-old or older. Does she love reading at home?' Miss Kay had short dark hair and a hint of moustache on her upper lip. She was still young enough to be enthusiastic about her work.

Wanda smiled. 'Yes, Anna reads all the time. She takes after her aunt and her grandmother. I'm so grateful to God for that. She is a clever girl.'

'She certainly is that. She's quite exceptional in my experience. I wanted to let you know that there is a gifted and talented programme you could put her in for. That means at age 11 she could be eligible to get a free scholarship to a private school. It's very hard to get a place but I think Anna stands a good chance.'

Wanda walked out of St Joseph's elated. Nothing else mattered except that Anna would achieve something in her life. She would be the Zosia who lived. I've done it, thought Wanda, I've produced something worthwhile.

Wanda didn't want to go home yet. Pawel wasn't there and her father had had to start work on the Canal apartments without him. He was probably working late as the project was behind schedule. Wanda looked at her watch. Anna would be in bed by now and Helena would no doubt be in her study, getting out books and starting on her research. She wasn't a good conversationalist these days.

Wanda wanted to talk to people, to sing and shout about her wonderful daughter. She headed for her brother's house at Derwentside. Even the thought of seeing Maxine had its charms.

She caught the bus and made her way to the house, walking up the drive to John's front door. The huge magnolia tree at the side of the house was in full bloom, the rhododendron bushes gave off a sweet scent from their pink and white flowers. She rang the bell. It played the first few notes of Green Sleeves. John opened the door.

'Hello little Brat, just thought I'd pop in as I was passing.' She knew that was a silly remark as she made it. The house was in a private cul-de-sac so no one was ever just passing.

'Wanda,' said John in surprise giving her a hug. 'Nice to see you – come in.'

He led the way into the sitting room. Wanda looked up at the large, tangerine-coloured draped curtains that covered the full-length windows. Tart's knickers, Pam always called them.

'Hello, Maxine. Oh, Derek, you here too? We could have a little party – live it up.' Her eyes met John's and they gave each other a little smirk.

'We were going through some business accounts,' said Derek. 'It's nice to see you Wanda. It means we can stop now.'

'We were just about to have a gin and tonic, do you want one?' John asked.

'Does Rose Kennedy have a black dress? Of course I'd love one.'

Wanda sat down next to Derek. He began eating some peanuts from a bowl on the coffee table. His glasses kept slipping down his nose and he constantly pushed them up again. His gingery hair was getting thinner and his collar was stained with a little blood where he'd cut himself shaving. Poor old Pam, thought Wanda.

How are Mum and Dad?' asked John scooping up some ice from the bucket and putting some in her drink.

'OK. Mum's engrossed in her nutters, as we sympathetically call them. She's lost in a world of her own most of the time. She keeps using jargon like 'life events' and 'outcomes'. I wish she'd speak normal English. It's getting hard to talk to her – she hangs around with too many academics with pointy heads these days.' John laughed.

'And Dad has just been given some of the renovation work at the old mill site. Did you know the development is called 'The Canal Apartments'? Sounds classy, doesn't it? Can't think why they didn't call it 'Babcock's Flats'.'

'And how is your lovely little girl?' asked Derek. 'Pam was telling me what a bright child she is.'

'Funny you should say that. I've just come from a parents' evening at St Joseph's and - I hate to brag but I'm going to anyway - the teacher said she should be put in for the gifted and talented programme. She said she may get a scholarship to a private school'

'Fantastic,' said John. 'She has brains that one, she'll go far.'

'We'll be sending Clarke to Repton prep school. It's expensive but worth it. His name is down already,' said Maxine.

Wanda smiled at her. You can't make a silk purse out of a sow's ear

'Anyway, hasn't she done well,' said John. 'Let's raise our glasses to Zosia,' there was an awkward pause, 'I mean Anna.' Maxine laughed nervously. 'So Pawel wasn't at the parents' evening with you?' John added quickly.

'No, he's gone to London to see an old friend. Very mysterious but it's someone over from Poland. He left yesterday morning and said he would ring when he got there. He hasn't yet – rung I mean, I assume he got there.'

'Oh, you're on your own like me – Pam has gone to London to see her cousin for a few days,' said Derek.

Chapter 20

Aleks wasn't used to feeling nervous. It wasn't his natural state. Even when he had got mixed up with that gang of thugs in Gdansk, he'd played it cool. He thought he was just helping them lift a little cash from the payroll train – he had no idea these people were involved in drugs and sex trafficking too. He had got out as soon as he realised. Aleks was only into small-time theft and only when absolutely necessary. Drugs, sex crime and associated violence were not his thing at all. Still, he had kept his cool on that occasion and it was his level headedness that always saved his life.

But this meeting with his own flesh and blood was quickening his heart. He'd been in England for six months already and he had put off this day as long as possible. The problem was, it had the potential to go badly wrong. He wandered around the top room of Roger's house and started rehearsing what he was going to say.

Standing in front of the wardrobe mirror, he practised, 'My dear son.. dear boy… Pawel, my dear…' None of these terms came easily to him at all. Also he had to remember Pawel was not a four-year-old boy but a man of, what, 33 or something like that.

Pawel had telephoned him two days earlier, sounding curt on the phone. His voice was deep and he spoke well – just like his mother. He was coming round to the house at 4pm and staying for dinner – if things went well, of course.

Aleks had spent the day walking round Camden Town buying food and drink to welcome his only son. He went into Marks & Spencer on the High Street and bought bread, cheese, grapes, three bottles of red wine and some expensive chocolates. He usually shopped at the market but he decided his son deserved quality and M&S represented quality to him. He took it all back to the house and laid it out on the kitchen table. It looked good. Aleks sat at the table smoking, but he couldn't settle. He had to move, do something, get outside.

He walked over to Regents Park to take in some sunshine and have a think. Sitting near the rose garden, he smelled the rich perfume from the flowers filling the air. Some men dressed in brilliant white were playing cricket on the grass. Aleks watched and tried to work out the rules. There was a good deal of standing around, waiting, shouting and laughing. Aleks decided it made no sense. He couldn't tell who was winning and who was losing as there was no celebrating and no jeering. They all shook hands afterwards. It was almost as if it didn't matter who won.

Aleks turned his attention to the girls walking past in their summer dresses. This was one of the best things about summer – the pretty girls in their bright, scanty dresses. He bought himself an ice-cream from the van parked near the zoo and wandered in to the Japanese garden. It was all so beautiful, so relaxed but it was displacement activity – he should be thinking about more important issues, such as his son. Aleks forced himself to think how the proposed visit with Pawel might turn out.

He imagined many different scenarios, the three most popular were:

a. Pawel would hit him and then storm out of the house.

b. they'd have such a blazing row, and there would be so much noise and violence that Roger would kick them both out of the house.

c. Pawel would take a sawn-off shotgun out of a carpet bag and gave him both barrels in the stomach.

Aleks wandered back to the house. He called from the hall but no one answered. Good. Roger and Eunice were still out at a fundraising event for Amnesty International so he had the house to himself. Aleks was just about to pour himself a vodka when the doorbell rang. He felt his stomach lurch and had a sudden urge to use the toilet.

The front door was solid and heavy. Aleks pulled it open. On the doorstep he found a man with fair hair, green eyes, wide Polish features and high cheekbones. Next to him was a woman with shoulder length red hair, slim figure – very good-looking.

Aleks stared, not knowing which one to look at first. He backed away allowing the couple to enter into the hall. Composing himself, he held out his hand to Pawel.

'Son,' he said. There was a pause as Pawel looked at the proffered hand for a while and finally put his hand in that of his father. Aleks glanced sideways. Wanda was beautiful. Well done to his son bagging such a lovely creature.

Aleks smiled and took the woman's hand. He bent down to kiss it and said, 'I am so pleased to meet you at last.'

The woman smiled at him and said nothing.

'I'm delighted to welcome you here.'

She didn't say anything but looked over at Pawel who said, 'She doesn't speak Polish'.

'Yes she does, I spoke to her on the phone,' said Aleks smiling.

'What?' said Pawel frowning. 'You spoke to Wanda? She knows you're in London? She never told me, you never told me. What's going on?'

'Wanda wrote to me before I left Poland – in very good Polish I might add. She found me because of that famous Shipyard Worker photo. Do you know the one? Not many people realise it's me.' Aleks turned toward the woman again and addressed her. 'So you see I know you speak Polish, Wanda.'

'This isn't Wanda,' said Pawel.

Aleks looked at his son. Oh, shit - yet more complications, he thought. Had Pawel left his wife? Was this his mistress he liked to tout around? Aleks decided he needed to play it cool, not be judgmental. He must be accepting of his son whatever was happening.

'Ah! Good, Come into the sitting room,' he said in English.

They followed him in. Pawel said in Polish, 'OK, she's not my wife and before you start lecturing me...'

'Pawel, I am the last person on earth to lecture anyone about anything,' Aleks replied in Polish. Then he switched back to English.

'So who are you, my dear?'

'I'm Pam. Pawel's… friend. We are having a few days holiday in London. I didn't quite realise he was taking me into the middle of a family feud,' she laughed nervously.

'No, that fine Pam. It's just that Pawel and I haven't seen each other for nearly 30 years so this is all a little strange.' He turned to his son. 'I did hear about you from your mother of course. How are you, son? Please sit down.'

Pawel gave a cynical laugh and shook his head.

'I'd rather stand. You're unbelievable – you know that? Truly unbelievable.'

'It has been noted before. I hear I have a beautiful granddaughter. Do you have a picture of her?'

Pawel started to speak, then stopped and stared out of the window, biting his fingernail.

'Have you any idea – have you the slightest notion what you put me through? Have you any idea how hard my mother had to work to look after me? You never sent any money – she told me that. You sent a card about every four years, I think I got a present from you when I was 10, you never visited me. You just don't give a shit do you?'

'I am a little…' he looked at Pam, 'haphazard.'

Aleks could almost hear the tears in his son's voice – the same little boy as before. He'd always tucked away feelings such as guilt, regret, remorse where he could never find them. This meeting, though, was very difficult and the feelings hard to avoid. He must let his son say his piece.

'Growing up without you, in a tiny flat with my mother crying herself to sleep, and my grandmother who was neurotic and doted on me but couldn't exactly discuss football, or car engines,' shouted Pawel.

'Well, neither can I – I know nothing about either topic. How old is your daughter, Pawel?'

'She's seven,' Pawel yelled and the roar of his voice reverberated round the room. Then there was silence and Pawel frowned and stared at the carpet. Then he abruptly sat down on the sofa. Pam followed suit, sitting on a nearby armchair.

Aleks reverted to Polish,' So, your wife and child are at home and you are in another city with another woman. Who is she? What's going on?'

'She's a friend – actually a friend of Wanda, sort of. She doesn't know about it. I thought Wanda didn't know about you either but it seems she is hiding things from me too.'

Pam stood up. 'Look, I think you two need to sort things out between yourselves so I'm going to sit a little café I noticed down the street and have a cup of coffee.'

'Pam, no, we're going now. I…' said Pawel.

'No you stay, Pawel. You need to speak to your dad, have it out with him. It will do you good. I'll be back later.' Pam got up and walked out. They heard the front door shut downstairs.

The two men sat there. A long silence ensued. Why had Pawel brought this woman, Aleks wondered. Was it a deliberate ploy on his son's part. A way to show his father he could get a good-looking woman. Aleks guessed Wanda was not so pretty.

'When I look at you I see a strange amalgam of my mother, of Irena and Mira. It's difficult – seeing you again after all these years. I don't know what to feel,' said Aleks.

'Guilt perhaps?'

'What is the thing you are most angry about, Pawel?'

'Why is my wife writing to you behind my back?'

'Why are you screwing this woman behind her back? Wanda told me she was afraid to let you know she'd contacted me. That doesn't sound like a very good relationship to me. No communication. She said she knew you were unhappy and she thought it was a deep psychological problem because your daddy left you.'

Pawel gave a bitter little laugh.

'No, Dad, it's not really to do with you.'

'It's connected with this Pam woman is it?'

Pawel got up and walked round the room gazing at the pictures on the walls.

'Whose house is this? How come they let you stay here?'

'Roger Elliott is the photographer who took the Shipyard Worker photo. I met him in Gdansk in 1980, helped him out. The success of the photo has been a godsend for me.'

Pawel took out some chewing gum and put a piece in his mouth. He picked up a large coffee table book from the shelf. It was called *My Best Shots: Photographs* by Roger Elliott. He began to flick through the pictures.

'Have you left Wanda?' asked Aleks.

'No, I'm just – on holiday. I..' he paused staring down at the book. 'This girl here, this picture taken in – 1971 – amazingly it looks, well, quite like Wanda.'

Chapter 21

Wanda loaded the washing into the machine. Her routine every day was taking Anna to school, shopping on the way home then starting house work after her elevensies of tea and chocolate biscuits. Day melted into depressing day, all the same, the routine unchanging. She was the mother, the cleaner, cook and housekeeper. Helena often worked at home, busy in her study, typing up her interviews or researching from weighty academic books. She didn't have the time or inclination to chat. On this particular morning, however, Helena had left early to conduct an interview in Macclesfield. Tadek had already to gone to the Canal Apartments to start work.

The phone rang and Wanda rushed over to answer it, hoping it would be Pawel at last.

'Is that Ted's wife?' said an unfamiliar voice.

Wanda paused, trying to work out who was talking. 'No, it's his daughter.'

'Oh, your dad has been took poorly, love. He fell off his ladder at work and the ambulance is here taking him to the Derby Royal Infirmary. I'm Terry Conway, the work supervisor. I'm going with him. Could you meet us there, love?'

Wanda rang for a taxi and rushed over to the hospital. Sitting in traffic on the London road, she watched passersby rushing along the street, cowering from the rain. They were shopping, going on their lunch break, leading their lives. They were all carrying on as usual – yet her father was so ill in hospital that he might die. She stifled the urge to scream but asked the driver to hurry as calmly as she could. The car came to a standstill next to the statue of Florence

Nightingale outside the hospital. Wanda stared at it for a while, the stone arm raised, the comforting lamp was missing. She suddenly thrust some money at the driver, got out of the cab and ran the rest of the way.

Wanda found the reception desk and asked which ward her father was in. Nightingale Ward, she was told. A nurse directed her to a waiting room where a large man with a florid face came forward to greet her.

'You must be Ted's daughter – you look like him. I'm Terry.'

'How is he?' she asked urgently.

'The doctors are with him, love. The nurse said we should wait here and they would let us know what was happening soon.'

'He fell off his ladder, is that what happened?'

'Yes, but I think the reason he fell was because he had a heart attack. He was on the floor clutching his arm. I recognised it because I had a heart attack myself, two year ago, like.'

Wanda twisted the strap of her handbag round and round her wrist.

'The doctors know what they're doing, love,' said Terry stroking her arm. 'He'll be ok. Don't go fretting.'

Wanda went into the corridor to find a pay phone so that she could leave a message for her mother with the university. She fumbled with the change, trying to get the coin into the slot. Her voice trembled and shook as she explained to the department secretary what had happened. Wanda went back to find Terry.

'Listen, love, I'm sorry but I must get back to work now but here is the phone number at my office. Do you need anything? Here is some money for the pay phone.' He plunged his hand into his trouser pocket and brought out a handful of change.

'You take this, love. I wanted to get rid of all this shrapnel anyway. Call me if there is any news, ok?' He pressed her arm and went out of the room.

Wanda felt dazed, alone. She tried to think rationally. No one had told her brother what had happened and someone needed to pick up Anna from school. She went back to the phone and called Maxine.

'Yes, of course, I'll pick her up don't you worry,' said Maxine. 'I'll bring her here and give her a meal. I'll phone John right now and he'll come over so you won't be on your own for long.'

Wanda put the phone down. Maxine's brisk kindness threatened to bring tears to her eyes again. She noticed a vending machine a little further down the corridor. She bought a Twix, a Bounty and a bar of Cadbury's Dairy Milk. Opening the Bounty, Wanda went back to the waiting room. No one was there. With her mouth full of chocolate and coconut, she burst into tears. Bits dropped out of her mouth and she struggled to find a tissue in her bag. A nurse came in and asked if she could do anything. Wanda asked about her father and the nurse said she would find out and be right back.

Half an hour went by. Wanda picked up some old copies of *Woman's Weekly* on the table. Michael Parkinson was smiling on the cover of one, another had a girl wearing a hat and scarf (the pattern for which could be found inside) and the coverline, *Betrayed: read our exciting new serial,* while the other had a picture of a cherry tart dripping with thick cream. Wanda stared at the covers, not reading.

The nurse came in and told her that her father had been sedated and was resting. The doctors were discussing what action to take and they would let her know as soon as possible. She went out, leaving Wanda alone again.

She looked round at the NHS information posters stuck on the faded yellow walls: *Have You Washed Your Hands? AIDS Is Not Prejudiced, anyone can get it!* There was a picture of woman with a bruised face underneath the headline, *She Didn't Walk Into A Door.*

Wanda felt her depression deepening. The room was very hot and she couldn't see a way to open the windows. She looked at her watch, 2.20pm. A large, black woman came into the waiting room dragging a boy of around eight by the arm. She sat down and put the boy in the seat next to her. He started scraping his feet on the floor.

'Don't do that,' the woman said crossly, smacking the boy's arm. Then he began banging his hands on the arms of the chair.

'I told you, stop it' said the woman. 'Will you keep still and be quiet?'

Poor lad, thought Wanda, he's a young boy but she expects him to sit absolutely still and do nothing. She smiled at him but he just stared back at her. Then he sighed in an exaggerated fashion, leaned back and started pulling at the yellow curtains behind his chair. Wanda saw his mother start to raise her hand to hit him and she jumped up, 'Would you like some chocolate?' she said offering the bar to the boy.

He smiled and nodded then looked at his mother. She smiled too.

'Say thank you to the nice lady.'

'Thank you,' said the boy, taking some chocolate.

'It's boring in here isn't it?' said Wanda to the boy.

'We're always having to wait here while they do tests on my daughter,' said the woman. 'She's got leukaemia.'

'Oh, I'm sorry,' said Wanda.

'She is only two years old...'

The door opened and to her relief Wanda saw her mother and brother come in. Helena, white faced, wrapped Wanda in her arms. John went to talk to the doctors to get some information. He returned with an Indian-looking man in a white coat.

'Mrs Baran?' he said. 'So sorry to keep you waiting. We've assessed your husband's condition and he has had a major heart attack. I have been having a discussion with my colleagues and we have decided to try a new heart procedure if you are in agreement.'

'What is that? How serious is it?' said Helena.

'Your husband is very ill but there is a chance that this will save him. It's called a heart bypass. We take a vein from the leg and replace the blocked vein supplying the heart with blood. This operation has been done many times in the USA and in London hospitals but this will be first time it has been done at this hospital. I have to warn you that we are untried. We discussed sending him down to London but decided it would be safer and quicker to perform the operation here. We have little time and must act soon.'

Wanda blurted out, 'Then you must do it straight away. If it could save his life…'

'We need permission as well… Your husband is awake. We'll need him to sign the forms.'

Chapter 22

'Stay for dinner. Roger and Eunice will be back soon and my friend Bronek is coming over.'

Aleks looked at his son who was sitting silently, tapping his thumb on his hand. It was hard for him to know what to make of this man. He seemed so angry, so rigid yet he had come here with his mistress. What was that gesture meant to prove?

'What about Pam?' asked Pawel.

'She's invited too, of course.'

'What will you introduce her as? My wife?' asked Pawel.

Aleks spread out his hands. 'You can call her whatever you want – mistress, girlfriend, colleague, therapist, supermarket checkout girl – it doesn't matter. It's your life.'

Pawel looked round the room, his eyes resting on the large portrait photographs on the walls, some brightly coloured, Andy Warhol style.

'All right – we'll stay for dinner. Who's this Bronek?'

'I met him in Warsaw back in 1970. He's about your age, an English Pole. He came to find his roots – or some such nonsense. He taught me English actually.'

Pawel nodded slowly.

'If you don't mind me asking, what's Wanda like?'

Pawel pursed his lips. 'She had a sister, Zosia, who died. Died in my arms as a matter of fact.'

'In your arms…?'

'I didn't kill her, don't look so horrified. She was staying with us for the summer in '71. She and I had been to stay with friends in Krakow and she died from botulism from bad meat. It was the most horrendous event in my life.'

'Yes, I heard about the death but I didn't realise you were there.'

'Yeah, I was there. Zosia was gorgeous – long dark hair, great figure, beautiful face.' Pawel looked up at the ornate chandelier hanging from the high shabby ceiling. 'I still have nightmares about her death. I keep dreaming that I pick her up and she is fine, she comes back to life. But later I meet her walking in a corridor and she suddenly vomits all the black bile from her mouth as she comes towards me, her arm outstretched. The dreams have been so vivid lately.'

Pawel looked at his father as if he had suddenly realised who he was talking to. He looked away, out of the window to the house opposite.

'Things might have been different had she lived – different for me I mean. I could have won her over,' he continued.

'Ah, you were in love with her. So the marriage to Wanda was one of convenience, then? A visa marriage.'

'No, no, not convenience. I just ... I don't know. In some ways she's too good for me.'

'She's scared that you're following in your father's footsteps. She thinks you're going to run away too. Are you? Have you?

'No, I haven't, I came to see you, didn't I?' he paused, a look of huge sadness on his face. 'I don't know what I'm doing, not really.'

'You're going back to Wanda then?'

Pawel looked at his father but then the door opened and Roger and Eunice came in. Aleks stood up.

'How was the meeting?'

'Yeah, good,' said Roger and looked at Pawel.

'This is my son Pawel,' said Aleks.

Dinner consisted of hard bread that Eunice had made, a vegetable stew, red wine, cheese and biscuits and fruit. Aleks was standing behind his chair at the table and Pam brushed against him on her way to the next chair. Aleks made an exaggerated move and stared at her.

'You do that and you have to marry me,' he said.

Eunice laughed, Pam blushed very slightly and Pawel looked cross.

'So Pawel – have you been following the situation in Poland?' asked Bronek.

'Same as everyone I suppose. My mother is back there so I worry about her. The letters are still censored so I don't really know what hardships she's suffering as she can't say. She worked all her life for the bloody communist party but she never got anything out of it – not really.'

'She was always like that,' said Aleks. 'When I first saw her at a meeting of the Communist League I couldn't believe my eyes. She was so beautiful, so radiant, so eager. She was so serious, never laughed but what did it matter. I was in love.'

'She must had a little humour – she married you. It's true though and she never lost her idealism with age as most people do,' said Pawel. 'She is a true believer, like the horse Boxer in *Animal Farm*. She always thinks if she just works a little harder, then everything will work out fine. She believes in the cause and she must work for it.'

'A dreamer. She doesn't see the reality,' said Aleks.

Roger laughed. 'Is she one of those people who think *Imagine* is the best song ever written and full of profound political thought?'

'She's probably never heard of it,' said Pawel.

'All we ever hear about Poland is trouble and strikes and food shortages,' said Aleks. 'But it is actually a real country where things happen – music, laughter, love. I could tell you some stories.'

'What stories?' asked Bronek.

'Well, I'll tell you about my grandfather. He spent most of his life in a small village in Western Poland but before he died, he said he wanted to be buried in the village where he'd been born which was about 300 kilometers away. The trouble was, when he was actually laid out on his death bed, they didn't know how to get the body back there.'

Pawel was smiling, his face suddenly looking so much younger, and he was looking at his father with expectation. Aleks realised the lad didn't know any stories about that side of his family. He continued embellishing as much as he could.

'So my two uncles decided they would take my grandfather's body back to his village on the train. Obviously the train company wouldn't take corpses so they decided to dress grandfather in his best suit, pull his hat down over his eyes and take him to the railway station in his wheelchair. They bought three tickets and somehow managed to prop him between them and get him onto the train.'

Eunice began laughing, her hand over her mouth.

'Anyway, they dragged him along the corridor, found an empty compartment and propped grandfather's body up in the corner. They pulled down his hat over his face to make it look as if he were asleep. The train set off and all was going well. After an hour, my uncles began to get thirsty. They decided it would be all right to leave grandfather for a while so they went to the restaurant car for a beer.'

Aleks looked round the table. Roger was peeling a satsuma but listening intently. Eunice was grinning broadly, Pawel and Pam were both leaning forward with their elbows on the table, taking in every word. Bronek was resting his chin on his arm, a slight smile on his face.

' So they had a nice beer and wandered back to the compartment but grandfather was - gone! My uncles couldn't believe it. He had just disappeared. A soldier was now sitting in the seat opposite. So they asked him, 'Comrade soldier, have you seen our father who was sitting in the corner here?"

'The soldier said, 'Yes, he was here but he said he was going to the restaurant car for a drink.'

My uncles looked at each other, turned to the soldier and said, 'We're quite sure he didn't do that.'

Everyone at the table laughed.

So my uncles explained to the soldier what they were the doing and the soldier said, "Thank God for that." He told them he'd come into the carriage and put his heavy bag on the rack above the seats. The train jerked and the bag fell down and hit the man sleeping on the seat below. When the soldier checked he found the man was dead and thought he had killed him. He panicked and dragged the body to the door, opened it and threw the body out.'

Eunice shrieked with laughter. 'Did they get his body back?' asked Pawel.

'History doesn't relate,' said Aleks.

They all started laughing. Then silence fell.

'So, Pam, how did you meet Pawel?' asked Eunice.

Pam paused, 'I went to school with his wife Wanda.'

Everyone looked down at their plates or started to take a great interest in their napkin. Roger looked round the table with a half smile.

'That's killed the atmosphere stone dead,' he said.

'No, it's fine really,' said Pam quickly. 'It's just Pawel wanted to meet his father and I said I'd go with him, that's all.' She shrugged. 'These things happen – it's no big deal, I'll be back with my husband tomorrow.'

Chapter 23

Tadek lay in the intensive care ward hooked up to tubes and drips. A machine monitored his heart rate. The whole effect was surreal, thought Helena, as if they were in a television drama. She sat next to her husband, holding his hand. Janek and Wanda sat on the other side of the bed. The ward was dark with lamps over individual beds casting shadows over melancholy faces. There was a vague hum from the large, old fashioned heating system, a smell of antiseptic in the air masking the stench of urine.

'We need you to sign these permission forms, dad,' said Wanda waving them in front of his face. 'The doctors have to operate on your heart soon. Mum, he needs to sign them.'

'Wanda,' Helena closed her eyes, 'please, leave it to me.'

Tadek smiled at his daughter and she dropped her arms to her sides.

'Don't worry, I'll take care of things,' said Helena. 'Why don't you and Janek go and get yourselves a meal. You've been here for hours, Wanda, and I'm sure you're hungry. Also you need to phone Anna and reassure her that everything is all right. You have to think about her Wanda.'

'I should stay here,' said Wanda, but looked more doubtful.

'Come on,' said John. 'We need to leave mum to talk to dad for a while. We can go and eat. There's the Raj King just opposite here – let's get a beer and a good hot curry.'

John took his sister firmly by arm and Helena watched them leave, Wanda's heels clattering down the hard tiled ward floor, past the duty nurse and through the huge swing doors at the end of the corridor.

Helena stroked Tadek's forehead and kissed his hand. He smiled at her.

'Helenka' he whispered in a hoarse voice.

'Are you in a great deal of pain?' she asked.

'Not so bad. But it does feel as if a huge weight is sitting on my chest - like an anvil perched on my ribs. A strange, strange feeling.'

'This operation they're talking about involves putting a new artery to your heart – one that isn't clogged. The doctor said they take an artery from your leg. They want to operate tomorrow but they say it has an excellent chance of success. I think it's a good idea, don't you?'

Tadek closed his eyes. Helena gripped his hand tighter. She knew the doctors here had never done the operation before and perhaps they just wanted to experiment, as a medical curiosity. She felt sick with fear, terrified she would recommend the wrong action.

'I was thinking about my father,' Tadek said, breathing heavily through his nose. 'He was a blacksmith. Maybe that's why I see an anvil. He was always red faced from the heat of the furnace, he had huge, powerful hands and his arms were covered in little burns from the flying sparks.'

Helena stroked his arm. Tadek rarely spoke about his parents, indeed neither spoke much about the past. Yet emotions they had repressed for years were always threatening to overflow like boiling pots with the lid on, waiting to spill over.

'My father learned the trade from his father. He tried to teach me but I hated the heat, hated the noise of the clanging metal. I just wanted to be outside growing vegetables and looking after the animals.'

'Blacksmithing wouldn't suit you – it's too aggressive, too loud.'

'I used to hold the horse's reins while he put on the shoes. I was good at calming the horse, keeping it quiet. My father was so strong. You know, when you pick up a carthorse's leg to put on the shoe, it tends to put its whole weight on you. He had to be strong.'

Helena tried to imagine Tadek's upbringing in a small, country village, so different from her own early sophisticated life in the city.

'You're Mother Nature's boy. You belong with the plants and animals.'

'I learned that from my mother. She knew all about herbs, roots, wild mushrooms. People in the village would come to her for remedies. They used to say she was a bit of a witch. I wonder what she would prescribe for Coronary Artery Disease – nettle soup probably'.

Helena smiled.

'When you get older, there are more dead people in your mind than living,' Tadek continued. 'My grandparents, my father and mother, my sisters, the schoolfriend of mine who lay down on the railway track when he was 14, the girls from a school near my house who were all shot by the Germans in retaliation for something or other – and of course, my dear, sweet little Zosia.'

He turned his head slightly towards his wife. 'If it's true, if there is a heaven I will see her again. What are the chances of it being true do you think?'

Wanda and John took their seats in the Raj King Indian Restaurant. The lighting was gloomy, red flock wallpaper, black tablecloths, portraits of Hindu gods and a soundtrack of Indian music depressed the atmosphere further. Wanda felt so far removed from her father, her family in this place, she didn't want to be there. How could she stop Janek bossing her around. A young waiter approached, wearing a white waistcoat, his black hair greased down on his head. He looked nervous, inexperienced.

'We'll have a vindaloo, boiled rice, two naan bread, and a sag aloo,' said John loudly adopting a condescending tone. 'Also two beers – or do you want a soft drink, Wanda?'

'I don't mind, really I don't,' said Wanda looking at the red carpet. The young man bowed and walked away.

'There are so many Pakis in Derby now,' said John before the waiter had gone too far. 'I hope that one who is going to operate on Dad knows his stuff.'

'Pakis? That's rich coming from you – Janek Tadeusz Baran! Just because you call yourself John Allsop doesn't hide the fact that you are an immigrant too,' said Wanda. 'Anyway, this is an Indian restaurant not Pakistani. What if people said to us, Polish, Russian, Ukrainian – it's all the same.'

'Ok, it's just when we were little everyone was white – they might have been Irish, or Polish, or Italian but at St Joseph's they were all white.'

Wanda shrugged and looked away. The drinks arrived and John took a gulp of beer.

'I should really phone Anna,' said Wanda checking her watch, 'although she's probably in bed by now. Is Maxine ok with having her?' said Wanda.

'Yes, don't worry. She'll be fine.'

'I can't worry about more than one thing at a time and my head is too full of worry about dad at the moment.'

The waiter arrived with trays full of food – hot steaming spice smells filled the air. John breathed in deeply, took a poppadom and crunched it in his mouth.

'This new heart bypass operation sounds good, though, doesn't it?' said John, bits of poppadom falling out of his mouth.

'I know but these particular doctors haven't done it before. I'm a bit worried that they are experimenting on our father.' Wanda watched her brother eat, wondering how he could be so casual, so hungry!

'Well, they probably want to try it from a professional point of view but it will notched up as a success if they save his life. He's - what is he now – 60 this year.'

Wanda looked at the little bowls of brightly coloured food and watched John pop a dollop of saag aloo in his mouth. A blob of spinach fell onto his tie.

'I really don't feel like eating, Janek,' said Wanda miserably, letting her fork clatter down on her plate.

The heat was stifling in the ward forcing Helena to take off her coat and then her cardigan. The elderly man in the next bed was moaning and plucking aimlessly at his covers, his eyes shut. His face was sunken. No one took any notice.

Helena looked round at the other beds, she could almost feel the years of pain and grief fill the Victorian rooms. A hundred years ago it was a workhouse, full of separated families, hungry children, forced labour. The nurse at the end of ward was sitting at her desk, writing, her face illuminated by an anglepoise lamp. She was tapping her flat black shoe rhythmically against the leg of the chair.

Helena bit her lip and looked down at her fingers stroking her husband's hand.

'I have been thinking about my father a great deal, just like you. I want to know him better. When you don't have a father in your life – there is a gap,' said Helena.

'I'm a very lucky man,' said Tadek, looking at the ceiling. He paused and closed his eyes. 'You know what I was also thinking about just now? The aliens' registration office in south London when I first saw you, I think it was 1946. You looked so beautiful but thin and tired. I gave you my sandwich and you smiled at me. That was heaven.'

Helena felt tears come to her eyes and she blinked them away. 'I remember looking out of the window of that horrible office and seeing some children playing on the bomb site opposite,' she said. 'I realised more than anything I wanted children, many children. After everything we had been through, I knew that having children was so vital.'

'I thought English children were the most beautiful in Europe,' whispered Tadek. 'I was so used to seeing ill, hungry, thin children in war torn countries that the children here looked so healthy. No one was starving. Everything seemed so peaceful here despite the bomb craters and the rubble. Astonishing.'

'When you said to me you thought the children were beautiful, I knew you were a good man. I was right of course.'

Helena bent down and kissed Tadek's hand again.

'Do you remember that shabby flat we had just after we married,' said Helena. 'That strange group of Polish refugees we lived with: aristocrats, farmers, soldiers, policemen – none with a penny to their name. We had fun at our wedding reception, though, didn't we? We were all so relieved the war was over, we had survived that we were all a bit hysterical, I think. Or traumatised.'

Tadek's eyes closed again and he made a grimace of pain.

'I'm tiring you, we should stop talking,' she said.

'No I want to talk – I may not get the chance again.'

Helena couldn't bear to hear that, she convinced herself that it could not be true. She had married a man who she knew was steady, reliable, who loved her. It was what she'd needed at the time but she wasn't in love with him. Love grew later but there had never been any passion. Helena looked down at her hands in guilt.

'The NHS will save your life – I'm certain of that,' said Helena. 'We don't think about it until we're ill and then you cling to it like a child to its mother.'

'Zosia used to dig in the garden, do you remember, and find little bits and pieces. Her special things. I came across her box of treasures the other day. Did Wanda tell you? I thought we could give it to Anna when she is a little older – something to know her auntie by. Do you think that's a good idea?'

'Yes, that's a very good idea,' agreed Helena.

Tadek rested his head on the white pillow stamped with a read motif that read, Derbyshire Health Authority.

'Come on, just try a little bit,' urged John. Maybe the pain of the curry would take his sister's mind off what was happening to their father. He watched her put a little in her mouth. She quickly took a drink of water.

'This vindaloo is burning my tongue, it's probably made a hole right through my skin. Why do men think it's so macho to order curry that's too hot – there is no taste, only pain,' said Wanda.

'It's not that hot, you exaggerate.' John looked at her. It was so funny watching her eating curry – she really wasn't in her natural habitat. Suddenly he felt a pang of sorrow. A few days earlier, Maxine had seen Pawel holding hands with Pam in Markeaton Park. He couldn't say anything to his sister. He couldn't say anything to his office manager either.

'Is Pawel back yet?' he asked.

'No and he hasn't phoned either but I do know where he's gone and I know exactly who he is seeing.'

John sat forward, his heart fluttering. He felt his mouth go dry. 'Do you?' he said nervously.

She leaned forward. 'He's gone to meet his long-lost father,' she said.

Chapter 24

Wanda slowly walked up the couple of steps to the front door of 16 Porton Crescent with Anna by her side. She put her key in the door and went into the hall.

'Put your coat on the hallstand, sweetheart,' Wanda whispered. She stood for a few minutes looking at her pale face in the hall mirror then glanced up at the staircase. She saw 10-year-old Zosia sitting on the middle step her hand on the banister, wearing her red dress with the tulip decoration. Zosia was just staring straight ahead, she wasn't crying. Then she suddenly looked down at Wanda, her face expressionless.

Wanda closed her eyes for a moment and her sister was gone. There was a suitcase on the bottom step. She stared at it for a while then opened the door into the sitting room. Pawel was sitting on the sofa, drinking a beer. He had his bare feet on the coffee table and he was watching the football, the volume turned up loud.

'Where have you been?' he shouted over the roar of the television. 'I came back this morning and no one was around. I was just about to phone Janek to see where everyone was.' He belched loudly. Anna came into the room and sat on the armchair.

'Hello, Daddy,' she said, pulling her skirt over knees.

Pawel looked at her. 'And where have you been all this time?'

'Staying with auntie Maxine' said Anna.

'Where's your babcia?'

'Still at uncle Janek's and auntie Maxine's.'

'She must be desperate for company. Wanda, make me a bacon sandwich, will you? I'm exhausted, there was so much traffic on the M1 I was almost stationary for about an hour. I think you know who I met in London.'

Wanda went into the kitchen without replying, took some bacon out of the fridge and laid three rashers in the frying pan.

'Why didn't you tell me you wrote to him? I wouldn't have been angry. He is my father after all,' Pawel called. 'Anyway, do you want to know what my father – this man of legend - is like? He looks like an older version of me, I suppose. Greying hair and plenty of it, round gut and quite tall but not as tall as I remembered. Although the last time I saw him, I was only four and I thought he was as high as the ceiling.'

Pawel got up and went into the kitchen. He watched as Wanda cracked an egg into the pan, sliced some bread and put it in the toaster.

'He has reinvented himself as some kind of artist, can you believe it?' Pawel continued. 'The only artistic thing about him is his creative accounting. He was in prison for two years for embezzlement, my mother told me that. I'm sure he's conning these people he's staying with. They are artists and they're putting on this exhibition called 'Stories from Behind the Wall'. They think he will contribute to it.

Wanda took out the butter and put the kettle on.

'His friends think he was imprisoned because the authorities didn't care for his 'art'. It's such a joke. My mother was always too good for him – I told him that and at least he had the decency to agree.'

Wanda turned the bacon over and added some tomatoes and mushrooms to the pan.

'Funny, isn't it? I spent so many years wanting my father, praying he would come back, imagining I saw him in the street, replaying the last time he walked out of the flat with me running to the window and waving to him down in the courtyard.'

Wanda spread butter on the toast and poured the boiling water in the teapot.

'And now I've met him again and I realised – nothing. Do you know what my mother once said to me, 'W'rk hard and do your best or what happened to your father will happen to you." And I said, 'What happened to my father?' And she said, 'Nothing".

Wanda set two mugs of tea and the plate of bacon, eggs, mushroom and tomato on a tray along with the plate of toast. She carried it to the dining table. Pawel followed.

'I used to hero-worship him. I cried for hours at night for him to come home. Now I've met I just want to tell him – 'Too late, it's too late – just fuck off.' I don't know if I even want to see him again.'

Wanda sat down at the table and took a sip of her tea.

'So that's fathers for you. Good riddance to bad rubbish.'

Pawel began to eat his meal.

With his mouth full he asked, 'Where have you been anyway. I rang last night and no one answered. I told you I'd ring.'

Wanda put down her tea cup and looked at Pawel. 'My father died yesterday,' she said.

Chapter 25

Derby, 1983

It was one of those days rare days in England when the clear blue sky was so perfect, so unalloyed that it seemed a sin to remain indoors. John stood in his garden looking up at the cloudless sky criss-crossed only with aeroplane vapour trails. He noticed the lawn was starting to yellow due to the lack of summer rain. He must remind the gardener to water it tomorrow. John was proud of his land, the grass sweeping down before him towards a wooden fence with the river Went beyond. The gazebo, ornamental fountain and sundial, all installed by Reg back in the 1970s, were still the main features of the garden. John had bought a new table and garden chairs so they could eat out on the patio.

He checked the yellow roses trained to grow over the sidewall. Their nodding heads gave off an uplifting perfume. He thought of his father and Tadek's meticulous care for his garden. Last time he was at Porton Crescent he noticed the garden was looking unkempt. He made a mental note to send his gardener over sometime to tidy it up.

John touched a velvety yellow rose petal and decided he would cut some roses to put on his father's grave. They had buried Tadek with Zosia and Babcia: his daughter and mother-in-law, three generations under one turf. His mother had been distraught when she was told three was the limit in one plot. 'Where will I go?' she'd asked plaintively.

John looked at his watch, it was 12.30. Derek had told him the invitation was from 2pm. The dress code was, apparently, 'smart casual'. He went into the sitting room, his eyes unaccustomed to the gloom. Lily was sitting in her usual chair, watching *Countdown* on television.

'Oh, I don't know how they get those long words,' she said not looking away from the screen. 'I can't do them big sums either come to that. I do like that lovely girl what puts the letters out. And she can do the sums so quick. How did she learn that?'

'I think she went to Cambridge. Where's Maxine?'

'Upstairs. She's reading *Buxom Belles*, whatever you call it. She's been reading it all morning.'

At that moment Clarke came running and bashed his father hard between the legs. John felt tears come to his eyes as he fended the boy off.

'Clarke, don't hit me,' said John holding his son away. 'Bloody thug' he murmured under his breath.

'I'm Luke Skywalker. Mummy bought me a light sabre and white costume.'

'That makes me Darth Vader, does it?' said John. 'We need to get you washed and ready. Let's find mummy, shall we? Amber is having a nap I suppose.'

He went up to his bedroom. Maxine was sitting on the bed blowing her nose on a tissue and wiping her eyes. Sheets of paper were spread out around the bed.

'What the matter?' he asked.

'This story is so good, it's so sad.'

'What, *Buxton Belles*? Do you really like it?' He picked up a sheet and looked at it incredulously.

'It's fantastic. I found it on your bedside table yesterday and thought I'd have a quick look. I haven't been able to stop reading it.'

'We should be getting ready to go to Derek's.'

John picked up the papers and put them together in a pile and secured them with the rubber band.

'I think I'll take this to Wanda and see if she likes it,' she said.

'I want to go up to Buxton and see all the places she describes. Were these families real?'

'I think it's fiction but you can ask Samantha if there's any truth in any of it. Get changed, we must go.'

Dressed in a smart suit, John waited in the car for Maxine and the children. Clarke was fighting as usual but Maxine had got him into clean trousers and a white shirt. Amber had a pink dress with a pink elastic band and bow round her head. John looked at her and his first thought was that the pink dress exactly matched the huge pink, raised birthmark on Amber's face. He said nothing. Maxine hated anyone to mention the disfigurement so they all pretended it didn't exist. All except Clarke who constantly shouted about Amber's 'strawberry.'

'How many people are coming to this party, do you know?' asked Maxine rubbing at a strain on her white skirt. She was wearing a blue and white striped blouse that was too small for her and it gaped open in the front and showed her bra. John wondered if he should mention it but decided it wouldn't be worth the aggravation.

'About 20, apparently. Derek is so proud of this child, he talks about nothing else. So we have to say the baby is beautiful even if it's ugly.'

'Of course he won't be ugly – what a thing to say. He has a beautiful mother. I'm sure he's a lovely little baby.'

Mm, a gorgeous mother, thought John.

'Wanda will be coming but she says Pawel is working.'

'Working? That's unusual.'

'Yes, amazingly. He's got some work in a private house he has to finish. The couple there are divorcing and they want to sell it quickly. So he's working Sunday to get it done.'

'We could pick up Wanda on the way.'

'I suggested that but she said she would make her own way there. She says Anna loves going on the bus.'

They drove to Derek and Pam's semi-detached house in Belper. A bunch of pale blue balloons, fluttering in the breeze, were tied to the front gate.

'Ah, look, blue for a boy,' said Maxine, getting out of the car. She carried the champagne and presents – two pairs of little blue trousers and an activity board from Mothercare. The card read, 'Welcome to baby Ben. Love from John, Maxine, Clarke and Amber.' The bottle had a blue ribbon round the top and the presents were wrapped in paper decorated with rattles and drums.

Derek, beaming from ear to ear, greeted them at the door. He was wearing an apron that said, *Stand back, Dad is cooking.* John thought he had never seen him look so happy. He seemed years younger and appeared to have a completely new lease of life. He even gave John a hug – unheard-of behaviour. They followed him into the dining room.

Derek handed them both a glass of champagne. John looked round the room. Mr and Mrs Haines, Pam's parents, sat in the corner. Mr Haines, now retired, was smoking his pipe.

He raised a glass to Mrs Haines. 'Congratulations to the proud grandparents.'

Pam walked in radiant in a red flowered Laura Ashley dress with wide white collar and belt. She had on matching red high heels and a white flower in her hair.

'John, lovely to see you.' She bent forward to kiss his cheek but John went for her other cheek and accidentally kissed her on the lips. He felt a frisson of excitement at the touch. Pam's eyes shone, she touched his arm. 'Thanks so much for the present,' she said smiling at him.

'And where is the little fellow?' said Maxine, her plate piled high with vol au vents, sausage rolls and crisps.

'He's having a nap at the moment,' said Pam. 'The excitement got too much for him. We just had a little blessing at St Joseph's with my parents and Derek's mum and he was so good. Come outside to the garden when you're ready. It's such a lovely day.'

John piled his plate with salad and wandered outside. Clarke was already in the garden sword fighting with another little boy, and Amber was on the swing being pushed by a little girl with long, blonde hair. Pam was laughing loudly with a woman John vaguely recognised but couldn't quite place. Pam saw him staring at her.

'John, do you remember Lydia? Her dad used to be the manager of the Polish club.'

'Oh, Lydia, yes of course. You went to school with my sister.'

'Yes, with the lovely Zosia. Is Wanda here? I'd love to see her?'

'She's on her way with her daughter, Anna.'

'Late again,' laughed Pam. 'I'm sure there was some hilarious mishap she'll tell us all about.'

'And you have children, don't you, Janek? Are they here?' asked Lydia.

John pointed out his children and asked about Lydia's son.

'That's Tomasz over there – he's nearly 6 foot tall. Can you believe?'

John looked over and saw a young man helping Derek with the barbecue. That was the baby who caused such a scandal when Lydia, aged only 17, had become pregnant. That baby was now 14 years old and looked about 20. Some noise and excitement from the kitchen heralded the arrival of Wanda and Anna.

'Ah, here she is,' said Lydia.

Wanda appeared, clutching a champagne glass filled with bubbly.

'Sorry, I'm late, folks. The heel of my shoe broke as I got off the bus. Look, I have it here. It snapped right off. I had to lurch up and down as I came to the door. It looked like my Richard III impression,' said Wanda holding up the heel.

'Bring the other shoe here and I'll snap that heel off so at least you'll be the same height,' shouted Derek. John was amazed – he'd never heard Derek make a joke before.

'You're all right, Derek. I've embarrassed Anna enough. I hope to borrow some slip-ons from Pam for the way back. Can't wait to see your little son. He was only two days old when I last saw him in the hospital – having a nap, is he?'

'Anna, you little darling,' said Lydia. ' Oh, God love her, she's the spitting image of her auntie Zosia. Aren't you, my darling?' She gave Anna a hug.

'I don't know,' said Anna stiffly. 'I never met her.'

'No, of course you didn't.' said Lydia.

'She's her own person, aren't you, sweetheart?' said John.

'Who wants some badly cooked meat?' asked Derek.

'Don't say that, Derek. It's finest quality from Marks & Sparks,' said Pam.

'It's the cooking technique, not the meat,' said Derek's brother Cliff. 'Is it burnt on the outside and raw in the middle in the finest barbecue tradition?'

Perched on garden chairs, kitchen high stools and camping chairs, everyone began to eat. Glasses clinked and the children screamed and shouted at the bottom of the garden. Anna sat next to her mother, carefully eating a beefburger in her fingers. From an upstairs window came the sound of wailing.

'Baby's awake,' said Derek.

'I'll go and get little Ben everyone,' said Pam. 'Time the party boy was here to meet everyone.' And she disappeared into the house.

'Ben Hoar,' whispered Wanda to John. 'Perhaps he'll turn out to be good at chariot racing.'

John sniggered. 'I said to Maxine the other day, 'I'm just off to visit the Hoars.'

'She should have said, 'Don't let them overcharge you'.

'I know, but that's not Maxine's style. How's mum, by the way. She seems to be coping well. Keeping busy.'

'She's working on her thesis. She's done about 50 interviews I think. She's also researching the life of this uncle of hers, Dr Nathan Weinberg. I'm not sure why. He was an early psychiatrist or something. She keeps going through a folder of his full of bits of paper and documents. She seems very wrapped in her own world. Sometimes I think it's just something to do rather than spending time grieving for dad.'

'I'm glad she's doing work she loves,' insisted John. 'I think she always…' His voice trailed away as he saw a strange expression come over Wanda's face. She became suddenly very still, her eyes widened and she reached out and grasped John's hand. He followed the direction of her gaze.

Pam was standing by the back door holding her son Ben who was blinking in the sunlight and rubbing his eyes with his tiny fists. Everyone was crowding round, taking his chubby little hand and declaring how much he had grown.

John gave an involuntary intake of breath. A feeling of dread came over him. He squeezed Wanda's hand as they both stared at the baby.

Couldn't everyone see it? Wasn't it glaringly, stunningly obvious? Ben had bright green eyes, a wide Slavic face and blonde hair. He was the absolute image of Pawel.

Chapter 26

Sometimes you reach the stage where there is nothing left to fear. It's all gone so wrong, so monumentally wrong, that nothing matters. You can say and do exactly as you wish.

Wanda was sitting in her father's favourite brown-coloured armchair in the sitting room at Porton Crescent. The lights were off. A thin, muted light came through the windows — the dying light of an English summer's day. It was around 9pm.

Wanda had asked her mother to take Anna to Janek's house. She told her she needed to speak to Pawel and she didn't want anyone else there. Helena tried to question her but Wanda was saying nothing and Helena could see her daughter was in no mood to be crossed. She packed a little overnight bag for herself and Anna and left.

Wanda poured herself a large whisky. She didn't know why she was drinking whisky, she hated it. Why was there even any whisky in her father's cabinet – he'd never drunk it either. Where had he got it from? Stupid how mundane thoughts came to her even at times like these. She picked at loose threads on the arm of the chair, feeling more and more light-headed. Pam had once said Pawel looked like Michael York. How flattered Wanda had been by that comment, flattered that her husband looked like a handsome actor. You stupid idiot, she thought bitterly. You stupid, stupid fool.

Half an hour went by. Pawel's van pulled up into the drive. Wanda heard his key in the lock, and his boots scraping on the mat. He dumped his bags of tools with a clang in the hall. Wanda clenched her fists, her heart thumping in her chest. Zosia, aged about 13, dressed in her

Pinecrest uniform, was sitting on one end of the sofa. She pulled up her white socks and looked at Wanda, a slight smile on her face.

'It's not you I have to worry about,' whispered Wanda fiercely. 'It's not the dead who are the problem, it's the bloody living!'

Wanda watched the door – soon it would open. She felt oddly calm, powerful, in control. Her resolve faltered a little when she heard Pawel whistling. He was happy? She saw the door handle move and he came in.

'Why are you sitting in the dark?' He reached out and put on the light.

Wanda took in a deep breath as light flooded the room. She said nothing.

'Did you have a nice day?' asked Pawel, after a confused pause.

'I went to Pam and Derek's baby's christening party.'

'Right, so I suppose you've eaten already.' He turned to leave.

'They are so very, very pleased with their new baby. Do you realise how delighted they are with him?' said Wanda. A deathless hush filled her body.

Pawel turned back again and stared at Wanda in confusion. 'That's good,' he said finally and laughed. 'Perhaps being a mum will make a decent human being of Pam.'

'Will it? Do you think so? Do you really think so?'

'I'd better get changed,' said Pawel nervously.

'No, stay where you are. I sat in Pam and Derek's garden. Derek was at the barbecue. He had on an apron that said 'Dad is cooking.' John, Maxine and the kids were there. Anna was there. Lydia from school was there. Family, friends, so many happy, drunk, well-fed people.'

Pawel frowned but was starting to look frightened.

'The baby – his name is Ben by the way – was having a nap. He is nearly six months old. So everyone was laughing and joking then Pam eventually brought Ben down to show him to the audience of, let me think, about 20 people.'

Wanda glanced at the sofa and saw Zosia looking at her. She had that superior, I-told-you-so expression on her face, a slight smile playing round her lips.

'Stop it, stop it, stop fucking laughing at me. You're always making fun of me,' she screamed at Zosia.

'I'm not laughing, I swear….' stammered Pawel.

Wanda stood up and walked towards him.

Her hair was dishevelled where she'd been running her hands through it. Some mascara had smudged beneath one eye, her neck was bright red with emotion, her fists clenched.

'Let me describe the happy parents to you in detail. Pam has pale skin, dark red hair and blue eyes, Derek has light ginger hair, pale skin, blue eyes, a round nose and a thin face. Ben, on the other hand, has deep green eyes, olive skin, blonde hair, a wide face and Roman nose.'

Pawel swallowed and stared hard at this wife. He began to breathe heavily.

'Janek noticed straightaway. He grabbed my hand. We were both thinking the same thing. Ben looks exactly like his father, he's the spitting image of his father.'

'I don't know, I don't know anything about…'

Wanda was now standing right in front of Pawel. She could smell the whisky on her breath. The words came flooding out of her.

'Derek is infertile, he is firing blanks – Pam told me that two years ago. How can Pam have a baby if her husband is unable to have children? How, Pawel? How?'

Pawel began to back away a little. Wanda moved forward.

'I am so sick of the world and his wife treating me like a piece of rubbish, like shit,' screamed Wanda. 'Good old fat Wanda, stupid Wanda, you can always rely on her to make a fool of herself. Well, I suppose I should expect that from others but when my husband… If my father was here…'

Finally, tears came to Wanda's eyes and chin began to wobble uncontrollably.

'Pam is a bitch, I'm sorry – I didn't realise what she was like. She is evil, evil.' Pawel spoke quickly.

'Oh, she forced you to sleep with her. Is that it? She put a gun to your head.'

'No, but I didn't know she was... I had no idea that Derek was...'

'...that she was using you as a stud?'

Pawel dropped to his knees. 'I'm so sorry, I honestly didn't know. Please, please forgive me. If I had known that, I would never...' Tears were pouring down his face, he was down on all fours, dribble falling from his mouth.

Wanda stopped and looked down at him. Part of her wanted to kneel down next to him, to put her head on his shoulder, to ask him to hold her. But she didn't. She stood there looking at him grovelling on the floor.

'Go upstairs, Pawel, and pack a suitcase. You can keep the van. Get out of my house. I don't ever want to see you again.'

'Wanda, I love you. I never realised how much but Pam is so evil. I didn't know how much I wanted you.'

'Pam isn't evil, she just takes what she wants. But she couldn't do that if people didn't give her what she wants. She uses people but they let themselves be used.'

'Don't send me away. Anna needs me – is she asleep? I want to see her. I want my daughter.'

'Don't give me that crap – you never wanted her, you were only interested in yourself, you always have been.'

All Wanda wanted now was to hurt him as he had hurt her. She wanted to be as cruel and as vicious as she could be.

'No, it isn't true. I love her, I want to be her daddy.' Tears and snot fell on the carpet from Pawel's face.

'And what about your son – do you want to be his daddy? Are you going to challenge Derek?'

'No, I have only one child, that is Anna.'

'Pawel, you are only interested in yourself, you take what you want. You only married me so you could stay in this country. You know what, actually you and Pam would make a good couple. Trouble is she wants a wealthy man – not a lazy, useless, pointless painter and decorator. That's so annoying isn't it?'

Zosia sat smiling on the sofa, doing an ironic slow handclap.

Chapter 27

Bronek leaned over and opened the passenger door. Aleks got in and slammed it shut hard.

'Careful! You'll shatter the windscreen,' said Bronek. 'Look, Pawel wants something.'

Pawel was waving his arms above his head at his father. Aleks slowly wound down the window. Pawel leaned into the car.

'I bought these for Wanda. Please give them to her. And this is a book for Anna.'

'Ok, Pawel, see you in a few days. I'll ring you when we get there.'

'Yeah, thanks, Dad.'

Aleks took the things and put them on the back seat. Pawel backed away and Aleks wound up the window again.

'Did you hear that? He called me Dad,' said Aleks looking at Bronek.

'Poor bugger, he looks so upset. And look at those pathetic presents. He really is in a bad way. You're supposed to plead his cause with those things.'

Aleks looked at the presents. There was a small bunch of freesias, a box of Ferrero Rocher chocolates and a copy of the children's classic *The Secret Garden*.

Aleks tutted. 'Idiot,' he said under his breath.

'This is the second time I find myself driving you around, trying to solve your problems. Why do I do that?' asked Bronek.

'Because you have nothing better to do in your tedious life,' said Aleks.

Bronek started the engine. 'I suppose it's true - you make life interesting.'

They drove along Arlington Rd up to Parkway, past the Spread Eagle pub where Aleks had taken Pawel the evening three weeks previously when he'd turned up on his doorstep. His son had stood on the threshold, dripping wet in the pouring rain, his face etched with misery.

'Can I stay here tonight?' was all he'd said. Aleks could guess the rest of the scenario.

They drove along to Regents Park, Swiss Cottage and up to Brent Cross where they joined the motorway.

'I don't think I've been to Derby, before although I think I went through it on the train when I was going to the Peak District for a holiday when I was at school,' said Bronek.

'Well, it will be the first time for both of us.'

They drove in silence for a while.

'So Pawel's wife found out he was having an affair with that girl Pam, did she? Is that what happened?' Bronek said eventually.

Aleks sighed. 'It's even worse than that.'

Aleks told him about Wanda going to the christening party, seeing Pam's baby son who was the image of Pawel and working out what had happened.

'Shit – how terrible.'

'Yeah, a red haired, blue-eyed English couple apparently have a baby who looks like a little Polak.'

'Jesus, this is a bad idea going up there. It's going to be really heavy seeing your daughter-in-law. She won't want to see you,' said Bronek.

'I'm going to meet my granddaughter – that is all. I have a right to see her.'

'Do you? I'm not sure. I suppose that is the only card you can play with Pawel's wife. It might bring her round. Unlikely, though.'

There was another silence.

'You could also meet your grandson,' said Bronek pulling a face.

Aleks shook his head. 'God, don't.'

They stopped at Watford Gap services for coffee. Aleks looked round at the red plastic chairs and the glass cabinets full of greasy sausages, chips and baked beans.

'You know everyone laughs at English food,' said Aleks. 'The worst cuisine in Europe.'

'If you think it's bad now, you should have tried it 25 years ago,' said Bronek. The school dinners they served us when I was a kid were disgusting. I think people got used to rubbish food in the war with the rationing but they never thought to improve it afterwards.'

'And baked beans – how can people eat those? What's that?' said Aleks pointing at some black circles nestling among the baked beans.

'We're getting nearer the north – that's black pudding. It's made with blood and guts I think. I don't eat it.'

'And the toast is so pale and soggy,' continued Aleks. 'And look at that...'

'Ok, ok – you know what, if things are better here than Poland stop complaining, if they are better in Poland, then go back there. End of story.'

'Sorry, I didn't mean to offend your nationalist pride.'

They found a seat on the plastic chairs and put their drinks on the table still piles with dirty plates and spilled food. Aleks looked out of the windows at the traffic roaring up the M1. A family of four with two small children sat nearby drinking Coke and eating chips. Bronek looked at them.

'Have you noticed people are getting so fat these days,' he whispered.

'I can't comment,' said Aleks patting his gut.

'No, I mean young people, children.'

'It's the good life I suppose.'

'It's cheap, bad food I think.'

'During the war, I saw people starving. I saw dead bodies on the street, people who were just a pile of bones with a little skin stretched over them. In comparison I don't mind fat people.'

The mother of the young family opposite poured Coke into her toddler's bottle. Bronek turned back to Aleks.

'Are you still working at the Docklands project?'

'Yes,' said Aleks lighting a cigarette. 'It's going to be a huge complex, like a mini Manhattan in London. I'll get Pawel some work there when his mind is in a fit state to do something.'

Bronek pointed at the *Coal Not Dole* badge on Aleks's lapel. 'Did Roger give you that?'

'He likes to wear his opinions on his lapel. It means he pays lip service to his cause without actually having to do anything.'

'You seem to doing well out of Thatcher's policies. Lots of work, plenty of money,' said Bronek.

Aleks shrugged. Life was ok, there was no denying it. Long may it last.

'You know, I suspect people like Roger secretly love Mrs Thatcher,' Bronek continued. 'She really gives them a rallying point, someone they can all happily hate together. She's caused such camaraderie. They'll miss her when she's gone,'

'I wear the badge to please Roger since I'm living in his house and don't want to be thrown out. It's probably a good thing Mrs Thatcher is getting rid of all those old communists but I really don't have an opinion on it all.'

'Mrs Thatcher supports trade unions in Poland but wants to crush them in Britain. I'm sure the irony is lost on her. She's not known for her sense of humour.'

Chapter 28

John looked at the balance sheets with satisfaction. There had been a huge turnaround in the business and profits were rising fast. The workforce had been pared down and new technology put to good use. Orders were flooding in – things were booming. They had more work than they could handle. John wasn't sure how, but he had done it.

He leaned back on his leather, swivel chair and looked up at Reg Allsop's portrait on the office wall. I'm going to outdo your record, he mused. But I don't just want to have a small printing firm, I want to do more. I want us to be famous. I want to make a mark on this world. He picked up the manuscript. *Buxton Belles by Samantha Foy*. He was going to do it, he was going to publish the stupid novel. He'd use all his contacts to get the book reviewed, the author interviewed, get her on Radio Derby, in the *Derby Evening Telegraph* – then go national, get mentions in the broadsheets, get on Breakfast telly.

Maxine had loved the book so much she had gone on a trip to the North Derbyshire town with Samantha to look at the places mentioned. John had given a copy to Wanda and she told him it had helped her get over her depression about Pawel. John had even seen Lily looking through it so they must be easy to read, addictive. That's what I want, books that are the equivalent of crack cocaine, thought John.

The door opened and Derek walked in, holding a copy of the book. John looked at him.

'Did Pam like it?'

'She absolutely loved it. Read it in one sitting. We've got to get the rest of the series out.'

John grinned. 'That's exactly what I think. Let's take a punt on this thing. Publish and be damned. The ladies love it – so we're going to make money. Even Wanda came out of her depression for a while to read it.'

Derek paused. 'John, I've been meaning to ask you. Do you know why Pam and Wanda had a falling out? Pam just said they're no longer friends but when I asked why, she said it was just a silly little argument.'

John looked at Derek and thought, there are none so blind as those who will not see. He had to play things carefully.

'I don't know what the argument was about, Derek. Wanda is having a bad time with her husband leaving her. She's so touchy at the moment that perhaps she took something Pam said the wrong way. Anyway, least said soonest mended. The best thing is to let it all blow over and don't pry.'

'No, I wasn't prying,' said Derek looking shocked. 'I just hope it doesn't mean there is any problem between you and me.'

'Of course, not Derek. It has nothing to do with us so we should just carry on as normal.'

John smiled reassuringly. How on earth could Derek imagine that baby was his? Pam had brought the child into the office last week and every day he looked more and more like Pawel. She had looked definitely at John as if challenging him. She knew he knew, but no one was saying a word.

Aleks and Bronek drew up outside 16 Porton Crescent. They both sat and stared at the house.

'I think I should wait in the car – she doesn't know me from Adam. You can call me in later if she agrees,' said Bronek.

'No, come on in. I don't know how long we'll be. She might slam the door in our faces or invite us in for an hour. Let's see.'

They walked up the path to the front door. It looked like a typical English house to Aleks, he'd seen row upon row of them on the way up. They were so different from the soulless blocks of flats he was used in his native country. He rang the doorbell and they waited. There was a little plot of land in front of the house, a small lawn bordered with a flowerbed of lavender, azaleas and daisies. There were empty milk bottles on the front step and a mat with the word 'welcome'.

The door was opened by a little girl of around eight years. My granddaughter, thought Aleks with a sudden rush of emotion. What a beautiful child.

'Hello, is your mummy at home?' he asked.

Anna nodded and called behind her shoulder. A woman walked down the hall towards the door, wiping her hands on a tea towel. She looked tired and had deep, dark bags under her eyes. She wore no make-up, her blonde hair was uncombed and she was dressed in a baggy shapeless blue dress and old carpet slippers. Her clothes hung off her as if she had lost weight.

'Can I help you?' she asked looking at them. Then she paused and stared harder at Aleks. He bowed.

'I am Aleksander Lato. You must be Wanda. I have come to beg a favour. I would so like to talk to you and meet my granddaughter. Please?'

He looked imploringly at her. Wanda said nothing, her face a mask of blank indifference.

'This is my friend Bronek Olszewski,' continued Aleks. 'He gave me a lift from London. He is British but his parents were Polish. I met him in Warsaw. He was my first English teacher.'

Bronek smiled and nodded. There was a long silence.

'Well, you had better come in,' said Wanda turning her back on them and walking back down the hall. Anna was looking puzzled, staring from Aleks to her mother.

'Kochana,' said Aleks bending down towards Anna. 'I am your grandfather. I'm so happy to meet you.'

Anna backed away slightly, looking worried. Aleks stood up straight and decided to take things slowly. They walked into the hall and closed the front door and followed Wanda through to the kitchen.

'Do you want a drink?' she said sullenly.

'Coffee for me,' said Bronek, 'if it's not too much trouble. Do you want tea, Aleks?'

'Lovely,' said Aleks. 'Anna, I have brought you a Rubik's Cube. Have you seen one before? I can't work out the mechanism it uses, it's ingenious. You have to get every side the same colour. Do you think you'll be able to do it?'

The little girl took the multi-coloured cube and started twisting it. She wandered off to another room with it leaving Aleks, Wanda and Bronek in the kitchen.

'Thank you for inviting us in,' said Bronek. 'It's really generous of you.' Without waiting to be asked, Aleks took a seat at the table. Bronek followed suit. Wanda said nothing but turned her back on them and put on the kettle. She took three mugs out of the cupboard. As the kettle boiled and filled the kitchen with the steam, the silence grew more intense.

Aleks noticed she had a hole in her tights. He looked around the kitchen. The calendar on the wall showed Polish cityscapes – September was Lodz. A notice board next to it was covered in postcards, electricity bills and flyers for takeaway restaurants. There was one envelope with a Polish stamp.

Wanda put the drinks on the table with a plate of biscuits. Aleks noticed Bronek's mug carried the slogan *World's Best Dad* in red lettering. Wanda sat down.

'Did Pawel send you?' asked Wanda brusquely in English, looking at the table.

'No,' replied Bronek also in English. 'Aleks wanted to visit you and I agreed to give him a lift here. I seem to be his chauffeur these days.'

Wanda raised her eyebrows.

'We escaped together across the border together from Poland,' he explained. He took a biscuit and offered the plate to Wanda who shook her head.

'Why were you living in Poland?' asked Wanda looking up at him, puzzled.

'I studied Polish language and literature and spent some time in Poland during my degree. Then I went back afterwards intending to stay for a year. That was in 1969 and I didn't return until '81.'

Aleks looked at Wanda. 'It must have been the stress-free, luxurious life in Poland that kept him there so long,' he said.

'Actually it was Ania. I married a Polish girl.'

Wanda looked at him frostily. 'So you have left her, have you?'

'No, no,' said Bronek. 'I nursed her through terminal breast cancer for a year until one day she died in my arms. I decided then it was time to come home.'

Wanda closed her eyes, put her fingers to her head as if they were a mock gun and pulled the trigger. 'I'm sorry,' she said.

'It's understandable,' said Bronek. 'You've probably had enough of Polish men.'

Wanda looked at Aleks and shrugged.

'It occurred to me today that I've spent so much of my life listening to English spoken with a Polish accent,' said Wanda stirring her tea. 'Sometimes I think I've had enough of it.'

'It's a little clash of cultures,' said Aleks. 'I have felt that since I've been in England.' He'd actually found it less of a little clash and more of a head-on collision. The thick, slang-spiced speech of his fellow construction workers and the cold reserve of the bosses took some getting used to. However, he was starting to understand their sense of humour. When a hugely fat woman had walked past them the other day and fallen heavily on the pavement, one yelled, 'If we'd wanted a hole there, we'd have dug one.'

Bronek said, 'It was always embarrassing at school to have a 'funny' name and to speak a different language at home from school. For years, I would reply in English to my parents, much to their anger. Not that they were very rational people. They had both been in concentration camps and they had no idea how to be parents, or how to overcome their trauma. When I think about my childhood now, I realise Social Services should really have taken us away. My parents were completely crazy.'

Aleks looked at his friend in surprise. He'd never heard him mention this before.

'That war not only damaged those who were directly involved, but they passed it down to us long after the war was over', he continued. 'My sisters and I are still suffering from it.'

Wanda looked thoughtful. 'My parents were good – I mean they were hurt by the war but they didn't pass it on to us, not to a great extent anyway.' She looked back at Bronek. 'What made you go to Poland?'

He laughed. 'I now realise it was partly to anger my parents. They had risked so much to get away and they never wanted to go back. I don't know – I was just being bloody-minded I suppose.'

'But you married there?'

'Yes. Ania never spoke English so we always communicated in Polish. It's funny because although I'm fluent, I'd still rather communicate complex ideas and emotions in English. I don't know why.'

'I know. I agree with you,' replied Wanda. 'Polish was my first language, but I think and dream in English.'

'I dream in English now, but with Polish subtitles,' said Aleks smiling. He also realised the headaches he used to get with the strain of speaking a foreign language had gone.

'It's hard being married to someone from a different culture,' said Bronek. ' As we both know. Despite our names, we are English – you and I, aren't we?' said Bronek.

Aleks waited for her reply, willing her to open up. Finally she said, 'We are and we're not. When you're a child what you want more than anything is to fit in, to be part of the prevailing culture. If you're different – you might be a target. The main way you and I are identified as different is through our names. I actually changed my name for about five years in my effort to fit in - embarrassing.' She laughed bitterly.

'What did you change it to?'

'Jean Stapleton.'

Bronek snorted. 'Well, Wanda Baran is not that difficult a name for people to pronounce. I had to get people to pronounce and spell Bronislaw Olszewski! No wonder I became Craig Steed for two months in 1965.'

Wanda looked at him for a while and they both burst out laughing. Aleks wasn't sure what they were laughing about but he joined in. It was good that were getting along so well – even if he felt left out.

'You see,' said Wanda, her face suddenly falling back into her sullen expression and turning to Aleks, 'Pawel would not have found that funny. He never found the same things funny that I did.'

'Yes, it's hard to explain why something is funny. They say analysing a joke is like dissecting a frog – nobody laughs and the frog dies.'

They sat for a while in silence. Aleks looked out at the garden through the kitchen window. Someone had once carefully tended it. Roses climbed along the wall and he could smell the scent through the open window. A beautiful, peaceful home – Pawel had thrown it away.

'My sister wanted to study Polish at London university.' Wanda fiddled nervously with a teaspoon.

'Oh, which college did she go to?' asked Bronek.

'She didn't. She died of food poisoning when she was 18.'

No one spoke. Aleks knew Irena, in whose flat the death occurred, had been so distraught at the time she'd even phoned him. He'd tried to comfort her but it was useless – there was no comfort to be had. It was an unmitigated tragedy.

'That was a great tragedy for your family. Actually I did hear about it,' said Bronek.

'Who told you?'

Bronek paused and looked at Aleks. 'It was Pawel.'

Aleks remembered Bronek had visited him one day not long after Pawel had arrived following his break with Wanda. His emotions were so high he couldn't stop talking. Pawel had described Zosia's death to them both in detail and told him how he still thought about her and had recurring nightmares about her death. Pawel had been a man in free-fall, he was letting everything out.

Wanda closed her eyes and rubbed her face. 'I suppose news of my humiliation has already reached London.'

'His humiliation, not yours,' said Bronek. 'He's an idiot that man.'

'I agree with you,' said Aleks.

'Giving up someone like you and that lovely little girl. I would have cherished that,' continued Bronek.

Wanda felt tears come to her eyes.

'You didn't have any children then?' she said blowing her nose and wiping her eyes.

'No. Ania and I did try but no luck. Then she became ill and we were in and out of hospitals while the cancer retreated and advanced and finally won. But it was Aleks here who introduced Ania to me. Maybe that's why I tolerate him,' said Bronek.

'Ha,' said Aleks. 'I add spice to your very dull life, you know that.'

'Pawel looks quite like you,' she said looking at Aleks.

'I'm better looking.'

Wanda smiled. 'What do you do?' she asked, turning to Bronek.

'I work for BBC radio in Bush House. The Eastern European section. I was doing some broadcasting in Warsaw so I got a job with the BBC when I got back to London. It's pretty busy at the moment with so much happening in Eastern Europe.'

Wanda raised her eyebrows and nodded slowly.

Aleks looked up and saw Anna was standing at the kitchen door.

'Hello, sweetheart. Come and sit on my lap.'

She approached shyly and put something on the table in front of him.

'I did all the colours on your little box,' she said.

Chapter 29

'I've just heard the news,' John said grinning and rubbing his hands together as he walked into the office at Allsop's. 'Congratulations Samantha, you're a star.' He gave her a kiss on the cheek.

Samantha Foy was sitting with a copy of *Buxton Belles* on her lap. The picture on the front of the novel showed two ladies in 18th century dress strolling along the famous Crescent in the spa town of Buxton. Samantha looked up.

'Thank you for believing in me,' she said. John could never reconcile her fragile beauty with her broad accent.

Samantha showed him the letter she had received that morning.

Samantha Foye has been nominated for the Isobel Collins Romantic Fiction Award, 1985 for her novel Buxton Belles. The winner will be announced at the Grosvenor Hotel on September 24

'The prats spelled my name wrong!' said Samantha.

'So they did! Never mind – it's the nomination that counts. We'll put that on all the publicity material.'

'Will you come with me to the award ceremony?'

John couldn't believe it was all happening so fast. The thought of a literary event in London, his name lights. It was amazing.

'I'd be honoured. Even if you don't win the award, it will be a fantastic do.'

Samantha looked down at the novel. 'You know, what still annoys me about the cover is that Abigail had black hair, I specifically say so in the story but the artist drew her with blonde hair. Also Peter Radley doesn't look tall enough. And I'm not really sure the Crescent in Buxton looked like that in 1802,' said Samantha.

'I think it looks great,' said John. 'And it's helped sell the book. A certain bottled water company may be interested in sponsoring us.' He turned the novel over. 'And this picture of you on the back – well, you look like a model.' Samantha was shown in a frilly dress with her abundant curly hair flowing over her shoulders. 'When Nigel Parks came to interview you he commented that you looked like a Buxton Belle yourself. All these things help in marketing, you know.'

John looked at the books piled high on his sideboard. He had paid for its publication, used all his contacts to get reviews and interviews and he was taking 50 per cent of the profits. It was Samantha, though, who had sent it in for the award without telling him.

The second novel, *Abigail Alone*, was already on the presses. Little old ladies in libraries would be champing at the bit, thought John.

'There is something else, John. I should let you know I've had a letter from Crawthorne's asking me to come to a meeting.'

John broke off from his reverie and looked at Samantha. He noticed she called him John now and not Mr Allsop or Sir. This was the shy girl who he'd employed as his proofreader and taken a punt on her novel. Did she just say that major London publisher Crawthorne was interested?

'You're meeting them, are you?' asked John. ' Do you mean they want to publish the novel? But I gave you the break. You signed a contract with me. Why are you seeing them?' John's smile had disappeared.

'It's probably nothing,' said Samantha going a little red. 'But I should check out what they want.'

'Only if you're thinking of taking the books to them, otherwise there's no point.'

John clenched his fists. He had put the firm's money in the venture and against all the odds, it had paid off. He tried desperately to think if there were any loopholes in the contract they'd drawn up. Frankly, he hadn't paid much attention to it as he hadn't thought it would be important. If there were get-out clauses, Crawthorne's would find them.

'There is such a thing as loyalty,' said John. 'You're not going to dump me now, are you?'

'Oh, I don't think so,' said Samantha smiling. 'I just want to meet them because they are a big London publisher. It's all part of the experience.'

Wanda was at home waiting for Bronek to arrive. They were going out to the Assembly Rooms to see Ben Elton's latest stand-up comedy routine. Wanda was standing in front of her full-length mirror in her bedroom wearing a new dark blue dress she'd bought from Debenhams. In fact, all her clothes were new because the old stuff didn't fit her anymore. She'd lost an impressive two stone in weight since Pawel had gone and it hadn't been that hard actually as for months she'd found it almost impossible to eat. She'd taken to eating soft stuff such as breakfast cereal but although she could get the cereal on the spoon and put it in her mouth, she found it almost impossible to swallow. The food just wouldn't go down – it dribbled down the side of her mouth and back into the bowl. The weight fell off her and stayed off. She had stopped feeling hungry but felt fitter, lighter. She had decided to do the things she had been too scared to try before. She was taking driving lessons, she'd taken to colouring her hair ash blonde and was buying more stylish clothes.

Wanda took the amber necklace that had belonged to her grandmother and held it against the dress to see if it would go. She frowned and stared at her image. In the reflection she could see Zosia, aged about 18, looking as she did the last time Wanda ever saw her. Her long dark hair was hanging round her shoulders, her slim figure in a geometric-patterned top and dark brown trousers. She looked beautiful.

'You old fraud, Wanda,' she murmured to herself. 'Trying to be the pretty sister – it'll never work, you know. No one will ever fall for that.' The doorbell rang and she hurried downstairs to let Bronek in. She opened the front door with a smile on her face. There on the threshold stood Pawel.

Wanda groaned. 'What are you doing here?

'I came to see you and Anna. Can I come in?' He looked thin too and his face seemed more lined and drawn than previously. Wanda stared at him, unsure what to do.

'You look very nice. Are you going out?' asked Pawel.

'Yes, going to see some comedy at the Assembly Rooms so I can't talk.'

'Can I stay with Anna?' He gazed up the stairs.

'My mother is with her. Anyway, what are you doing here? I didn't know you were in Derby.'

'I'm up for the weekend seeing some friends. I keep trying to get work here, to be near you but there is so much more work in London. Can I see Anna?'

Wanda looked over his shoulder and noticed Bronek's car had drawn up in the street.

'Ok, I'll just go up and say goodnight to her.' She left Pawel in the hall and went to kiss Anna and tell her that Daddy was here. Anna jumped up and raced down the stairs to him and flung herself into his arms.

Wanda grabbed her handbag and jacket and hurried out of the door.

Wanda and Bronek walked from the Assembly Rooms along Irongate. The cathedral rose before them in its floodlit splendour and the bells pealed out 10 o'clock. They passed the artist Joseph Wright's house, the 17th century buildings and walked through the alleys of Derby Cathedral quarter to The Fighting Cock pub.

Bronek had to stoop because of the low ceiling. They found their reserved table and sat down. Each table had a Chianti bottle with a candle stuck in it. Layers of wax had dripped down the side of the bottle. Wanda couldn't resist picking pieces of it off. Bronek looked round at the low, Tudor beams, horse brasses hanging from the walls and old pots and warming pans decorating the ceiling.

'Funny place – are they going for the chic Italian look or olde English?'

'OK, don't come all London over us, we might have our confused provincial ways, but by gum we're 'appy,' said Wanda.

Bronek laughed. 'So, what did you think of the show?'

'After years of going to church and having to genuflect when you come out of the pew, I always want to do the same when exiting a row of seats. I sometimes go to the cinema then half kneel towards the screen and make the sign of the cross when I leave the seat.'

Bronek laughed and nodded. 'I do the same.'

The waitress arrived with the menu and took their drinks order. Bronek ordered a bottle of Italian red.

'Ben Elton was good. I know he annoys a lot of people but I thought he was really funny – but then I'm not cool,' said Wanda.

'No, if it's funny, you laugh. It would be ridiculous to sit thinking whether it was permissible to laugh or the correct thing. Either you laugh or you don't.

'Well, I laughed and didn't think. That's the story of my life.'

Bronek took her hand. 'You look really nice tonight. I like that dress.'

Wanda took her hand away and stared at her wine glass. 'Pawel turned up just as I was leaving.'

'Really? I thought he was in London working with Aleks.'

'He's here for the weekend, says he's trying to find work in Derby.'

'Well, it doesn't really matter, does it? Does Anna want to see him?'

'Yes, she does and it's wrong to keep her from her father. She doesn't know why we split and hard though it is, I want it to stay that way.'

'That must take a good deal of will-power'

'You have no idea.'

'You're such a nice person, Wanda,' said Bronek.

Wanda smiled and picked some more wax off the wine bottle. The drinks arrived and they clinked glasses. *Na zdrowie.*

'Aleks once told me that he left the family when Pawel was little and the child raced down the stairs and clung to his leg as he was going,' said Bronek.

'Really?' said Wanda. 'Pawel told me he just watched him go from the window and waved. He didn't know it would be last time. But I know how hard it was for him when his father left. I'm so sorry I had to put Anna through the same experience.'

'Children are resilient. I think Pawel's version of events is probably more accurate. Aleks is not the most trustworthy of people. He's great fun, witty, charming but a bit of a rogue and a thief if truth be told.'

'A thief? What has he stolen?' said Wanda with astonishment in her voice.

'He did some time in prison for fraud. He is not a violent man in any way but his morals are – well pretty fluid.'

Wanda smiled. 'It's annoying how much I like him. Pawel is like a watered down version: not so tall, not so handsome or witty or intelligent or charming. A pale reflection. Is Aleks really an artist?'

'This photographer friend of his put on an exhibition at the Whitechapel Gallery called *Behind The Wall*. Aleks had some monstrous piece of metal there which he calls art. It took four men to manoeuvre the thing onto its plinth but then it fell off on the opening day of the show and made a huge dent in the floor. They decided to leave it be and pretend it was intentional – empty plinth, artwork in distress on the ground. Such bollocks!'

Wanda laughed loudly and almost choked on her wine.

'He does some writing as well. Did you see his piece in the *Daily Mail* – *The Walesa I Knew*. It's pretty ridiculous – I think he only spoke about three words to Walesa ever.'

'He told me he went to the Lodz Film School with Roman Polanski – is it not true?'

'Well, he did go the film school for a year and Polanski did too but not at the same time.'

'He a bit of a fantasist, then.'

'I don't know if he actually believes the lies himself. But it's all part of the charm.'

'His son is the same but without the charm'

Chapter 30

Canary Wharf in London's Docklands was rising from the ashes of wartime bombing, disused docks and social deprivation. There were to be new offices, shops, ornamental pools and riverside pubs. The docklands project provided huge amount of work for construction workers, brickies, hod carriers. Aleks had been working on the site for two years and he'd found Pawel work as a plasterer there too. They were earning very good money although the work was hard. At the end of the day, they made their way home by tube.

'Perhaps we can find a place to live in London during the week. I've been living in Roger's house for nearly a year now and you've been there much longer. Doesn't he want to get rid of us?' asked Pawel.

'He doesn't seem to mind. If we get a place we will have to pay rent and rents are very high in London. Anyway, you're always going back to Derby at weekends to see Anna. It's not worth getting a place.' said Aleks.

'Yes, but I don't want to annoy Roger and Eunice. They are really good to us.'

'Eunice is from a rich family – I think they are some kind of aristocrats. Her parents have a mansion somewhere in the country. I've seen pictures of it. She goes there are at weekends sometimes. She has the money to be magnanimous. Anyway, I think we are their pet project.'

'Plenty of people with money are not generous,' said Pawel.

They got off the tube at Mornington Crescent and walked towards the house. Tired and grimy, they let themselves in and wiped their mud-caked boots on the mat. They plonked their tool kits in the cupboard under the stairs before heading to the top of the house to wash and change.

Wandering back down, they found Roger and Eunice in the sitting room. Eunice was kneeling at Roger's feet holding a packet of frozen peas against his face.

'What happened here?' asked Aleks.

'I was hit in the face with a brick,' said Roger. 'There was a bit of scrum up in Orgreave and I seem to have landed in the middle of it.'

'You were supposed to taking photographs from the sidelines not fighting in the middle of it,' said Eunice.

'I did manage to protect my camera though,' said Roger leaning forward and picking up his Canon T70. 'Got all my film safe.'

Pawel sat down on a stool. 'It is getting very nasty, this miners' strike,' he said. 'In Poland, if there was this level of violence they would just put the ringleaders in prison, bring in soldiers, have a curfew and use water canon to stop it all.'

'The miners are fighting to protect their jobs, their communities and their way of life. I saw police gallop past on horseback and hit the men with their truncheons,' said Roger.

'The police have to keep order, don't they?' said Pawel. 'Did a policeman hit you?'

'I was hit by a brick that was flying past.'

'Thrown by a miner?' asked Pawel.

'Probably,' said Roger. 'But that's not the point. Sometimes you have to use violence to get what you want and the miners are justified in fighting,'

'It can be very foolish to use violence. Walesa is achieving more in prison and becoming a symbol of hope, a martyr to the cause then going out creating mayhem,' said Aleks. 'Like that man in South Africa, Mandela.'

'That's true,' said Eunice. 'The trouble is, the miners' leader Arthur Scargill doesn't look like a martyr – he has weird hair, a silly baseball cap and he doesn't inspire confidence. At least I don't think so.'

'Is that what your father said?' asked Roger examining the cut under his eye in a small hand mirror.

'Daddy says Scargill has a really annoying way of hectoring people in meetings. He won't listen to anyone.'

'Your dad would say that, wouldn't he?' said Roger.

'Does your father know this Scargill man?' asked Aleks in surprise.

'Not socially,' said Eunice laughing. 'Daddy is a minister in the Department of Trade and Industry so he had to chair meetings with Scargill before the strike started.'

'Your father is a minister in this Conservative government?' said Aleks. 'Really – I never knew that,' He threw his head back and roared with laughter.

'We can't choose our parents, can we?' said Roger putting the frozen peas back on his eye. 'Could you get me a whisky, Eunice, I feel a bit shaky. I was ok coming back on the train but now I feel sick.'

'Delayed shock, probably,' said Eunice.

'I wonder, does this Scargill man support Solidarity in Poland?' asked Pawel.

'He should do. Daddy told me the communist government in Poland is sending in cheap coal to help Mrs Thatcher break the strike,' said Eunice. 'The Polish government have outlawed Solidarity and put the leaders in prison. That means Scargill and Walesa should be on the same side, doesn't it?'

Aleks grabbed the whisky bottle from Eunice as she went by and poured himself a drink.

'You would think so but I heard that Walesa had condemned Scargill saying he should not use violence and he shouldn't demand so much that he destroys his employers,' said Aleks.

'It's a crazy situation' said Eunice. 'By providing cheap coal, the Polish communist government under Jaruzelski is helping a right wing prime minister in Britain to destroy a strike by miners. Some of those miners, including Scargill, are communists. Jaruzelski has put those wanting a free trade union in Poland in prison and those strikers are not communists but free trade capitalists. Walesa condemns the violence of the British miners and says they should not bankrupt their employers.'

'So,' said Aleks. 'That means Jaruzelski is on the side of Mrs Thatcher and Walesa is also on the side of Mrs Thatcher.' He roared with laughter. 'It's the world turned upside down. Who is on whose side?'

'Actually, I am on the side of Mrs Thatcher,' said Pawel. 'These miners are idiots. If a mine is not economically viable it should close otherwise you just have loss-making industries supported by the state as in Poland. That situation has to collapse at some point. How can it be sustained?'

Roger stared at Pawel with his one good eye. 'Do you wish to remain living in my house?' asked Roger.

'Actually, it's my house,' said Eunice.

'Actually, it's your father's house,' said Roger looking round at her.

'Ah, so we are all living at the generosity of the Conservative government,' said Pawel smiling.

'Isn't all property theft?' said Aleks draining his whisky glass and holding it out for a refill.

Chapter 31

John Allsop and Samantha Foy got out of the black London cab. John handed the taxi driver a huge amount of cash and rashly told him to keep the change. Samantha was fiddling with her tiny bag and pulling her long green dress straight.

'Bloody hell, that was expensive,' said John. 'It's mad in London, the prices they charge for everything. I hope we get a good supper to make up for it.'

'Look at the door man,' whispered Samantha. 'He's got a top hat. Do we tip him and all?'

'I hope not,' John pulled at his collar. 'This tie is strangling me. You look great, love. If you win, it will be fantastic to see you go and get your award. You'll knock 'em out.' Until you open your mouth and all these soft southerners laugh at your accent, John thought.

They went into the foyer, the doorman tipping his hat to them. Inside, it was all red carpets and chrome fittings. They entered a huge room with a massive crystal chandelier.

'Oh, my God – Catherine Cookson is here. Do I dare say hello?' Samantha gripped John's arm.

'Why not – seize the moment, I say. What's the worst she can do?'

John watched as Samantha went to talk to her heroine. He wandered over to look at the seating plan. The tables were decorated with flowers, balloons and glitter on the tablecloth. John looked at the other names. Next to him was a man called Austen Talbot from *The Daily Telegraph*. There was also Phyllis Frost, novelist, Toby Letchworth of Collins, Letchworth and Harper, then Coleen Richards, Romantic short story writer. His own place setting said John Allsop, Publisher.

Samantha came weaving her way back through the crowd, her face flushed with pleasure.

'Catherine Cookson said she loved my novel, she actually said that.'

'Did she know who you were?' asked John.

Samantha smacked his arm. 'What do you mean – that she says it to everyone?'

The speeches began when they were half way through the main course. Some fellow from Crawthorne's Publishers, who were sponsoring the event, made a speech. Then a woman from the estate of the late Isobel Collins told them how the award had come about through Miss Collins' generosity. It took ages to get to the results.

John looked at the other four contenders. They were all female and all considerably older than Samantha. John decided it went on a rota basis and if these old biddies had been nominated a few times, it was probably their time to win. He started playing with his cutlery as the speeches droned on.

Samantha was talking and laughing with the man next to her. Then the climax was upon them, the winner was to be announced. John stared at the chandelier and waited for one of the old women in their synthetic dresses to go up. He was still looking into the middle distance when the announcement was made, 'The winner is Samantha Foy for *Buxton Belles'*.

Before John had time to react, Samantha was on her feet and heading for the stage. Everyone was craning to look at this tall, slim girl in a green dress, her red hair cascading down her back. There were murmurs of surprise, whispers of, 'look at her hair.'

John watched her in amazement. Where had all her confidence suddenly come from? She would have to make an acceptance speech. John waited in trepidation. Oh, God, had she prepared anything? He had forgotten to mention it. He'd been sure one of the old ladies would win. His heart beat fiercely with fear and excitement. Samantha stood at the microphone and was handed the award by last year's winner.

Next morning, John lounged on his London hotel bed. Samantha had left early to be interviewed on Breakfast TV. He'd offered to come with her but she'd refused. He switched on the television and while waiting for *Good Morning Britain* to start, flicked through the newspapers. Opening one broadsheet, he found a small section on page 10.

The Daily Telegraph, 3 March 1986

Pepys Modern Diary,

To the Grosvenor Hotel where I'm invited to an awards ceremony to anoint the 'Romantic Novelist of the Year'. This would normally be a more fitting outing for Mrs Pepys who is a martyr to Georgette Heyer. But as there were rumours of cake and champagne I decided my presence would be called for. I took a seat next to a dull-looking cove accompanied by a glorious creature with a crown of bright red, pre-Raphaelite hair. She smiled at me and I'm put in mind of the recently appointed Duchess of York, Sarah Ferguson as was – except with beauty, grace and breeding. After we'd had our snouts in the trough for an hour, the winner was announced. 'Samantha Foy for Buxton Belles'. At this, said beautiful creature got up from her seat and headed for the stage. We were entranced, bewitched, besotted. She took the microphone and started to speak. The roof flew off the place with hoots of laughter. She sounded exactly like Norah Batty. Splendid!

John looked up as the theme music to *Good Morning Britain* came on. A woman with big hair, far too much make-up and a bright red, shoulder-padded dress came on the screen. She was sitting on a blue sofa with a large vase of flowers on the coffee table in front of her. She was holding a book in her hand and John could clearly make out the familiar cover of *Buxton Belles*. He sat nearer to the TV and turned up the volume.

Hello, I'm Cynthia Turner and the time is coming up to 8.45. We're delighted to have Samantha Foy, winner of this year's best romantic novel award, in the studio this morning. Samantha, first of all many congratulations for winning the award. I read Buxton Belles and it's a delightful story. It really makes me want to visit the High Peak area of Derbyshire. Where did you get the inspiration?

Well, it were me nan really who started it. She were from Buxton and her nan were a maid in this big hotel what catered for the rich folk coming to take the waters.

Yes, because of course Buxton is a famous spa town rather like Bath. Abigail Cunningham is a heroine for our time. How did you get the book published?

I got a job at a printers in Derby called Allsop's. There you go, John, got a plug in for yer (thumbs up at the camera). Well, I thought a printers was a publisher. They told me I was going to work as a proofreader and I thought I'd be checking the spelling in novels and romantic stories and such like. I were only 16 and pretty stupid. But it weren't books I were proofreading it were stuff like, 'Mr and Mrs Widget request the pleasure of the company of whoever,' you know that kind of thing. Or 'Poonas for great tasting curry.'

[Cynthia is laughing and John felt his face colour] So you realised they just printed wedding invitations and flyers for curry houses.

Too right. Then I thought to meself that I could write me stories in the dinner break so I did that. Then Derek, me boss, says one dinner time, what are you scribbling all day, miss. And I say just little stories. And some of the other blokes pinched me book and read out the stuff. I was using things they'd just said, for the dialogue like.

And how did you persuade - is it Allsop's? - to publish the book.

Well John Allsop, the owner, invited me to his fancy house. I overheard him say to Derek that maybe I was the new Emily Bronte.

Well, yes, I can see that.

Actually, I think it was just the way I looked. You know my stuff is nothing like Pride and Prejudice or what not.

Wuthering Heights. No, but the Sunday Times Magazine took these pictures of you [holds up magazine to the camera] standing on, I think, High Tor in the Peak District with your hair blowing in the wind and this cloak – fantastic.

It were bloody freezing, let me tell you. They dressed me in this wool thing with a big hood and I had to stand on the edge of this cliff. And there were a storm brewing behind me. I could of got struck by lightening.

They are fantastic pictures though – you could do the cover of Vogue or Vanity Fair next.

I'm doing Derbyshire Life next week.

Fantastic. Anyway, Buxton Belles by Samantha Foy is out now at £3.99. The time is nearly 9 o'clock but stay with us, Samantha, because after the news we're going to be talking to a man who trains peregrine falcons.

Chapter 32

Wanda couldn't sleep. She woke up at 3am, 4.30am and 6am. By 6.30 she decided she might as well get up. She went downstairs wearing her dressing gown and waited in dread for the postman. She looked at her watch – the mail usually came around 8am.

She made some toast and went to sit by the window in the sitting room so she could see the postman come up the path. The sun was coming up and casting a strange yellow light into the sitting room. Wanda thought she could vaguely make out the faint outline of Zosia standing by the end of the sofa, doing up the buttons on her brand new Pinecrest blazer, pulling down the sleeves to make it fit. Wanda remembered her sister trying on her grammar school uniform. She had watched with jealousy and anger. Zosia had passed the 11+ and was going to a good school. Her life and career were mapped out for success. Wanda's was not.

But the jealousy she had felt about Zosia, was now translated into hope for Anna. Not just hope, but huge ambition, desperate desire, longing.

'There won't be any bullying at the school I've chosen for Anna. I promise you that,' she whispered to her sister. 'She won't suffer like you.'

Zosia stared back at her and stuck out her tongue.

'Don't mess this up for me, Zosia,' Wanda whispered. 'Please let Anna go to a good school. Please let her achieve what you didn't. It's the only way you can do it now, isn't it?'

Wanda closed her eyes and leant her head back against the chair. I feel sick, she thought. If Anna doesn't get into this school, I don't know what I'll do.

Half an hour later, the whistling postman made his way toward the door and the letterbox in the hall snapped open and shut. Wanda hurried out. There was the letter from the school on the mat. She felt as if she was going to vomit. She tore open the envelope and began to read, 'We have pleasure…'

A year earlier, Wanda had gone along to meet the headmaster when she'd applied for the place. She had told him she was a single mother, she'd never gone to university herself, her own mother was a widow and they didn't have much money. She could not afford to pay for her daughter to go to a private school, but her primary school had recommended she apply for the 'gifted and talented' programme.

As a result, 11-year-old Anna had been invited to sit an intelligence test. Wanda had taken her along to a little room at the school where she and another young boy sat a two-hour exam. Wanda had hardly dared ask her daughter how it had gone when she picked her up again. Anna had seemed just as carefree as always.

'Did it go well?' asked Wanda.

'It was fine,' said Anna and they spoke no more about it.

Now Wanda had proof in her hand that the exam had gone extremely well. She ran up to Anna's bedroom and shook her awake.

'You got into Derby School, you got in!'

She ran into Helena's room and thrust the letter under nose.

'This is marvellous. Did you show Anna?'

'Yes, but she just said, 'Good', and went back to sleep.'

'You should ring Pawel,' said Helena. 'He needs to be told. He will be thrilled.'

Wanda nodded and went downstairs to the phone. It was Aleks who answered the phone.

'*Kochana* – so good to hear from you. How is my intelligent and lovely Anna?'

Wanda found it slightly annoying how much she liked her father-in-law. He was unpretentious and charming and although she didn't trust him, he made her laugh. He spoke to Anna like an adult and she enjoyed his company, always asking when he was coming.

'I was phoning you about your intelligent granddaughter – she's been given a scholarship to a really good private school in Derby.'

Wanda heard a yelp of joy on the other end of the phone.

'I knew, I knew she was a genius. Takes after her grandpa, obviously.'

Wanda laughed.

'I want to come up and see her next weekend. Can I bring a present?'

'That would be lovely,' said Wanda.

'I'll bring Pawel along as well, he will be so happy.'

Chapter 33

John stood in his sitting room eating a piece of toast and marmalade. It felt dry and stuck in his throat. He should have been heading for the office but he couldn't summon up too much enthusiasm for that or indeed for anything. The sun was shining but it was raining in his heart. He looked at Maxine and her mother who were watching breakfast television. Christ, if they knew how depressed he really felt.

Lily sat back in her armchair. 'I do like that Cynthia girl on *Good Morning Britain*, only I read in the *Express* or was it the *Mail*, no it was the *Express* that she is walking out with some footballer who has a wife and three kiddies at home and that's not right. She took a sip of her tea and reached for a Bourbon biscuit from a plate on the small table next to her. The little table came in a nest of three: the next size down was in easy reach of Maxine who was sitting on the sofa, and the smallest one was supporting the aspidistra plant next to the television.

'Put the telly box a bit louder, Maxine, I can't hear what the girl is saying,' said Lily settling down into her chair and popping her slippered feet up on the footstool.

Maxine searched around among the cushions for the remote control. John closed his eyes as the noise blared out, assaulting his ears. He raised his voice to match.

'What did you think of Cynthia's interview with Samantha, Lily?' he said.

'Well, that girl has done well for herself. She used to work for Allsop's didn't she?'

'Yes she was our proofreader. She resigned last week, to become a full time writer.'

'The little madam,' said Maxine. 'You gave her her break, John, and now she's swanning off, going on telly and hobnobbing.'

'Oh, she's a fast one, no doubt,' said Lily. 'But you loved her stories, didn't you Maxine? You said she was a nice girl and her stories were compulsory.' Lily pulled her blue housecoat over her knees.

'Yes, the books are good but now Samantha's got too high and mighty'.

High, mighty and very, very rich. John had heard about the large advance Samantha had been given by Crawthorne's for her next six books. He'd worked himself in a rage when he'd discovered that. How stupid he'd been. He should have checked the small print on that contract. They could have made so much money. There was even talk of it being made into a mini-series for the telly. Now Crawthorne's were touting her around like she was their discovery. It made him sick to the stomach.

'Do you think Cynthia is looking a bit tired these days? They put too much make-up on the young girls. They're a strange orange colour.' Lily dunked her Bourbon biscuit in her tea and took a bite.

John had even hired a lawyer to look again at the contract he'd signed with Samantha but, after examining it, the lawyer had said it leaked like a sieve and there was no redress. Shit, shit, fuck fuck.

'They have to get up really early for these morning shows so that's probably why she looks exhausted,' said Maxine. 'The make-up hides the bags under their eyes. Do you think they make fun of Samantha's Derby accent in London? But then she doesn't hide it, in fact I'd swear she puts it on even more when she's down south.'

'They all think she's wonderful in London,' said John. 'That beautiful face with that accent goes down a storm with the literati.'

'I liked that chap what used to do the morning TV show with Cynthia - what were his name, Elvis or Elvin or whatever,' said Lily. 'They were a nice couple. I hoped she would marry him but she seems to like this Liverpool football player better.'

John had heard that Samantha was doing a talk at Buxton Opera House about her novels. He had a little fantasy about going along and sitting in the back row. Then at the end, when the time came for questions from the audience, he would stand up and ask her about loyalty, gratitude and the meaning of a business handshake.

'His name was Melvin, Mum, but Cynthia wouldn't marry him – he's queer, isn't it obvious?' said Maxine.

'There was a girl called Cynthia what used to live next door to us during the war,' said Lily. 'She wore lots of red lipstick and her hair up in a bandana. She used to work in a factory that made shells.'

'You don't make shells – you get them from the beach.'

Samantha had put, 'To all at Allsop's' in the acknowledgments for the first book, but John had felt insulted with that. It should at least have said 'To John Allsop, the man who discovered me.' Even that wasn't enough, nowhere near enough.

'I mean bombs not shells on the beach. She wore a bandana because you had to have your hair tied up in case it got caught in the machinery,' said Lily. 'Cynthia always used to say, 'After Coventry, us here in Derby will be next. They will bomb us to pieces. You mark my words'. Of course folks in Coventry didn't think they'd get smashed to pieces like that. I remember, before it happened, our milkman, Alfie, said his brother lived in Coventry and he said they won't bomb the city because it's in a hollow covered in fog and they will never be able to find it. Ha, they didn't stop the Germans though, they bombed the whole city flat.'

'Do you think Samantha is really pretty?' said Maxine. 'They keep calling her a Northern Beauty in the press. I always think she looks a bit too pale and ill. I heard a rumour that she didn't really write those books – they were written by her nan and she found them after her nan's death and decided to publish them as her own. Did you hear that, John?'

John shrugged his shoulders. He didn't care who wrote them, just that fame and fortune had slipped from his grasp. He was so stupid, stupid.

'So we waited in Derby for the bombs to fall and waited to be just like Coventry,' said Lily. 'Every night we had the air raid sirens going off and we went to the shelter. When we were kids we lived in a two-up, two-down house in Agard Street at the back of Friargate and our shelter was in the cellar of Pickford House because their garden backed onto our yard. It's a big old house and we hid in its old wine cellar. When I was a girl, I used to think when I grow up I want to live in a big house like this.'

'It could be true that her nan wrote the books because she doesn't seem clever enough to have done it,' said Maxine. 'I mean, whenever I spoke to her she seemed a bit dim.'

If only she were dim, thought John. The problem is she is really very clever indeed and quite ruthless. She outfoxed me.

'Anyway, the joke was that Derby never was bombed. Not once!' said Lily. 'We waited in them cold, damp shelters night after night and they missed us! The Germans didn't get us. It was a miracle, really.'

'Her books are in a big display in WH Smith and they say she is coming to do a book signing,' said Maxine. 'She has her face all over the shop with signs saying, 'Come and meet bestselling Derby author Samantha Foy.'

Perhaps the Telegraph could write a piece on 'The Man Who Discovered Samantha Foy?' thought John.

'Cynthia had a fella called Edwin,' said Lily. 'He had black, greased-back hair and thick glasses. He was what we called in them days a spiv. He didn't join up and he always had chewing gum and chocolate and stockings. When Cynthia was out he always used to hang around my sister and me. He used to say he'd give us a shilling if we'd kiss him. He was disgusting.'

'I don't think I'd give her the satisfaction of going to her book signing,' said Maxine. 'She should have stayed with Allsop's who gave her the break. Anyway, I've got a signed copy.'

Perhaps he should go round and see Samantha, thought John. Take a present, no hard feelings – that sort of thing. Make her feel bad by being generous.

'Once this Edwin got hold of my sister Pauline, she were only eight, and he put his hand up her skirt. I called him a dirty bugger,' said Lily. 'There was a blackout during the war – you couldn't have a light on and your curtains open. They'd send a warden and he'd shout, 'Put that light out.'

'Wanda liked Samantha's books, didn't she John? I went over there to get my signed copy back because she had borrowed it and she has this new fella who comes round now even though she's not divorced Pawel. This new one is quite posh and works for the BBC. He has a nice car and comes up from London on weekends. You think he's a cut above Pawel, don't you John? Maybe Wanda should marry this one.'

Perhaps Bronek could get him some recognition on the BBC, thought John. That might work.

'All sorts of things went on in the black out – you'd be amazed, you'd be absolutely amazed. It covered a multitude of sins.' Lily laughed a throaty laugh.

'Do you think Wanda will go and live in London with him, John?' said Maxine. 'He has a university degree and everything. But she wouldn't want to leave your mum or have Anna change schools.'

'I don't think she will,' said John. 'Anyway, Pawel seems to there most weekends too as far as I can see. She has two men dancing at her heels.'

'It was the blackout that covered up a lot of goings on,' said Lily. 'Anyway, they found him one morning dead in the road. He'd been run down. He was flat as a pancake.'

'Who?' said Maxine and John together.

'Edwin – I can't remember his surname now. He was lying squashed in the street. Mrs Reynolds who lived the other side of us said, "Good riddance to bad rubbish."'

'I don't know any Edwin,' said Maxine.

'The policeman said someone had driven over him in a car, then reversed and driven over him again.'

'Why would they do that?'

'To make sure he were dead, I should think.'

'What's that got to do with Samantha Foy?'

'Nothing – I was just remembering, thinking about when I was a girl.'

'Mum, you keep going off talking a load of nonsense. Pay attention to what's happening now.'

Chapter 34

Anna Zosia Lato sat on the coach with her school friends and listened to her teacher, Miss Everest, telling them they must be on their best behaviour in town as the reputation of the school was at stake and everyone would know them from their school uniforms. Miss Everest was what was known as a 'woman of a certain age'. In other words, the girls guessed her to be anything between 30 and 60.

'She is a 'Miss',' whispered Lucie Berenger to Anna, 'That means she is probably a virgin. Do you think any man has attempted to conquer Everest?'

Anna smiled. 'When he was asked why he wanted to mount Everest, he replied, 'because she's there.'

Lucie laughed.

Anna looked out of the window as the coach drove down The Strand and pulled into the car park near the Derby Museum and Art Gallery.

'Now girls,' said Miss Everest, 'We are starting with a lecture by Dr Michael Walker who is an expert on our own Derby artist, Joseph Wright. After the lecture there will be time to look round the rest of the museum and the shop before we head down to the Riverside Gardens where we will eat our packed lunch. All right, girls, single file and off the coach. Mind the step.'

Miss Everest counted them off the coach. They made their way into the museum and up to the Joseph Wright Gallery. The girls' shoes squeaked and clicked on the polished wood floors. They pushed the doors and entered the gallery. Anna had seen Joseph Wright's pictures in books and magazines but never before had she seen the real thing. She looked up in amazement – the pictures were absolutely enormous and so beautiful they took her breath away. The other girls were arranging themselves on the benches or the floor but Anna was lost in wonder.

These pictures were painted in the 18th century but they appeared so bright and fresh. And the colours, the faces, the way the light fell on the subjects – they could easily have been huge photographs.

A man with a grey beard, drip-dry trousers and brown Hush Puppy shoes stood in front of one of the paintings. 'Welcome to the Joseph Wright Gallery, my name is Michael Walker and I want to talk to you today about our town's own son, the wonderful artist, Joseph Wright. He was born in 1734 just a stone's throw from here in Irongate...'

Dr Walker's voice drifted away as Anna looked at the pictures. Each had a central source of light and the artist had shown with exquisite accuracy how the light fell on the faces of the each of those depicted.

'... his was an age of enlightenment, of rational thought, of experiment. He talked with men who wanted to know how the universe worked and what our place was within it.'

Anna looked at the painting called The Orrery – the device which shows how the planets revolve round the sun. In the painting, a lecturer is telling his audience how the model works, a young man is making notes, a women with a flowery hat stares intently at the device, two children giggle and embrace each other while two other men look at the model and the lecturer. The source of the light is unseen but its effects in the darkened room are astonishing.

'...Wright employed the chiaroscuro effect – the difference between dark and light. Look how he illuminates his subjects – the depth of colour, it could be a photograph couldn't it...?'

Anna for the first time felt she was in the presence of genius. She looked round the room at the other paintings. These enormous, glorious canvases had actually been painted, by his own hand, by a man born in Derby 250 years previously.

'...Wright is called Joseph Wright of Derby to differentiate him from another painter also named Wright of that time. He studied in London and went on a tour of Italy but he came back to his hometown and spent the rest of his life here. He was friends with the leading industrialists, thinkers, philosophers, painters, inventors and landed gentry of his day...'

Anna felt uplifted, inspired. When she looked at these paintings, she felt her life was full of infinite possibilities, she could achieve anything. The spirit of Joseph Wright – painter, philosopher, seeker of knowledge, friend of the curious – was filling her very being.

'...after periods of depression, asthma and lethargy Wright died in his Queen St house in 1797, his daughters by his side. He was buried in that wonderful Anglo-Saxon church, which along with so many things in our city, the town council saw fit to demolish in 1970. Vandals!'

Everyone clapped politely and Miss Everest instructed the girls where to gather and where they would be going next.

Anna stood up to leave the room with her classmates. She felt as light as air, she wanted to paint, to write, to study, to meet the great intellectuals of her own time. She felt flushed with enthusiasm. Anything was possible, even if you came from a provincial backwater, even if you came from Derby...

Lucie bent towards her and whispered, 'Christ, that was boring wasn't it?'

Chapter 35

Derby Evening Telegraph, March 21 1989

Polish Club to close after 35 years

Dom Polski, the Polish Club on Osmaston Road, is to shut its doors for the last time after nearly 40 years. The club was founded in 1952 by members of the Polish squadrons of the RAF. The former servicemen bought the property to provide a social centre for members of the Polish community in Derby. The club was famous for its Saturday night dances, restaurant and Polish school. Mr Nowak, long time Polish School teacher said, 'Since manager Mr Batorowicz died, the club has suffered from falling attendance. The older generation are dying out and the younger people are not so interested in their heritage. We are becoming assimilated – the third generation can't speak Polish any more. We have disappeared.'

The premises are now up for sale. All enquiries to Burkett and Webb, Estate Agents

Wanda read out the article to Lydia as they sat in the kitchen of her house on Kedleston Road.

'How long did your dad run the club? I only ever remember him doing it,' said Wanda.

Lydia looked thoughtful, trying to work it out.

'Well, I was born in 1954, the year the club was founded, and I think we moved in there when I was about five. Dad had set it up with his colleagues in the RAF and he was managing it from around 1959 to when he died last year.'

'I always thought you had the best of both worlds with a foot in each camp, your mum being English,' said Wanda.

'Oh, my mum isn't English – she's Scottish, get it right.'

'Yes, I mean Scottish.'

'We used to go to Ayr to see my cousins in the summer. When my Polish cousin came to stay once, she asked if my mum was German!'

'Does the Scottish accent sound German? I never thought about it. But I did wonder how your parents communicated when they first met. I presume your dad couldn't speak English when he arrived here.'

'No he couldn't. I think they had great difficulty. We kids always used to say he didn't understand what mum was talking about when she told him to be at the church on a certain day – then he found himself married.'

Wanda laughed. 'It is strange having a cross-cultural marriage. Pawel and I always spoke Polish to each other at first because he couldn't speak English and even when he learnt it we stayed speaking Polish. I wonder if we both lost out on the nuances of the language – he probably said things I didn't get the full meaning of.'

'I always felt I missed out too because I couldn't speak much Polish – with mum not being able to speak it. I always thought I only understood half that was going on. I was even more conflicted than you. That's probably why I managed to get myself pregnant at 17 – stupid child that I was.'

'Tomasz is a lovely boy – you wouldn't be without him now, would you. Take what you can get, I say. Look what happened to Zosia – you just never know.'

'Anyway,' said Lydia patting Wanda's knee, 'talking about taking what you get, I hear you have a new man. Do tell.'

'News travels slowly - I've known him a couple of years now. His name is Bronek, he lives in London so I don't see him that often. We go to the theatre and cinema but, I don't know, he's just a friend.'

'No plans to move to London then?'

'No, no, I can't move Anna and I don't to leave Mum.'

'How is Anna getting on at her new school?' asked Lydia.

Wanda face brightened. 'Fantastic.'

Lydia smiled with a relieved look on her face. 'I'm really glad because I did worry for a while that she might be bullied - like Zosia was.'

Wanda sat up straight and stared at Lydia. 'Did you know Zosia was bullied at school?'

'Yes. I still feel guilty that I didn't intervene but I didn't want to get picked on myself,' she looked down at her hands, 'I was a coward. Also, Zosia and I were not really going around together any more. I was interested in music, discos and boys – too interested in boys as it turned out. Zosia was always into history and art. You know what she was like, sometimes a little – I don't know, odd.'

'Why did they bully her?' asked Wanda. 'Who was it? I found some spiteful notes in her school bag after she died but of course there were no names on them.'

Lydia's face went red. 'Oh, no. What did they say?'

'Nasty poems and comments. I threw them away.'

'Some older girls started bullying her when she seemed to be alone. Also she was clever and pretty and some people hate that, don't they?' said Lydia.

'It wasn't because she was Polish then?'

'I don't think so. She must have suffered a good deal but I knew she was going off to university in London so I was glad everything had turned out well - so I thought at the time. Compared to me, a young girl stuck at home with an illegitimate baby she seems to have it all. I envied her.'

'No one in the family realised Zosia was suffering at that school,' said Wanda. She tried to think back to those days but she had been away working in London then. Her mother knew nothing about it so Zosia had obviously never confided in her. 'Hopefully nowadays we talk about things more. Back then it was very much stiff upper lip – you just got on with things and didn't complain.'

'Don't ask, don't tell.'

'Anyway, Anna is doing fine. I was worried she wouldn't fit in with those rich, confident girls but she loves it there.'

Chapter 36

Helena was holding in her hands a copy of her book for the very first time. She stared at it, felt its smooth pages, held it to her nose to smell the binding. *The Fragmented Mind by Dr Helena Poniatowska and Dr Nathan Weinberg.* She looked at the synopsis on the back, the bar code, the price (expensive at £20 but it was an academic text). It would probably only sell to libraries and those with a specific interest in schizophrenia but Helena didn't mind. The book was out.

She had invited her son and daughter out for dinner to celebrate its release. They sat in the Standing Order wine bar in the Cornmarket waiting to be served. The high ceilings were imposing. Portraits of Obadiah Stepp and other Derby worthies decorated the walls.

John had ordered champagne and it was sitting in an ice-filled bucket next to the table.

'This used to be the NatWest bank,' said John. 'And before that, the Corn Exchange. Now it's serving Pinot Grigio and posh fish and chips.'

'I've heard it's very good,' said Helena, a little surprised at her son's abrasive attitude. He seemed to be in a bad humour quite often these days.

'OK, let's have a look at your book, Mum.'

Helena bent down and fished it out from her handbag. She gingerly handed it over to her son. He stared at the cover.

'Why did you publish it under your maiden name?' he asked, flicking casually through the 460 pages.

'I just thought it would be correct as a professional name – you know, my father's name. You don't mind, do you?' said Helena.

'He's got no business minding,' said Wanda. 'After all, he officially changed his name from Baran to Allsop.'

'All right,' said John. 'What's in a name. A rose by any other name would smell as sweet as someone once said.'

'I think he was wrong, names are very important,' said Wanda. 'I've considered changing my name back to Baran but I don't want to upset Anna.'

John shrugged. 'How much of this work is from Dr Weinberg?'

'The first few chapters are taken from his notes. There are some of his interviews there and his comments. I suppose about a third. The title is his and I know he wanted to write a book so I'm fulfilling his dream as he is no longer in a position to do it himself,' said Helena.

'Do you actually remember meeting him?' asked Wanda. 'I mean before the war, was he around much?'

'I've tried again and again to remember but I don't think I ever met him. My mother didn't see much of my father's family after his death. I keep trying to remember but I don't think I ever saw him or his wife, my father's sister,' said Helena.

'That's strange behaviour, don't you think?' said John. 'You'd think they'd want to see their dead brother's daughter.'

'Knowing my Babcia,' said Wanda, 'she probably had antagonised or offended them in some way. So what was the relationship between this Dr Weinberg and your father?'

'I don't know really on a personal level but Nathan was interested in him from a psychological standpoint. I think it was his first experience of schizophrenia.'

John and Wanda stared at her in shock. 'You mean, our grandfather was a schizophrenic?' said John.

'Babcia always said he was a war hero,' said Wanda, frowning.

'That was one of my mother's little fantasies. The poor man suffered from hallucinations, disordered thoughts, insanity. Nathan included him in his case histories.'

Wanda swallowed. 'And this disease is hereditary, is it?'

'It possibly is but fortunately it hasn't shown itself in me or you two. Neither of you see things that aren't there, do you? Don't look so worried Wanda.'

'No, I'm seeing things in all their grim reality at the moment,' said John. 'But let's drink a toast.' He took the champagne and poured a little into the fluted glasses.

'To our wonderful, brilliant mother. Much success with her erudite book. May it prove more fruitful than my attempts at publishing.'

Helena smiled as they clinked glasses.

John glanced up at the newspaper rack on the wall. He rose and took a copy of the *Times* newspaper.

'Look at this picture. It says, 'Westward bound: East Germans in their two-stroke Trabants formed a four-kilometer jam at the Czechoslovakia-West German border, through which some 12,000 passed at the weekend.

Helena took the paper and looked at the picture. She shook her head in amazement.

'It's actually finishing. The Berlin Wall is coming down. People are free to go. I never thought this would happen in my lifetime.'

'Now Poland is free, perhaps we can finally visit,' said Wanda. 'What do you think, Mum. Would you like to go back?'

Helena sat and thought. She had last seen the land of her birth when she was 16. She has been in England since 1946 and she now spoke English with very little foreign accent. When she tried to think about Poland, she remembered her mother's discipline, their small flat, her cousin Irena but the main memory was of being thrown into a German truck with scores of other strangers and forcibly removed from the country. That trauma, that memory almost obliterated anything else.

'I don't know yet if I want to go back. Although I'd like to see the places where my uncle lived and perhaps find out exactly what happened to him.'

'The end of communism,' said John. 'It couldn't last, it was a fatally flawed economic system. We've won!'

'I wonder how Irena is taking all this?' said Wanda. 'She must be heartbroken. All her ideals and beliefs have failed.'

'She will think of a way round it. She's probably thinking it didn't work because they didn't follow it properly, didn't stick to Marx's ideas,' said Helena.

'That's true,' said John, 'but human nature being as it is, it was never going to work anyway.'

'Let's go and see her, Mum,' said Wanda. 'Take Anna to see her grandmother. I'd love to see Poland too. We could go, the three of us. It would be an adventure.'

Chapter 37

Derby, 1991

Wanda felt a little knot of fear uncurl itself in her stomach. Aged 41 she was going abroad and flying for the first time in her life. She'd applied for her passport and booked three tickets with British Airways for a flight to Warsaw.

She put her clothes in careful piles on her bed, selecting cool summer dresses, sandals – yes, she must remember the insect repellent because she'd heard the mosquitoes were bad this summer.

If Wanda was a little nervous, her mother was in a state of high anxiety. Helena was wiping down an ancient suitcase. Between bouts of frantic activity, she would suddenly sit down and twist her handkerchief round and round her fingers.

'I never thought I'd go back to the land of my birth, to my home city. I never thought it would happen. Tadek and I were resigned to never seeing Poland again. We thought the Iron Curtain was permanent. If only he'd lived to see this.'

Anna, calm and nonchalant, came into her mother's bedroom and flopped down on the bed. Her long dark hair spread out over the green quilt, her slim legs draped down the side of the bed. Wanda couldn't believe how tall and elegant her 14-year-old daughter was now – she was several inches taller than her mother already. She had also taken to speaking in a posh accent, copying some of the wealthy girls at school.

'I decided I was going to out-posh them,' she told her mother. 'I can do their accent, only make it even more elevated.'

'Your great grandmother would be so proud of you,' said Helena, smiling. 'You would be her little treasure.'

'You always told me Zosia was her favourite. People have told me that all my life that I'm like her but is it just wishful thinking? Do they just want me to be like her? I want to be taller than her, and much posher.'

'I think you are about the same height as she was, your hair and eyes are the same colour but you definitely win on the posh stakes,' said Wanda. 'Mum, should we telephone Irena again and let her know the time we are arriving?'

'I wrote to her last week and she sent a telegram back so it is all confirmed. She will meet us at Warsaw airport and we'll go back to her flat. Can you imagine, I haven't seen that flat since 1939 – I can't believe I'll be back there again.'

'Can we see where you used to live, Babcia?' said Anna.

'It didn't survive the war, I believe. I want to visit the flat where Nathan and Maria lived, though. I think that's still there. It would be wonderful to see their street. After reading about them, I want to see what they saw. Of course, it may all have changed out of recognition.'

Wanda saw her put her notes and academic books in her suitcase. She knew her mother would continue working even when they were away. Her book had been reviewed in *The Guardian*, *The Telegraph* and *The Spectator* as well as in a collection of academic journals.

Interestingly, Helena had also achieved that enviable balance of making the book academic enough for university libraries, yet popular enough for the layperson. It was selling well.

'I'll meet my other grandmother for the first time,' said Anna crunching on an apple. 'She said she would show me round the hospital. I told her I might study medicine too. She was really pleased.'

'It will be good to have your family all in one place together,' said Wanda.

'Yes, but when I told Lucie Berenger at school that my grandmothers were first cousins, she said she was surprised I didn't have two heads or six fingers on each hand.'

'She's talking nonsense,' said Wanda crossly. 'Your father and I are second cousins, there is no genetic danger in that. None whatsoever.'

'But it does make for an even closer family, doesn't it' said Anna squeezing her mother's arm.

Chapter 38

Aleks sat back in his airline seat and looked over at his son. Pawel seemed nervous, he was chewing his nails. The take-off had scared Aleks too but he hid his fear with a large glass of vodka. Looking down, he could see London spread out beneath them as the plane banked to the right. In two hours, they would be in Warsaw. He was coming home in a rather more elegant fashion to that in which he'd left.

Pawel hadn't been back for about 15 years and Aleks knew he was looking forward very much to seeing his mother again. There is nothing like a mother's unconditional love, something to wallow in like a hot bath. Pawel had been talking all day about the small flat where he'd been brought up, the dusty courtyard where he'd played football, the creaking lift with its metal lattice doors. He'd described with affection the echoes of the stairwell, the banging of the hot water pipes. Aleks smiled, thinking his son wouldn't be so nostalgic if he still had to live there.

They had told Irena nothing of why Pawel and Wanda had split, just that there had been arguments. When he'd phoned her a few days earlier, she'd asked him if there was any way the two could be reconciled. 'You never know,' he'd replied. It was easier if she had some hope.

The man in the other seat was a businessman looking to take up new opportunities in the brave new world of Eastern Europe. Aleks struck up a conversation during which he happened to mention that he used to work with Lech Walesa, now the President of Poland, at the Gdansk shipyards. The man was impressed and gave Aleks his business card. Aleks put his head back against the seat. This was a good life, he could get used to this.

They landed at Warsaw airport with the new duty free shops and luxury items on sale. Aleks looked around in amazement.

'Can you believe the changes to this country?' he said to Pawel. 'Your mother is going to hate this all this capitalism, consumerism. She'll be like a fish out of water.'

'It seems so weird,' said Pawel. 'I can hardly recognise it's the same country.'

They took the tram to Irena's flat. There was a new energy about the place, a new sense of excitement. The wall had collapsed, the Iron Curtain had rusted away. Aleks had seen on television the Berlin Wall being dismantled brick by brick but at the time he didn't really believe it. Now he was here and it was true. Everyone felt silly with freedom. It was like the wild west, everyone for themselves.

They had brought presents for Irena but when they arrived at her flat all she was excited about was seeing her son again. Aleks watched her hang round his neck as if she never wanted to let go. She even gave Aleks a kiss on the cheek.

Irena was in the kitchen preparing food. Pawel walked round the tiny flat examining everything.

'This place was my home for 25 years, my prison for 25 years,' he said. 'Look at these photographs: my grandparents' wedding, mother as a baby, me as a toddler. Look, here's a picture of my babcia.' A look of sadness came over his face.

Irena had prepared a beautiful meal: cold ham and salami, tomato salad, cucumber and yogurt, fresh bread, radish, and pickled herring. They sat down to eat. Aleks tucked his napkin in his shirt.

'Strange how things turn out isn't it? Meeting up with my own father in London of all places,' said Pawel. 'And after all this time, here we are, we three together again. I'm actually having a meal with my mother and father for the first time at age 42.' He put one hand on his mother's hand and the other on his father's.

'And to be doing that in a free Poland, who would have ever have dreamed that,' said Aleks. 'Momentous times, eh?

So many little coincidences and chances and here we all are, in the right place at the right time. '

'Is is all just coincidence?' asked Pawel.

'Why? Do you think it's divine intervention?' asked Irena laughing.

'No, of course not, but people make their own luck don't they?'

'We don't always have control over events. Sometimes a small thing can have dramatic consequences. A split-second decision can be fatal,' said Aleks. 'It can boil down to simply where you are standing. I was reading about this boy called Chris Gueffroy. He was only 20 and he tried to cross the Berlin wall and escape to freedom on the other side, but he was shot by the border guards and left to bleed to death. A commonplace event you might say but this happened in February 1989 – the poor boy only had to wait a few months and he could have walked safely through the wall with no problems at all. Now that's a tragedy.'

'It's Shakespeare,' said Pawel. 'Dramatic irony.'

'Tell that to his mother,' said Irena, shaking her head.

Outside they could hear the rattle of the trams on the street, a couple talking loudly in the corridor. Does the water still smell of chlorine, Aleks thought. He wanted a bath but the idea of that green water didn't tempt him.

'You are only here because your mother and I happened to meet and fall in love,' said Aleks looking at Pawel. 'A moment in time, a little sooner or later and it might never have happened. I was amazed because I knew I was never good enough for her but she still married me.'

'Foolish woman,' said Pawel. 'How did you meet?'

Irena tutted and looked away, 'We don't want to go into all that,' she said.

Pawel smiled, 'All what?' he asked.

'Your mother fell in love with me and followed me everywhere, I just couldn't get rid of her. In the end I said, all right woman, I'll marry you.'

'Nonsense. I was helping rebuild this city after the war. I was working helping load bricks to reconstruct the old town. Your father was busy pretending to be busy. He was

mostly sitting around, smoking and telling people what to
do.'

Aleks was enjoying this. He had had a hearty meal, there
was plenty of vodka, he had a receptive audience of people
he loved, yes he really loved them both. He felt a glow of
wellbeing.

'I was keeping morale up with my witty talk and jokes,'
said Aleks. 'Keeping people entertained is just as important
as working. During the first world war, some people said
Charlie Chaplin should have come back to Europe to fight
for his country but instead he stayed in America and made
funny films ridiculing the Germans. Surely you have to
admit he did the right thing. His films were more important
to the war effort than him dying pointlessly in a trench.'

'So you're the Charlie Chaplin of the construction
industry, are you?' asked Pawel.

Irena stood up and began clearing some of the empty
plates away. She brought out cake and the coffee pot from
the kitchen.

'Come on, eat up, I've been cooking all day,' said Irena.

'What a great cook you are, Irena. Nearly as good as my
own mother,' said Aleks.

'Your mother wasn't a great cook – she was too erratic. A
crazy woman. You take after her.'

'She was a little eccentric but funny and always
laughing,' said Aleks.

'I never knew her,' said Pawel. ' What did she do that
was so funny?'

Aleks lit a cigarette and leant back in his chair. Irena
fiddled with the cutlery and Pawel looked expectantly at his
father.

'Let me tell you a story about your grandmother, Pawel.
When she was a young girl, she was living in Warsaw and
she was asked by a young couple who were friends of hers
to look after their dog while they were away. They lived on
the fifth floor of a block of flats and they asked her to come
in every day and feed the animal and pet it a while to keep
it company. They told her she didn't need to take it for a
walk because it was very old and just liked to sleep.'

'How old was she, who were these people?' asked Irena.

'She was about 19 and it doesn't matter who they were. Let me finish the story for God's sake. So the couple went on their holiday and mum went to feed the dog. The second day she went up to the flat and let herself in. Horror of horrors - she found the dog dead in the kitchen. She didn't know what to do. She couldn't just leave it in the flat but it was a big dog so she couldn't easily get it out. She decided to find a big suitcase, put the dog inside and get it to the vet. She found a suitably large case and managed to push and pull the dog inside. Then she dragged the case over to the lift and took it downstairs.'

Aleks looked at his son who was sitting spellbound listening to the story. He had obviously never heard it before. He wanted to spin out the talk as long as possible, he wanted this evening to continue for ever.

'Anyway, she got the suitcase down to ground level,' continued Aleks. 'With a good deal of effort she pulled it out on to the street and stood waiting for a tram. When it arrived, she heaved the case aboard, found a seat and sat down with the suitcase near her.'

'This is going to end badly,' said Pawel, 'I can feel it.'

'Shush and listen. Anyway, a young man came and sat next to my mother. He struck up a conversation and was very friendly. After a while he asked what she had in her suitcase. Well, she didn't want to say 'a dead dog' so she said she was moving house and didn't want to entrust her valuable jewellery and art work to a moving company so she was taking the things herself. The man nodded and agreed that was a good idea. Then the tram paused at the next stop. The man suddenly grabbed the case, jumped off the tram with it and ran down the street.'

Pawel began to laugh loudly and Irena smiled. Aleks spoke over the laughter.

'The other people on the tram asked if they should chase him but mother said, 'No, don't worry about it.' Can you imagine the man's face when he finally opened that suitcase.'

They sat drinking vodka and eating cakes, talking, laughing. Aleks felt a wave of happiness sweep over him.

'I have some news,' said Irena. 'I think you will be pleased when you hear it.'

'Are you marrying a millionaire, Mother?' said Pawel.

Aleks stopped smiling, 'Over my dead body, Woman'

'We are having visitors the day after tomorrow.'

'What visitors?' said Pawel. 'They can't stay here, there's no room.'

'Well you and Aleks can stay at Bogdan's, can't you? You should make way for some very important guests.'

'Who?' said Aleks and Pawel together.

'My dear cousin Helena, her daughter Wanda and my darling granddaughter Anna. Isn't that wonderful?'

There was silence and Pawel closed his eyes and put his head in his hands.

'Come on, darling,' said Irena patting his shoulder. 'I want you and Wanda to make up. I don't want things to be like it was between me and your father for years. We can still be friends, spend time together.'

'Irenka, it's not that simple,' said Aleks. 'You don't understand.'

'I do understand, couples tire of each other and split up. I know that better than many people. But they can reconcile,' said Irena.

Pawel got up from his seat. 'Sit down, Son,' said Aleks. 'Irena, there are complications. You shouldn't have invited us at the same time. I assume you haven't told Wanda we'll be here.'

'No, I thought it would be a nice surprise. What's wrong?'

'Well, don't tell them. We will move out before they come and they can have the flat to themselves. You can't make things work just because you believe they will.'

'Oh, but I do believe they will,' said Irena frowning.

'Yes, you always did believe in things,' said Aleks. 'You replaced God by believing in communism. After living in the West, I now see things aren't perfect there either. That's just it - communism doesn't work, capitalism doesn't work, marriage doesn't work, work doesn't work – and forcing people to be together who don't want to be together doesn't work either.'

Irena got up and walked into the kitchen.

Aleks looked at his son and stroked his hand. Pawel looked round the room and stared at the old, brown sofa behind him.

That was where Zosia had died, screaming, crying out and spewing out black liquid from her throat.

Chapter 39

Anna Zosia Lato walked away from the plane at Warsaw Airport followed by her mother and grandmother. It was a day of firsts: her first time in a plane, her first trip out of Britain and her first taste of alcohol as she sipped a little of her grandmother's vodka mixed with apple juice.

After they had collected their bags and walked into the arrivals hall, Anna saw a woman who looked a little like her maternal grandmother – same eyes and nose but the shape of her face was wrong and her mouth was different. There was no denying – this was her paternal grandmother. For the first time it really hit Anna that her parents were related. They had no similarity to each other but seeing the resemblance between her grandmothers made Anna aware that her family tree was shaped more like a poplar than an oak.

The woman was holding red and white flowers tied with ribbon. Her face lit up with delight and she ran towards them, greeting them with hugs and kisses. Anna felt overwhelmed – this was her grandmother, the same but different. It was a very strange sensation.

Soon they were in the taxi heading toward Irena's flat. Anna listened to the rattle of Polish between her grandmothers. She had learnt the language in some isolation having heard it from her parents and grandparents., but she noticed Irena used words and phrases she had never heard before. This was going to be an exciting experience. She looked at her mother who wasn't listening to the conversation but was looking out of the taxi window and biting her nails.

Anna looked at the wide streets bisected by tram lines, the huge grey stone buildings and unfamiliar shops and kiosks. She thought about her father. She had phoned him the previous week and he'd told her he was going to Poland with his father to see his mother. She didn't know what to do with that information. She didn't tell him they were due to arrive in Warsaw two days later. She realised if she told her mother Pawel would be there, the trip would be off. As the child of separated parents, she was caught in the middle, not knowing which way to turn, not wanting to show disloyalty to either side. Anna had decided to do nothing and let events take their course. So far, Irena had not mentioned Pawel. There could be an awful scene if he was back at the flat. Hopefully, Irena knew that would be a terrible idea and would spoil the whole holiday.

The taxi stopped outside some old, brown blocks of flats about six storeys high. There were balconies all around the outside. Anna could see through the large entrance that the flats were arranged around a central courtyard with a tree in the middle. Some little boys were playing football in the courtyard.

They carried their cases to the lift, Helena and Irena keeping up a stream of conversation. Wanda was quiet, lost in thought. As they entered the lift, Anna suddenly realised that they were going to the room where Zosia had died. How terrible, she had never thought of that until this moment. She looked round at everyone else, wondering if that thought had occurred to them as well. Helena didn't seem aware of it but Anna had a feeling that Wanda was thinking about that. That was perhaps the cause of her apparent sadness. She had been addressing Anna as Zosia much more often lately – something she had always done in times of stress.

The lift was old fashioned, wood panelled. There were metal doors you had to slide across. Anna noticed a particular, familiar smell but she couldn't quite remember what it was. The lift shuddered and shook its way to the third floor. They walked along the corridor and Irena took out her keys and opened the door. Anna followed them inside through the hall into the main room. To her relief,

there was no one else there. The dining table was covered
with a lacy tablecloth, there were shelves with books and
ornaments, a television, a sofa, coffee table and a cabinet
with crockery. Sunshine streamed through the large
window and the branches of the courtyard tree waved in
the breeze.

Anna walked round the room, picking up the little
ornaments on the cabinet, looking at pictures of a young
and lovely Irena holding Pawel as a baby. She looked into
the small kitchen, the bathroom next to it and the bedroom.
That was it – the extent of the flat. It was crammed full of
furniture, boxes, and nick-nacks.

Irena was in the kitchen getting ready to bring out the
dishes. Anna slipped in next to her while Helena and
Wanda were talking in the other room.

'Babcia, can I ask you something?' she said quietly.

'Of course, *kochana*. Oh, you are a beautiful girl,' and she
squeezed Anna in a tight hug.

Anna smiled and waited for the embrace to end.

'I spoke to my father last week on the phone,' she
whispered, and he told me he and my grandfather were
coming. Are they here now?'

Irena looked toward the other room at Helena and
Wanda but they were lost in conversation.

'They are staying nearby with friends,' she said quietly.
'Your grandfather told me it was a bad idea to spring them
on your poor mother. They know you three are here,
though. What do you think?'

'I agree with grandfather. My mother would be so upset
if she suddenly saw my dad. It would ruin the holiday, so
please don't say he is here. I think she wouldn't mind seeing
granddad, though.'

Irena patted Anna's hand. 'Let's see how things go, shall
we?'

They all sat down to eat.

'I'm so happy to see my lovely granddaughter at last,'
said Irena. 'I heard news about you from Aleksander. He is
so impressed – tells me how intelligent you are.'

'You're going to say I'm just like Zosia, aren't you?' said
Anna with a half-laugh.

'Well, you are your own person and not your aunt. But let me tell you it is no insult at all to be compared to her. She was a delightful girl – also very beautiful and clever. I have to say there is a great similarity.'

'She stayed here in this flat with you, didn't she?' asked Anna.

'Yes, she spent a lot of time with my mother. They were great friends for the time they were together. They went to Lazenki Park to listen to the Chopin played there. Zosia told me she was disappointed because the pianist turned out to be an old woman and not a handsome youth.'

Wanda and Anna laughed. Anna looked at Helena who was smiling but there was pain behind her eyes and her brow was furrowed.

'Zosia was always a romantic,' said Wanda. 'She always thought she would marry a prince, her dream man was called Prince Frederick, and they'd live in a castle. She used to make Janek dress up as her prince but he didn't want to be romantic, just to hit people with his sword.'

'I'm sure she would have found a prince, just as her grandmother did,' said Irena.

Helena raised her eyebrows and said nothing.

'I always carry this picture with me in my purse,' said Irena, looking in her handbag. She took out a creased print and passed it round. 'It's of Zosia and Pawel feeding the pigeons in the market square in Krakow.'

Anna looked at the photo. Zosia was smiling at a pigeon on her hand while Pawel was leaning toward Zosia and staring at the camera. He looked so young, thought Anna and almost handsome. They had gone to Krakow all those years ago and Zosia had eaten contaminated meat at the house of the people where they were staying. Anna wondered if the picture was taken after Zosia had already eaten and her fate was sealed, or before and it still hung in the balance. If only I could shout at her, don't eat the meat, thought Anna.

Then a thought struck Anna and sent a shiver down her spine. She looked round at the sofa – she was probably going to sleep on the same sofa on which her aunt had died.

She looked at her mother and wondered if the same thought had occurred to her. That beautiful dead girl was the elephant in the room – they were all thinking about her horrendous death but no one wanted to mention it for fear of upsetting the others. Zosia still loomed large over all their lives. That night, Anna was indeed required to sleep on the same pull-out sofa, but in fact she slept peacefully, untroubled by ghosts.

The next morning Wanda and Anna went out to look round the shops, leaving Helena and Irena to have a chat at the flat.

'It was strange to walk into this place again after so many years. I never thought I'd see it again,' said Helena.

'You probably never thought you'd see Poland again, did you? I remember getting a letter from you once saying you could never come back. When auntie Barbara was living with you, there was no need.'

'I suppose not and also there were too many negative associations with the place.' Helena paused and looked out at the large tree out in the courtyard. She sat a moment collecting her thoughts. 'My childhood was not very happy – just myself and my mother and you know how difficult she was.'

'Yes, of course. My own mother didn't like auntie Barbara very much,' said Irena. 'But father always loved her and tried to protect her as a brother should. He had a difficult time, trapped between those two powerful women. You always spent a lot of time with us which was wonderful because as we were both only children, it was like having a sister.'

'It was, wasn't it? I never saw anyone from my father's family. I suppose they wanted to forget about him, given his mental illness and his death.'

'Yes, his suicide must have been so shocking,' said Irena.

Helena said nothing. She could not bring herself to talk openly about her father's death. Perhaps he had taken too much morphine himself but her mother's role in his death and indeed her uncle's could not be pushed aside. Her uncle supplied the drugs and it's possible her mother administered them with her father's knowledge. Did she need to find out the truth, or should it lie dormant?

'It was a terrible shock when you were taken by the Germans,' continued Irena. 'Your mother came to see us and she was hysterical. She was screaming and crying that her baby girl had been taken away.' I can see her now, standing at our doorway, her hair all over the place, her face white. She was just dressed in her indoor clothes – normally she would never go out without a coat, hat and gloves. That struck me at the time as the most terrible thing. The fact that you were taken as slave labour seemed less important than the lack of gloves.'

Helena sighed. 'Yes, it was traumatic - I was living the trauma.'

'Of course you were. Actually, my mother was very good with Barbara, despite their hostility. She said you were taken away to work so you must still be alive. She tried to give us all hope.'

'I was only 16 years old, a child. They took me and about 40 other people, complete strangers, to some kind of warehouse where we were separated into groups,' Helena continued. 'The old and infirm and the very young were taken away. I was put in the group with other fit, strong women. They herded us onto trains – we had no idea where we were going. Someone looked through the slats of the train carriage and said, 'We're heading west, into Germany.' Someone else said, 'Does that mean we're going to work, that we're not going to death camps?' We actually felt a little cheered by that. We were going to be slave labour not to be murdered in concentration camps. It's amazing what can make you hopeful, isn't it? When everything else is gone, there is always hope,' she said looking up a picture of her mother Barbara on top of the sideboard.

Chapter 40

The next day, Irena, Helena, Wanda and Anna set about exploring the city. They took the tram to Paweski Cemetery. Helena had a map detailing exactly where her father's grave was situated. Walking through the lines of gravestones, Helena eventually found his resting place. She remembered going there with her mother every year on All Soul's day until the war. She had bought some white lilies and Wanda and Anna watched in silence as she arranged them in the metal vase. Standing up, Helena kissed her fingers and placed them on the headstone. 'Sleep peacefully, Daddy,' she said.

They walked through the old town and adjoining streets. Helena gazed round at the city she hadn't seen since she was 16.

'I was so afraid to come here again, so worried of the memories,' said Helena. 'Strangely I feel quite calm and relaxed. It all seems so different.'

'Perhaps that's because there is a free government now. Maybe you wouldn't have felt the same if it was still communist,' said Wanda.

'Maybe that is why,' said Helena. 'I can disassociate the two – it's as if it were two different cities. I have put all the fear and hurt in a little box marked 'old Warsaw' and now I'm walking round 'new Warsaw' so it is just excitement and interest that I feel.'

Clutching a piece of paper with the address of Dr Weinberg's apartment, Helena told Irena about her uncle and aunt, the story of their lives and how her uncle had died in the concentration camp.

The buildings in that district were still intact. They got off the tram and walked along the line of grey stone buildings to find the flat. Helena read the names and numbers on the buildings and eventually stopped outside a door. They went inside the entrance hall. There was a desk and a young girl who was listening to a small radio and blowing bubbles with her gum.

Helena addressed her. 'Excuse me, I wonder if you know anything about the residents who used to live in these flats before the war?'

The girl stared and continued to blow bubbles. Eventually, she said her grandmother had been the concierge for most of her life but was now retired. She still often came in when she was out shopping. She couldn't keep away from the place.

'What time will she come, do you think?' asked Helena trying to hide her annoyance at the girl's surly manner.

The girl shrugged her shoulders and said in an hour possibly but she might not come at all. It was her mother who was now the concierge but she was ill that day.

'We will return in an hour. If she comes, can you tell her Dr Nathan Weinberg's niece would like to speak to her.'

The girl nodded and the four women went out to walk round the park and eat ice creams.

'Everything is changing,' said Irena nodding towards the huge advertising posters everywhere. 'I didn't think all this would happen in my life time. I imagine we cannot stop it now. It doesn't feel right but I suppose I am just old fashioned.'

Helena smiled. 'You will get used to it. We all have.'

'All the old certainties are gone – I don't know what to think any more.'

'You've been freed to think for yourself,' said Anna. 'And that can be a scary prospect.'

They arrived back at the flats about an hour later and saw an old woman talking to the young girl. Helena walked over and introduced herself.

'My uncle and aunt lived in this block before the war. Were you the concierge at the time?'

The old woman turned to look at her. She had lined skin, sparse white hair and a back bent from years of toil. 'Yes, I worked here from 1922 until 1962,' said the old woman. 'I remember all the residents. They used to say, "Pani Krystyna – how would this block run without you? Who would get the lift repaired, put new light bulbs in the stairs, clean the floors?" They all loved me and at Christmas they would buy me meat, fish, eggs and bread.'

Helena smiled. 'Pani Krystyna – I would be so grateful if you could tell me about my uncle and aunt, Dr Nathan Weinberg and his wife Maria. She was my father's sister. Do you remember them?'

Helena looked at the old woman's pale blue, runny eyes. Bits of white hair sprouted from her chin and her hands were bent into surreal shapes from arthritis.

'Let us sit down behind the desk and I will tell you. Bozena, please make us some tea.'

Anna called over. 'Babcia, we are just going to the shops down the road. Mummy has seen they sell some nice leather handbags and she wants to buy one. We'll see you back here in about an hour.'

'See you later,' called Helena and turned back towards the old lady whose crooked fingers were fiddling at the beads of her amber necklace.

'Do you mind if I switch on my little tape recorder. I'd like to get this information correct.'

'No, that's fine. Put on your machine – I will tell you all I remember.'

They settled down on two seats behind the desk and Krystyna began her story.

Chapter 41

You couldn't miss Dr Nathan and Pani Maria. They were the most flamboyant, most eccentric people who lived here. Everyone else was quiet, boring and ordinary but they – they were quite extraordinary, weird, exciting and possibly a little dangerous.

They came to these apartments in the same year that I did - 1921. I was only 16, it was my first job. They were a young couple. He was a Jewish man from a rich family. His father was a rabbi who was well known in the Jewish community. I believe there was some falling out with his family. The son took on all new ideas about atheism and communism. He never seemed to follow any Jewish traditions. I think he quarrelled with his father about that.

Then he married this young girl who was the daughter of Prince Olgierd Poniatowski – I say married but she still signed herself Maria Poniatowska. We would address her as Pani Weinberg but I don't think there was ever an actual marriage ceremony, at least that was the scandalous rumour at the time. She was supposed to marry some young noble fellow her father had selected for her but she refused. He said he would cut her off without a penny. I think that's what drew them together – they were both old-style communists, both from wealthy families, and both had been disowned by their fathers.

Dr Weinberg used to go to his surgery, which was just a few doors down on the left here. It's a hairdresser now. We all went to Dr Weinberg when we had coughs and colds. He treated me for free on many occasions – you could always rely on his kindness. Some people would pay him with food, or a bolt of cloth. One woman, who was a kind of gypsy I seem to remember, even told his fortune because she couldn't pay cash - he told me about it afterwards, he said it was hilarious. She had told him he would lead a long life and achieve success professionally. Ironic really, considering what happened.

Dr Nathan was always well dressed in a dark suit and small hat. His shoes were so polished you could see the windows reflected in them. He always had a kind word for me – he was the sort of person who noticed everyone even if they were cleaners, beggars, shop assistants. He didn't think he was better than everyone else. Of course, he got taunted in the street sometimes – all Jews did. They would knock his hat off or call him 'stinky Jew'. He never responded but would just pick up his hat and carry on walking.

She, Pani Maria, was a different kettle of fish. You could not call her kind and friendly. She wore strange clothes, clashing colours. She was fond of this hat with a peacock feather in it. Once, she came in from the street barefoot – her feet were filthy and we were all shocked.

She had a funny way about her, haughty and standoffish. She was a little peculiar too – people used to say she wasn't quite right in the head. She'd make strange comments sometimes. Once she came in late and I said, 'Goodnight, Pani Weinberg,' and she said, 'What do you know about it – you weren't even born then.' I have no idea what she meant. I heard she had a brother who was not quite the ticket – I never met him though.

Dr Weinberg was a chest doctor but he was interested in diseases of the mind as well. He told me he was writing a book. There were plenty of soldiers in those days who suffered from the shakes and bad dreams because of the war. Bad memories they had, poor fellows. He said he wanted to help them.

Dr and Mrs Weinberg were great friends with the Zabinskis, who were the directors of Warsaw Zoo. Pani Zabinski was a little odd too but a lovely woman. They were all – what's the word – bohemian. The Zabinskis were always putting on plays and revues at the zoo. All kinds of artists would go there – it was a great cultural centre. They used to speak French sometimes and Dr Weinberg would play his violin. Dr Weinberg often had colleagues from France over and he and Maria went at least twice to visit them in Paris. Perhaps they went more often, I don't remember.

They all loved animals – Feddi was Dr Weinberg's little terrier. He was devoted to it. Poor Feddi – the Germans threw him off the balcony when they were searching the flat during the occupation.

The Zabinski family were so upset when the bombs fell on the zoo. Many of the animals were killed. They tried to save the ones that were injured. The problem was, people were very hungry in those days so some took the carcasses to eat. Pani Goworek, who still lives here at number 245, told me her father brought back some meat he had found and it turned out to be a bit of zebra. She said it was strange to get a stripy steak on your plate. Anyway, the directors tried to save as many animals as possible. I heard they also hid some people in the zoo, hid them from the police. They were good people.

The Germans started rounding up the Jews in 1940 and putting them in the Ghetto. When it all started, I hadn't seen Pani Weinberg for a few days or maybe a week at that time. After the war, I heard her parents had kidnapped her and locked her in her room at home so the Germans wouldn't take her with her Jewish husband. Then Dr Weinberg disappeared. The day the soldiers came looking for him, the flat was empty except for Feddi.

After the Jews were all gone to the Ghetto, Pani Weinberg came back to the flat. She lived here alone for years. She had a huge scar down her face which she hadn't had before. She said Dr Weinberg had been taken to Auschwitz and died there.

She didn't tell me that her parents had taken her away – I heard that from old Lubek who lived next door to them. He said her father gave her that gash across the face when she was a prisoner at home and she tried to escape.

She lived here until – I think she died in 1975 or maybe 1974, I'm not sure. She was a mad, rude old woman by then and we avoided her. She spent her time looking for her husband – she was quite insane. Every day she would go out and say she was meeting him for coffee.

I never saw Dr Weinberg again, but then I never expected to. The last time I saw him he was going out of the main door with a little suitcase, his violin and Feddi under his arm. He smiled and nodded to me. I was surprised when Feddi turned up alone a few days later. I thought, Dr Weinberg is going to be upset that he has lost Feddi. I took Feddi up to the flat and fed him. He had a little bed he used to sleep in. I didn't know what to do. I suppose I thought it meant Dr Weinberg was already dead. What a shame, a nice gentleman.

I did go to Pani Maria's funeral - there were only about three people there. I'm not surprised by that. I was surprised, though, when her doctor came to see me and said she wanted me to have her husband's watch. It was a good pocket watch - Longines, Switzerland. The doctor also told me that Pani Weinberg, or Maria Poniatowska as he called her, was active in the Zegota during the occupation. Zegota was the part of the Polish resistance dedicated to helping Jews. They helped thousands to hide and escape. They sent Jewish children to live with Catholic families, arranged for people to get out of the ghetto and even to have plastic surgery if they looked very Jewish. I didn't know she was involved in that so I was surprised.

Anyway, I want you to have the watch. I want Dr Weinberg to know I'm sorry I didn't look after Feddi properly, I should have kept him downstairs. Dr Weinberg was always good to me but I let him down. By rights, your auntie should have given the watch to you.

Chapter 42

Krakow, 1991

Close to Krakow's huge main square, The Rynek, is The Grand Hotel located in Stawkowska Street. A young man dressed in hotel livery led Helena, Wanda and Anna through the faded grandeur of its corridors. The walls were pale green with a matching carpet on the floor. Helena had noticed a restaurant and bar downstairs with old black and white photos on the wall of past guests dressed in Edwardian finery.

The porter opened a panelled door at the end of the hall. It was a large bedroom with en suite bathroom. Helena looked inside.

'This is the double for you and Anna, is it?' said Helena. 'It's beautiful. Look, you can just about see the edge of the market square. Can we hear the trumpeter from here?'

'Yes, if there isn't too much noise from the street,' said the porter looking at his watch. 'If we wait a few minutes, he should be starting. Shall I show you the other room?'

Helena went to see her single room next door. It was darker and didn't have such a good view however Helena paid little attention to it. She gave the porter a tip and went back to her daughter's room.

Anna was lying on the bed, stretching her legs after their long journey from Warsaw.

'Look, a chocolate on the pillow,' she said unwrapping it and popping it in her mouth. 'This looks like a very posh hotel. The woman on reception was quite rude though, wasn't she?'

'It's funny, they have the nice porter in uniform and the flower displays but the old communist habits come through here and there,' said Helena looking out of the window again.

'I suppose it will take time to change,' said Anna leafing through *A Guide to Krakow,* a magazine she had found on the bedside table.

'There, did you hear that? It was the trumpeter,' said Wanda holding her hand up. 'It's quite faint. We can go into the square tomorrow and hear him properly. Do you know who he was, Anna?'

'Yes, yes he was the man who played his bugle in the tall tower to warn about an invading army back in, I think the 14th century, and he was shot with an arrow and died,' replied Anna flicking through the magazine. 'And every day since then, the trumpet player has stopped at exactly the same point in the tune.'

'I must ask at reception about trips to the salt mine Wieliczka and to Auschwitz,' Helena said. 'I assume we can arrange a tour from the hotel.'

'I'd like to go to the salt mine but do you really want to go to Auschwitz? It will be so grim and we are here on holiday,' said Wanda.

'I don't want to go but I think I should,' said Helena. 'I want to see the place where my uncle died. I want to pay some kind of tribute. I feel it's my duty. I can go alone, I'll be fine.' She was still in two minds about going, this could ruin the holiday.

'I'll come with you, Babcia,' said Anna. 'It will just be half a day and you could go shopping or have a lovely soak in that huge bath tub, Mum.'

Aleks and Pawel moved back to Irena's flat once Wanda and her mother and daughter had set out for Krakow. Pawel was enjoying his mother's care and cooking and catching up with old friends from school and college.

Aleks was restless though. He had arranged to meet some acquaintances so he could conduct a few business deals. There were always little arrangements to be made: selling T-shirts, bars of soap, jeans and videos of films. None of the stuff was totally legal, but it was a good way to make some money.

Aleks didn't want to tell Pawel too much about his activities. He found it all a little embarrassing but it had a peculiar kind of thrill. It was a little like low-level betting. He and Pawel were due to fly back to London the following day. In two weeks, Irena was set to join them for a holiday. Aleks set out that morning for a meeting – he'd off-loaded some pirated videos and he was meeting someone to get his cash. As Aleks stood out in the courtyard, he looked up at the window of the flat. Pawel was standing there looking down at him. Aleks, his cigarette clamped between his teeth, smiled and made a mock salute to his son. Pawel smiled and raised his hand in farewell. Their eyes met.

Helena and Anna boarded the train from Krakow station bound for Oswiecem, called Auschwitz by the Germans. As they sat back in their seats, Anna read information from the guidebook to her grandmother.

'Apparently, there is a canteen where we can get soup,' she said.

The mere thought of food made Helena feel a little sick. She was already afraid of what she would find, afraid of her reactions.

'I really don't think I will be able to eat there,' said Helena. 'Could you?'

'We can find a guide who will take us round. They are mostly retired teachers,' said Anna, still reading from the guidebook. 'Auschwitz I is the work camp then Birkenau is the extermination camp. This sounds too gruesome – can we handle this?'

'I don't know,' said Helena. 'I really don't know. I feel I want to put some memorial there to Nathan but I don't know if I can. Will there be a record of his name there? Are there any graves as such? I want to find out.'

'Let me look at his watch, Babcia. I remember how grandfather used to mend watches.'

'Yes, Tadek did that for years,' Helena smiled. 'Some people even paid him repairs as he was so skilled.' Helena took the watch from her handbag. It was quite heavy and

round with a gold-coloured case and large screw on the top
for winding it up. Anna took it and held it to her ear.

'It has a nice loud tick. I remember grandfather showing
me the insides of a watch like this.' She slipped her nail
along the side of the smooth back and it popped open. 'Look
at this!'

'Oh, it opens,' said Helena in surprise. Anna reached in
and took out a small lock of black hair tied in the middle
with a thin piece of red ribbon. She held it up for Helena to
see. Helena put her hand to her mouth, her eyes filled with
tears and she looked away, out of the train window. Anna
replaced the lock of hair and clicked the watch shut again.

As they left the train, the sun went behind a cloud and it
threatened to rain. Helena pulled her jacket round her
shoulders and shivered. The warmth seemed to have gone
out of the world. She stared at the famous gates emblazoned
with the lie 'Work makes you free', the train tracks, the
barbed wire and buildings behind. Could she really enter
this place? She felt sick at the thought. How much sicker
had Nathan felt on seeing these same gates? She had to be
strong for him.

Aleks walked away from Irena's flat and made his way
down Senatorska by tram. He was meeting Leon, someone
he'd met at a gambling syndicate two days earlier who had
bought a box of videos. There were copies of *Thelma and
Louise* and *The Silence of the Lambs* that Aleks had bought
from a man in a pub in London. He'd let Leon have a
sample to test that they were what he said they were and
that they worked. He had the rest of them with him and
they could finish the transaction. Leon said he would pay
him straight from his pay packet if they met at his place of
work, a warehouse on the outskirts of town.

Aleks had to take two trams and a bus to get there. He
eventually got off at a deserted stop. The only building
around looked like an old, closed down factory. Aleks
walked up the gate. It was fastened with a padlocked chain
and the perimeter had barbed wire all around. Aleks looked
down again at the address on the piece of paper and
wondered if this could be correct. Had Leon just brought

him here on a wild goose chase? He noticed a light was on in the factory so assumed somebody must be in. There was a gap in the fence and he threw the box of videos in firth then pressed through the hole himself. A piece of barbed wire caught on his jacket and tore a small hole in the back. Aleks swore with annoyance. Through to the other side, he picked up the box and made his way towards the factory building. Looking up, he noticed a German Shepherd dog prowling on the flat roof. It stared down at him over the edge but didn't bark.

Outside the death camp, Helena noticed groups of teenage school children, a party of elderly women who looked American, and some Japanese tourists. There was chatter, loading of cameras, shouted instructions. Standing alone away from the group, Helena noticed an elderly man. She approached him.

'Excuse me, Sir. How much does it cost?'

'There is no charge, Pani,' said the man. 'If you wish, I can be your guide.'

Helena nodded and beckoned to Anna. They followed the man, who had a pronounced limp, through the gate past the curled barbed wire. The man's name was Tomasz and he had been an inmate in the camp when he was a teenager.

'I want everyone, particularly the children,' he pointed to Anna, 'to know the truth about what happened here. I arrived here on my 14th birthday. There was a strange sweet smell, we all noticed it. We later discovered it was burning bodies.'

He walked quickly, stumbling on his damaged leg, as if a hurry to get somewhere. Helena and Anna hurried after him.They walked past the brick huts and parade grounds.

'The first thing I saw when I arrived here in 1943 was a smartly dressed guard with a beautiful German Shepherd dog. I always loved animals and I looked at the dog's shiny coat and its pink tongue hanging out of its mouth. I wanted to pat its head and stroke its glossy coat but it snarled at me. My father and I were sent to this hut. My mother and two sisters had been separated from us. I never saw them again. My father lived until two days before we were liberated.'

Tomasz wore a black, threadbare jacket, old dusty trousers and a light blue shirt. His shoes were scuffed and one lace was undone. He was far too lightly dressed for the weather but he didn't shiver. His wiry grey hair blew around in the breeze.

'How can you bear to come back here?' asked Helena.

'I don't know,' said Tomasz. 'Maybe because it is the grave of my parents and sisters, maybe because I can't forget what happened and what I saw with my own eyes. Maybe because this is where I lost my faith in humanity. I want to the world to know it happened and not to deny it or say we didn't suffer.'

He spoke almost to himself, as if he didn't register who he was talking to. It was as if the present didn't exist, all that mattered was the past.

Aleks wandered around the side of the brick building looking for an entrance. He called out Leon's name but there was no answer. He peered in at a dirty window but could see nothing. Eventually, he found a small side door. The blue peeling paint and loose handle seemed to indicate it hadn't been used in a long time. The door was not locked, though, and Aleks stepped into a huge, empty factory space. There was a smell of engine oil in the air and streaks of oil on the floor. Chains hung from the ceiling - it must have once been a hive of industrial activity.

'Hello, Leon,' he called, his voice echoing around the walls. Damn the man, Aleks thought, he'd been cheated. No one was here and he'd never get his money. There was some obscene graffiti on the walls and an ancient picture of Lenin on which someone had drawn glasses and black curly hair. Aleks smiled and looked round the vacant space once more. As he turned to leave, he heard a noise from a room in the far corner of the room. A door opened. There stood a short man dressed in an old suit. He was bald, pot-bellied and very ugly. He was flanked by two other younger, taller men.

'Lato – remember me? Komorowski,' said the short man and smiled.

In a blind panic, Aleks dropped the box of videos on the floor. Two tapes skidded across the concrete. Aleks turned, bolted for the door, grabbed the handle and pulled it open. He threw himself outside and began running across the courtyard towards the barbed wire fence. The dog jumped down from the low roof and chased him. Aleks could hear it barking and snarling behind him. The animal leapt at his back, latching its teeth onto his jacket. It began shaking him violently, dragging him backwards and Aleks could feel the jacket ripping. He looked desperately for the gap in the fence – where was it?

He ran towards the gate, pulling the dog with him until he managed to shrug off his jacket and launch himself on the gate. He began tugging desperately at the metal bars.

The two men caught up with him, grabbed him and pulled him to the floor. The dog was barking madly and jumping around in excitement. Aleks wrapped his arms round his head to protect himself and curled up in a foetal ball. The two men began kicking him as he lay on the ground. He felt a huge wave of pain in his back and blood poured down into his eyes.

'No one double crosses Komorowski' shouted the short man as he stood nearby watching the beating. 'Did you think I'd ever forget? Five years, 10 years, 20 years – I never, ever forget.'

'I can pay you,' shrieked Aleks between the blows. 'Call them off and I'll pay you back. I've been in England, I have money, plenty of money.'

'I don't want your money now,' said Komorowski, 'You will pay with your blood.'

Aleks back and legs now felt numb and there was no longer any pain. From the furthest reaches of his memory Aleks saw his friend Szimon's face, covered in blood, Szimon getting a beating. They had gone to school together, played marbles, football and cowboys together. Last time Aleks had seen him, they were walking back from school in a Warsaw street when Szimon was set upon by German soldiers who beat and kicked him. Szimon had looked at him, blood pouring down his face, his glasses smashed. He'd put out his arm towards Aleks and Aleks had turned and run home.

Aleks peeped up at the sky between his fingers. He saw how bright the sun looked, a giant yellow ball shining and gleaming in the sky. He heard a crack as his arm broke. How beautiful the sun was, how warm and golden. A kick behind him broke his spine. Did the sun look the same from every part of the earth; strange how it shone on everyone: Hitler, Stalin, Komorowski; weird to think the sun would keep shining for millions and millions of years. Then a heavy boot kicked him hard in the face and the sun went out.

Helena looked tentatively at Tomasz and broached the subject on her mind. 'I had an uncle who was here. He was a doctor – Nathan Weinberg. Do you think you might have known him?' she asked tentatively.

He stopped to look at her. 'There were no names here, Pani, only numbers.'

'Yes, but as he was a doctor I wondered if he had a prominent position in the camp. Is there anywhere I can find out when he arrived here and when he died?'

'They are compiling a list of all the inmates but of course the vast majority of Jews were sent straight to the gas chambers and were never documented. However, as your uncle was a doctor he may have been part of the team of Jewish doctors who assessed people. So he might have survived for a period of time. How old was he when he arrived here?'

'I don't know. I assume he was in the Warsaw ghetto for some years. He was probably about 45 I think, maybe a little younger,' said Helena.

'I have my mother's death certificate, all properly made out,' says Tomasz. 'She was in the resistance so they documented her fully. They did not do that to most of the others.'

They walked on round the camp. There were row upon row of huts, weeds growing between the paving slabs, signposts in German. The weather was getting colder, the sun had completely disappeared. A group of schoolgirls was giggling while trying to open some cartons of fruit juice. There were gales of laughter as the juice sprayed all over one girl's dress.

Tomasz remained fixed on what he was saying. 'This is the parade ground and every morning the orchestra would play. They played Mozart, Beethoven, Brahms – beautiful music filled the air competing with the screams.'

Helena sighed heavily. Then a thought occurred to her.

'My uncle played the violin. Do you think he might have played in the orchestra? Do you think that meant he could have been spared?'

The guide stopped and looked at her.

'Was he a very good player – was he orchestra standard?'

'I don't think so. I think he just did it for a hobby.'

'You have to understand there were many people among the thousands here who were very talented. They were the ones selected to play in the orchestra.'

Helena's spirits dropped again. She would have gone through this for nothing – she would never find him, never know his fate or be able to pay tribute to him. *The Fragmented Mind* would have to be enough. Tomasz looked back at Helena.

'Also, Pani, if your uncle had survived he would have gone back home to his family. You would know if he had lived.'

Helena and Anna went inside one of the huts. It was cold and bare, with three levels of wooden bunks. Helena touched the rough wood, someone had slept here, many had died here.

'There's a message written on the wall, Babcia,' said Anna peering at the graffiti, trying to make out what it said. An elderly overweight American woman with a walking stick, who was also in the hut, came to stand next to her and also stared at the wall. They had seen her outside the camp earlier in the day.

'Do you know what it says?' the woman asked Anna.

Anna peered at the writing, a long forgotten message in Polish, etched into the brick. 'I think it says, something like 'Life is full of thorns.'

Helena put on her glasses and approached the wall. 'It says, 'Life is full of thorns and you have to get through it as best you can."

'What language is it in?' asked the woman

'Polish,' said Anna and Helena together.

'Not Hungarian?' asked the woman stepping slowly from one foot to the other as if it pained her to stand up. 'My parents were from Hungary – they died here. I'm looking for something in Hungarian.'

'No, it's Polish. I'm sorry I don't know any Hungarian,' said Helena.

'I don't remember any either but I keep thinking there must be a letter to me from them. They wouldn't leave me without a message.'

'How did you get separated from them?' asked Helena.

She looked at the woman who wore a yellow synthetic top and beige trousers. She had thick white socks with brown sandals and leaned heavily on her walking stick.

'I was five – they sent me away on the *kindertransport* before the war so I would live. They could only send children, adults had to stay behind. I was sent to England. My father said he would write me a letter when I was settled. There must be something from them, anything. He promised faithfully he would write – there must be a message.'

She shook her head sadly and wandered out through the door of the hut, walking slowly and painfully, an elderly five-year-old still looking for her mummy and daddy.

Helena took Anna's hand and they went outside. Tomasz led them into another building which he said was the infirmary. Perhaps Nathan had worked here, Helena thought. Perhaps he helped people, made assessments, saved lives.

Another room contained a huge mound of spectacles, another heaps of human hair. Elsewhere, a tangle of prosthetic limbs.

'Babcia,' said Anna threading her arm through Helena's. 'Can we leave now? I hate this place. I want to go back to the hotel.' She looked at Tomasz feeling guilty.

'My father committed suicide,' said Tomasz as they walked back to the entrance. 'He ran at these gates one day and the German Shepherd dog chased him and bit his leg and pulled him to the ground. Then the guards beat him to death. Even though I'm allowed to leave now, I still can't.'

He put his hand to his mouth and looked around with the most distressing look of despair on his face.

Helena reached into her bag to get out her purse but Tomasz waved his hand at her and walked away towards the parade ground.

Chapter 43

The train from Krakow pulled into the station in Warsaw. Wanda, Anna and Helena hailed a taxi to take them back to Irena's flat. Their flight was due to leave for London at noon the following day, their holiday was nearly over. They made their way into the family block of flats and into the creaking lift.

'Is Babcia Irena at work?' asked Anna.

'I don't know but she gave me the key so we can get in whenever we want,' said Helena, opening the door.

The three women piled through the front door with their cases and took their coats off in the hall. They were talking happily, discussing their trip, announcing their need for tea and cake, Anna saying she was desperate for the toilet. They walked through into the sitting room and then stood still, open-mouthed in astonishment.

Pawel was sitting on the sofa, his head in his arms and Irena had her arm round him, kissing his uncombed hair. Irena looked up at them, her eyes red with crying.

Helena approached them slowly. 'What's happening? What's the matter? Pawel, why are you here?'

'It's Aleksander,' said Irena. 'He was attacked yesterday. We were at the hospital with him. He had internal bleeding.'

'Attacked? Who by?' asked Helena sitting down next to her cousin.

'We don't know, probably some gangsters, criminals. The police have taken statements but we don't know anything.'

'How is he?' asked Wanda, her voice shaking.

'He died this morning at 9.45am. He didn't regain consciousness,' said Irena.

Wanda sank down on the armchair and Anna hid her face in her mother's arm. The room was silent but for the gentle rocking of Irena against her son and his low sobbing.

'I will make us a drink,' said Helena. 'I'm so sorry, I don't know what to do. I will make some tea.' She stood up and looked around uncertainly.

'I didn't even know you were in Poland. Where did it happen?' asked Wanda gently. Pawel looked up at her.

'Some children found him yesterday on the ground outside a disused factory in the Eastern suburbs. We have no idea what he was doing there. We had a call from the hospital and we spent the night at his bedside. I kept talking to him and talking to him but he never woke up. He never looked at me, he never woke up.'

'He could probably hear what you said.' Wanda crouched on the carpet in front of Pawel and touched his hair. His face was buried in his arms.

'They'd beaten his face to pulp – it was swollen and purple.'

Irena brought her arm tighter round her son.

'Why did people do that to him? He never hurt anyone – he was a bit careless with money but he was never, never violent. He didn't deserve that.'

'Of course he didn't,' said Wanda. 'He was a lovely man.'

'The police must find out who did this,' said Irena. 'I knew this would happen in the modern Poland. Society has broken down, there is no rule of law. Gangsters roam the streets and criminals do anything for money.'

'Don't make this ideological, Mum,' said Pawel looking up. 'My daddy is dead and it's nothing to do with capitalism, it's evil men who did it and you get those everywhere.'

'Was it a random attack or did he know them, do you think?' asked Wanda.

'I suspect he knew them,' said Pawel wiping his nose on his sleeve. 'He said he was meeting someone who owed him money. Someone called Leon but we don't know any more than that. It might have been a trap. He said there were some scary people around.'

'Did you tell the police all this?' asked Wanda.

'Yes, of course we did, but there is not much they can do. We don't have any names or addresses. There were no witnesses - it was a deserted factory. There might be some fingerprints. I don't know.'

'At least we have the family altogether here,' said Helena. 'We all have each other, that's what matters.'

Pawel looked up, took Wanda's hand and placed it on his tear-streaked face.

Chapter 44

Paris, 1992

Helena stared out at the swelling, grey waves. The sky was low and overcast and the English Channel seemed inhospitable, dirty, greasy. The wind had picked up and the hovercraft was being thrown high up onto the waves and then crashing down into the troughs. People were being jolted in their seats and many of the passengers looked decidedly green with seasickness.

Helena was beginning to regret choosing the Hovercraft over the more stable ferry but it could cross over to France in only 30 minutes and she had opted for speed. She sipped some dreadful, scalding tea from a paper cup she'd bought at the kiosk and nibbled a Hobnob biscuit to calm her fear and seasickness.

It would be her first visit to the French capital and a huge honour to be asked to talk at the psychological conference at the Hopital de la Pitie Salpetriere. Freud himself had once attended lectures there. *The Fragmented Mind* had had very good reviews and since its publication there had been a growing stack of invitations for Helena to speak at conferences, attend lectures, even an enquiry from BBC Radio 4.

Despite all this, Helena had to continually convince herself it was all really happening. She worried that she would be found out to be a fraud by these eminent men when she stood up to speak. In her mind, she kept imagining someone would stand up and shout, 'She can't lecture us – she's just a little Polish refugee girl, a nobody.'

On top of this, Helena was wondering if she would encounter any language difficulties. The lectures were to be given by a group of international psychologists so proceedings would be in English. Nevertheless, she would need French for day-to-day encounters. She'd learned the language at school back in Warsaw before the war and had been considered a good student. But that was 50 years ago. Could she remember any of it? She'd been practising her French with Anna before the trip to try to bring back long forgotten words and phrases. She clutched her little French phrase book and hoped it would suffice.

Helena noticed a fellow passenger – a young man with black curly hair and glasses. He reminded her of her uncle. She had put thoughts of Nathan Weinberg out of her mind since her return from Poland but now she wondered what he would think of her achievements. Would he be proud of her, speaking at the conference? Did she need his approval? Was he her security blanket, some ideal she clung to when she was frightened?

Helena had put the folder containing the notes and papers of her uncle's life back in the drawer. Her search for the story of his life had come to an end. She had found no evidence of his life and death in Auschwitz. The last sighting of him on this earth had been by the concierge as he left the flats that day in 1940. After that – nothing. Her only hope was that in the future more documents would come to light and his name could appear on a list or in a chance comment from another inmate from the camp. There was nothing more to be done other than wait and hope.

When *The Fragmented Mind* had first come out, she had hoped for a while that including Nathan's name on the front cover and some of his case histories in the book would jog someone's memory. One of his colleagues, perhaps an acquaintance from France, would get in touch and tell her his story. After a year she had heard nothing and decided nothing was going to happen.

Docking in Calais, Helena walked through the arrivals hall and was met by a driver holding up a card that said *Dr Poniatowska*. He wore a chauffeur's hat and told her he was to drive her to Paris. Helena smiled and nodded, before getting into the back of the pale yellow Citroen. Again she felt nervous, again she had the feeling she didn't belong there. Someone would find out she was actually a machinist from Babcock's Hosiery Works who had spent years making pants, trousers and shirts. It was only a matter of time before she was rumbled...

But the drive to Paris was smooth, and she was dropped off at her hotel around five in the afternoon. The Modern Hotel was at the end of the Metro line at Mairie de Montreuil and was a comfortable, three-star establishment. Helena ate alone in the hotel restaurant and went to bed early. The next morning, she collected her papers and took the Metro into the centre of Paris. Clutching her map, she found her way to the hospital. The weather was cold and crisp but some hardy souls were drinking coffee outside on pavement cafes. The smell of roast coffee beans and sweet pastry filled the air.

Helena entered the hospital and was shown into a large room filled with the buzz of conversation and people who all seemed to know each other. As she passed through the crowd, Helena heard snatches of conversation: Americans talking to Hungarians, Germans talking to Italians, Swedes conversing with Spaniards – all speaking in English. For business and academia, English was used for communication but it was a kind of English that a native speaker would find unusual. In fact, Helena had been told, when an American or English person was added to the mix it slowed everything down as the real language seemed to sit uncomfortably with the invented model of communication.

Helena found a place near the table where coffee was being dispensed, swallowed the lump in her throat and fumbled with her lecture notes and box of slides. She thought pictures would be a good idea as they'd give her audience something to look at during the lecture and also would allow her to collect her thoughts if she were stumbling. Now she began to worry that the slide machine would go wrong, or she wouldn't be able to work it, causing an embarrassing silence. She took a cup of coffee and a pain au chocolat from the table and someone gave her a list of the day's lectures. She was number two on the agenda: *Dr H Poniatowska: Interview techniques for schizophrenia patients and coping with disorganised speech patterns*

Professor Jobert, who was organising the conference, caught sight of her and raised his hand in greeting. Helena smiled back and tried to make her way over to him but immediately someone else had taken his attention. Helena was jostled and spilled a little coffee down her white blouse.

Dispirited, she decided the best thing to do would be to take her seat at the front of the hall. The chairman took the stage with a welcome address and introduction. The first speaker talked about current developments in medication for schizophrenia and argued it was largely a biological illness. When Helena's turn came, she walked up to the stage, looked at the serried banks of eminent men and women, cleared her throat and began:

'Ladies and Gentlemen, before I say anything else, I just want to start by briefly paying tribute to my late uncle, Dr Nathan Weinberg, whose early research into schizophrenia first sparked my interest in the subject. His notes are incorporated into my book *The Fragmented Mind* which is why he is listed as a second author.

To her surprise, Helena thought the talk went extremely well. As it went on, she lost her fear and even managed to make a few jokes. The talk was well received, her audience seemed animated and never bored and there were a variety of questions at the end. The lecture even ran a little over time which Helena took to be a good sign. When she sat down afterward, she felt elated and relieved it was over.

They took a break at 1.30 for lunch. Helena found herself seated next to Prof Francois Jobert himself. She was happy, animated – and her appetite returned with a force. They discussed the methodology of recording case study interviews, the latest drugs and therapies and the difference in manifestation between men and women.

Helena was listening to Professor Jobert making an important point when an elderly, white-haired man walked behind her chair, leaned towards her and whispered, 'It's a great pleasure. I knew your uncle well.' Then he walked away. Helena turned and tried to look at the man. Prof

Jobert was still in full flow. She longed to follow the man out of the door but that was impossible without being rude. When she could excuse herself, she went out in the corridor but it was empty. She didn't see the man again.

At the end of the day, she spoke to Prof Jobert.

'There was an old gentleman at lunch today and he commented on my uncle Dr Weinberg. Did you see him walk past and speak to me? He had white hair, was small and very slim and aged about 70 or more.'

'Sorry, I don't know. There are so many delegates here that I'm afraid I don't know many of them personally.'

'He spoke as if he knew my uncle,' said Helena with a puzzled expression. She told Prof Jobert all she knew of her uncle's story.

'I can introduce you to the archivist,' said Prof Jobert. 'She should know who worked here or will be able to find out.' Helena nodded and decided to rearrange her plans. Back at her hotel, she arranged to stay an extra day and telephoned Wanda to tell her something had come up and she was staying on for a while.

Chapter 45

Derby, 1992

There he was, standing on the doorstep, a small bunch of drooping daffodils in his hand. Wanda tutted and held open the door for him.

Pawel came in to the hall and handed Wanda the flowers. He leaned to kiss her cheek but she turned away and the kiss landed awkwardly on her nose.

'I only got back from Poland last week. I stayed for two months to be with my mother and organise my dad's funeral.'

Wanda's face softened. Pawel looked childlike, a lost orphan.

'The police have got nowhere with finding the murderers – but I want, I need justice. By the way, did you see this? I picked it up at the airport.' Pawel handed Wanda a copy of *The Observer Magazine* and pointed to an article.

ROGER ELLIOTT: On the Psychiatrist's Couch

The award-winning photographer was born in 1948 and raised in London. He was educated at boarding school and attended Camberwell School of Art. His seminal news photographs from the late 1960s and 1970s led to him winning News Photographer of the year in 1981 for his iconic picture of The Shipyard Worker. His recent portraits of Diana, Princess of Wales since she separated from Prince Charles have put him in the top echelons of British portrait photographers.

When were you happiest?
That exhilarating charge towards the American Embassy with thousands of others during the anti Vietnam war protests in 1968
What is your greatest fear?
Losing my sight
Which living person do you most admire?
Nelson Mandela
What is the trait you most deplore in yourself?
Being shallow and insincere
What is the trait you most deplore in others?
Hypocrisy
If you could bring something back to life, what would it be?
Aleks Lato, the man immortalised in the photo The Shipyard Worker, who was pointlessly murdered last year.
Who would play you in the film of your life?
If Robert Redford wasn't available I could I do it myself
What is your most unappealing habit?
Calling people darling when I can't remember their name
What is your favourite novel?
The Collector, John Fowles
What is the worst thing anyone said to you?
I'm sorry but she died
What do you owe your parents?
I get my charming smile from my father and my sense of social justice from my mother
Who is the love of your life?
She knows who she is
Which living person do you most despise?
Mrs T
Who would you like to say sorry to?
A girl who misinterpreted the picture I took of her
Have you ever said, I love you, and not meant it?
Oh, yes
Who would you invite to your dream dinner party?
Julia Margaret Cameron, Cartier Bresson, Bill Brandt and Harry Houdini
Tell us a joke
Doctor: You have cancer and Alzheimer's
Patient: At least I don't have cancer

Wanda smiled and tucked the magazine under arm.

'Come on in and let's have a drink. Anna is in town at the moment but she should be back before long. Did you know she is going to apply to Oxford university?'

They walked into the sitting room.

'I'm so impressed with that girl, my wonderful daughter.' Pawel sat down in Tadek's old armchair and crossed his legs. Wanda sat down on the sofa opposite.'

'So what did the police say about your father's murder? How did you leave it?' she asked.

'The police don't seem too interested. As far as they are concerned, dad was just a petty thief. But I only realise now how much he meant to me...'

'Bronek says the police in Poland...'

'Bronek – that arsehole. Has he been here again?'

'Bronek was extremely upset about what happened,' said Wanda loudly. 'He'd known your father for a long time. He had helped get him out of the Poland during martial law remember.'

'I don't want to talk about him – his fancy car, his job with the BBC.'

Wanda got up. 'You're a child, Pawel. Listen, you can't dictate who I see or who I spend time with. I like Bronek, we have a lot in common.'

She got up and went to the kitchen. Pawel followed her.

'Like not love! I just don't want that man in this house, near my wife and daughter. I forbid him to come here. You are my wife – we are not divorced.'

'I know, that's something I want to talk to you about, Pawel.'

'Well I won't talk about it, never, I will not discuss that. My daughter remains my daughter, nothing can change that.'

'And your son?' said Wanda with a slight laugh.

Pawell clenched his teeth and shook his head.

'I don't have a son,' he said softly. 'Derek was there at the birth, he is bringing up the child, paying for his shelter, food, clothes – the child is his son and no one can say otherwise.'

'As if things can be swept away that easily, Pawel. I cannot forget about it. I saw Pam in town the other day and I had to run away because there was no way I could bear to see her or her child. It was too much for me.'

Pawel put his arm round her shoulder.

'I want to talk about Anna. Tell me about her university application.'

Wanda poured the boiling water into two tea cups.

'You feel jealous about Bronek. Can you understand how I feel about Pam? It's a thousand times worse. Whenever I think I am over it, something like that happens to bring it all back again.'

'What does Anna have to do with this Oxford application?'

Wanda paused as she added milk to her tea and lemon to Pawel's.

'She applied to Oriel College and has an interview next month. She has to go there for three days and stay in the college during the interviews. I can't believe it – it's so exciting.'

'It is wonderful. My mother was absolutely delighted with her. She does intend to come and visit. She can stay here, can't she?'

'Of course, my mother will want her here as well.'

Pawel ran his fingers through his hair.

'I want…' he began. 'I want more than anything to be forgiven, to go back to how we were when we first met. I want to turn back the clock and I want us to have a second chance at happiness.'

'I know you do. I just can't forget.'

There was a slam of the door and Pawel looked round to see Anna coming into the kitchen.

'Daddy,' she cried and flung her arms round him. He gently lifted her off the ground.

'Moja kochana Anna.'

Pawel lavished endearments on his daughter while she squealed with joy.

Wanda thought about her own father, how she had danced with joy when he came back from work, how he had made her a dolls' house, brought her soup when she was ill, sat her on his knee and read her stories.

Wanda turned away towards the sink. She could never have Pawel out of her life.

Chapter 46

Paris, 1992

The next day, after Professor Jobert's suggestion, Helena paid a visit to the archivist's office and soon found herself surrounded by yearbooks and lists of hospital personnel. She started with the records dated 1947. Turning the pages she looked at lists of names accompanied by black and white photographs. She went carefully through 1950, 1951, 1952. Two hours later, she was still checking indexes and leafing through pages.

It was boring work and she was starting to get hungry and tired. When she finally found what she was looking for, she was yawning and ready to give up. But there it was – the answer to all her research, dreams and yearnings. The photo showed the all too familiar curly hair, now pure white, and open-faced expression of Nathan Weinberg. He was standing in the hospital corridor with another man. The caption read, *Prof Nathan Bernard et Prof Jacques Lacan, 1957.*

Helena gave a little cry and brought her hand to her mouth. Despite the name change, she was certain this was her uncle. Her heart was beating so loudly she thought everyone could hear it. She took the volume to the archivist and asked about the picture. She was told Prof Bernard had worked at the hospital from 1948 until 1965 when he retired.

'I'm his niece. I've been trying to find out about him. When did he die?' asked Helena.

'Let me just check,' said the women. Helena stood by the counter, waiting. Nathan would be, she had to work it out, in his mid 90s by now. Surely he couldn't still be alive. In a

minute the woman would come back and say he'd died last
year or in 1966 or in 1986. Thoughts tumbled through
Helena's brain. He had got away. A wave of happiness
washed over her. Perhaps helped by Zegota. Perhaps by his
wife. But why hadn't he gone home?

The woman came back after a while and handed Helena
a piece of paper. Written on it was the address: La Retraite,
Parc de Garlande, 92220 Bagneux.

'Professer Bernard is in a hospice. It is about 10
kilometers from here.'

'How do I get there?' Helena was almost panting with
excitement.

'You can just get a taxi outside.'

It was a fairly short ride and the taxi left Helena standing
outside the gates of the hospice. She stood for a moment
looking up at the imposing building. It was situated in
beautiful gardens. She could see a nun wearing an elaborate
white headdress pushing one patient in a wheelchair about
the grounds. She made her way into the building and found
a reception desk, worrying her schoolgirl French would not
be enough to explain who she was. She wrote the name
Professor Nathan Bernard on a piece of paper and showed it
to the woman there.

'Please tell him his niece, Helena Poniatowska, is here to
visit him,' she said in English.

The woman looked puzzled and went to another room.
Helena waited. She looked at the brass crucifix on the wall.
The aroma from an enormous bunch of irises, lilies and
carnations in a vase on the desk filled the room. Helena
looked round at the white walls and a feeling of
extraordinary peace came over her.

A different woman came out.

'Professor Bernard is extremely frail,' said the
receptionist in perfect English with an irritated air. 'His
sight and hearing are very bad. He is bedbound. I told him
your name but I don't know if he understood what I said.
But please come in.'

She led Helena into a private room with a huge window
looking out onto the garden. The bed was raised high and
pillows supported the occupant to almost a sitting position.

Helena stood by the door and stared at him for minutes. She felt too shocked to speak. The old man was almost bald, just a few strands of white hair on his head. His skin was yellow and sagged in swathes below his eyes and chin. His weathered hands, covered in brown liver spots, were resting on the top of the white covers. Helena looked at the long, elegant fingers. They were the hands of an artist, a musician, a surgeon. She swallowed and felt her eyes fill with tears.

Helena looked round at the nurse who approached the patient and touched his arm.

'Professor Bernard, your niece Helena is here,' she said in French.

The old man opened his eyes. Helena approached.

'Who is it? Is it you, Juliet?' he said in French.

'No, it's Helena Poniatowska, Jan's daughter,' Helena said in Polish. 'You last saw me when I was a baby, I think, in Warsaw. That was in 1926. Do you remember?'

'Who – who is that?' Nathan said again in French. 'I don't understand.'

'You remember Maria Poniatowska, don't you?' Helena continued in Polish. There was a long pause.

'Poniatowska, yes of course,' Nathan finally spoke in faltering Polish as if struggling to find the words.

'Do you remember my father, Jan Poniatowski? He was one of your first case studies. He suffered from schizophrenia. You interviewed him and made notes. I read your notes. I have been looking for you for many years.'

There was another long silence. Nathan brought a shaking hand towards his face, then let it drop again on the sheets.

'The little baby – Barbara's little baby,' his voice shook with emotion. 'You survived. I thought the Germans had taken you, I heard there was a round up. I thought you had died.' He spoke Polish slowly, as if dragging the words painfully from his half forgotten memory.

'And I thought you had died too,' Helena said, her eyes full of tears. 'My aunt Maria said you were taken to Auschwitz and had perished there. I went to the death camp last year to try to find out what had happened but there was nothing.'

Helena sat down and took Nathan's hand.

'I read your notes, your case studies, letters – so many little pieces of your life that Maria had kept in a folder. I felt I knew you. Now I have solved the riddle. If only I had found you years ago.' Helena couldn't stop the tears flowing down her face.

'You became a professor of psychology – just as you wanted,' she continued. 'And you lived in Paris all these years and we didn't know. Maria didn't know.'

Helena looked at the large brown liver spots on his head, the white stubble on his chin. He breathed heavily through his nose.

'I wanted a new life so I changed my name and disappeared – we had all been through so much.'

'What happened after you left the flat that day? You had Feddi and your violin with you.'

'Feddi,' said Nathan then he was silent before speaking.

'I was warned I needed to hide. Maria had disappeared. I didn't know where she had gone. I went into hiding at the zoo. My friends, the Zabinskis, concealed me.'

He stopped and began to cough. Helena waited as he recovered his breath. He reached toward his water and Helena took the glass and helped him to a drink. He began to speak again.

'At one point, they even kept me in one of the animal cages. I slept in the straw where the lions had been sleeping days before. I even used their water bowl. Then I got new papers, I was given an new name and identity. I shaved my hair and told everyone I was French. The Zagota smuggled me on a train and I lived in the south of France during the war then came to Paris. I stayed here ever since.'

Helena smiled. 'I'm so happy you were safe.'

Nathan stared up at the ceiling. 'I'm sorry, Maria, that I didn't contact you. I couldn't face returning to Poland. I wrote many letters but I couldn't post them, I couldn't drag up the memories. Please forgive me. I wanted the old life to be over, forgotten and a new one to rise from the ashes.'

'I'm sorry, uncle, but Maria died in 1975. The concierge at the flats – Krystyna Nowicka, told me what happened. Maria had given her your watch, so she gave it to me. Here it is.' Helena took the pocket watch out of her handbag. Nathan turned his head and looked at it.

'It was a present from Maria. We bought it in Zurich. It was very expensive.' He smiled and closed his eyes, resting back on the pillow. 'I'm glad you have it. It must stay in the family.'

Helena nodded and sat in silence for a while.

'What did you think of my father, Jan Poniatowski? Did you like him – when he was lucid? Was he a good man, despite everything?' Helena looked hopefully at Nathan.

He opened his eyes and turned to look at her. 'He was a poet and a gentleman. The illness ravaged his mind but he was a true nobleman. It was so difficult. I tried to help your mother and you – in the end your father killed himself but you have to understand, it was the illness. The real Jan, the true man, he would not have left you. You must believe that.'

Helena squeezed his hand. The nurse approached and said.

'I'm sorry I think you must leave now. Professor Bernard's son and daughter and grandchildren are here to see him.'

Helena stood up quickly. 'I'm sorry – oh, I didn't realise. I'm so glad he has family.' She leaned over and kissed Nathan on the forehead.

'*Do widzenia, wujek*, - goodbye, little uncle,' she said. His eyes were closed but he smiled.

As Helena walked down the corridor, blowing her nose on her handkerchief, she saw a lively family group coming towards her, dark-haired twin girls aged about 12, a handsome older boy and two middle-aged couples. They were all chatting happily. Helena smiled at them and nodded as she walked out of the building. She phoned the hospice from her house a week later and they told her renowned psychologist Prof Nathan Barnard had died two days after her visit. She had missed the funeral.

Chapter 47

Dear Wanda

I'm the last person in the world you ever want to hear from but I hope you will read this letter before you rip it into tiny pieces and throw it in the bin.

I don't deserve to be forgiven for what I did but strangely I didn't realise at the time that I would be hurting you. I am stupid but all I could think about was my need, my overwhelming need for a baby. Nothing else mattered – not Derek, not you, certainly not Pawel.

You may be surprised to hear that I always envied you. You always inspired love in people that I never could. People sought your company, laughed at your jokes, felt easy and happy when you were around. I felt it too but never knew how you achieved it. You have great talents and the best thing is you have absolutely no idea you have them. You will probably ask: so why do people hurt me all the time? The truth is, they have no intention of doing that. You are so good to be around that they relax and forget to be careful of your feelings.

My father died yesterday. He had cancer of the pancreas and they sent him home from hospital because there was nothing more they could do for him. He wanted to die at home but was in so much pain we had to give him a huge cocktail of drugs every day. I nursed him day and night. By the end he was doubly incontinent, he didn't know me and he was in so much pain he kept begging to die.

My mother had started sorting out his books and papers. There were copies of letters he wrote to the Home Office regarding your grandmother being allowed to come to England. There were also boxes of his cine films. He was an enthusiastic amateur film-maker and was compiling a series called Derby Life. I have been watching the films again as I sat nursing him. They are amazing.

He started filming when he was 19 and had just come out of the army at the end of the war. There is footage of Derby on VE day – people dancing in the Cornmarket. He took film of the steeples of St Joseph's and St Wystan's opposite before St Wystan's was pulled down and they built that dreadful road. Can you remember those little medieval houses round there? A lost world all captured on his little film – raggedy children playing in the street, old women scrubbing their doorsteps, a rag and bone man walking down the street. Dad also took film of a military procession marching down Friargate, an archaeological dig on Chester Green, the Maundy Thursday ceremony at the Cathedral, the Queen making a speech in the Market Place for her Silver Jubilee, Brian Clough being paraded round the streets when Derby County won the championship. I think I should donate the films to the Local Studies Library or some film archive.

Anyway, among these films are personal records too. There are family Christmases, weddings, holidays at Skegness and these fragments of film I'm sending to you here. I've put them all on to videotape for you. This is one dad took at your house in 1962. I watched it with tears streaming down my face, regretting what I can never get back.

Anyway, Wanda, that's all I can say to you. It will hurt you to mention my son but he is the love of my life, the only reason to get up in the mornings. Forgive me.

Pam

Chapter 48

Derby, 1994

Anna sat on her bed, leaning back against the wall. She held Zosia's treasure box in her hands, running her fingers over the indents in its carved wooden surface. Turning the tiny key, she opened the lid and carefully took out the treasures, one by one and laid them on her bed. The shards of pot, the smooth pebble, the old penny, the note from Zosia to Wanda and Janek warning them not to pry – it always made Anna smile. She had no siblings and the rivalries, arguments and affections of those who did were a constant source of envy to her.

The box lay open and empty on her quilt. It had a decorated border round the base, jointed at each corner. Anna stared at the border and noticed a tiny gap in the joints. She picked up the box and examined it more closely. The inside was not as deep as the outside appeared to be. She fiddled with the base and realised it could slide outwards. There was a very shallow drawer underneath. As Anna pulled it out, she found a piece of paper folded in two. She took it out and read it.

To my father

Not the scuttling mouse, not the black-hand spider, not the smooth articulated snake. My secret fear, my panic-lurching, chemical-soaked dread is the bird trapped indoors.

Is the panic mine or his? In desperation he flings his fragile body against the pane – misunderstanding all he sees. His wings beat on the ceiling until, exhausted, he rests on the table and defecates on the white linen cloth.

I stand spread-eagled against the wall, the tiny blue missile between me and the door – the means of escape.

We are both trapped.

We look at each other. The black beady eye of the bird – my own wide-eyed dread.

You walk in, take the tiny creature in one hand and post it through the small upper window. You have set us both free.

Zofia Baran, 1968

Anna folded the note again and sat thoughtfully on her bed. She leaned over and looked again at the letter from Oriel College, Oxford offering her a place to read English in September. All her life, Anna had been told how much she looked like her aunt, how her character was similar, how she must succeed as Zosia did, how she must live to replace the one who died.

Anna leaned back against the wall. I cannot live for you, Zosia, she muttered. I am not you and I don't know what you wanted to do. I like your poem but you are a dead girl and I am alive.

'Anna, can you come down?' she heard her mother calling.

Halfway down the stairs, she heard her mother on the phone.

'...she's been offered a place at Oxford. Yes, she does need to get the grades but I know she will. Of course, she's delighted, we all are.'

Anna came into the sitting room. Helena threw her arms round her neck.

'*Kochana*, I prayed so hard they would offer you a place. I'm so pleased. Wanda, who are you phoning? Is it Pawel? Give me the phone. Pawel – such wonderful news, Zosia - I mean Anna - has a place at Oxford – isn't that the best news?'

Wanda hugged her. 'I have a bottle of champagne to celebrate.'

'But Mum, remember I might not get the grades, it's a conditional offer.'

'Of course you will – come on, let's find the champagne glasses,' said Wanda.

'Pawel is coming over in an hour. He just has to finish up where he's working.' Helena poured the frothing drink in the tall champagne glasses.

'I hope daddy is pleased,' said Anna.

'Of course, he's pleased,' said Wanda. 'That's why he's racing over here.'

'To Anna,' said Helena raising her glass.

'This will all look very silly if I don't get the grades,' said Anna.

'Of course you will – I don't have a single doubt,' said Wanda.

The three women drank a toast in the sitting room – giggling and chatting.

Wanda raised her hand and said, 'I have something to show you both. It's a videotape that came through the post. I was sent it a few weeks ago but I think we should watch it now,' said Wanda.

She went over to the cupboard by the television.

'I got this from Pam Haines,' she paused and looked at her mother. 'Her father died. Anyway, she was going through his amateur film collection and she found some of us. She put them on a tape and sent it to me.'

Helena was silent for a few moments. 'Did you reply to her?'

'No, Mum, I didn't but I did watch the tape and now we can all watch it.'

Anna looked from her mother to her grandmother, noticing what was said and unsaid but not understanding what lay beneath. Wanda put the tape in the video recorder and switched on the television.

The film had been shot on Super 8 so there was no sound. It opened with a handmade sign that read:

A Ronald Haines Production

Then it went into a colour shot of Pam and Wanda, aged about 12, standing in the garden at Porton Crescent eating blackberries from the bushes. Pam held a berry up to the camera then popped it in her mouth. Wanda was kneeling on the grass, pulling blackberries from the lower part of the bush. Then Zosia came into shot, shyly watching the goings-on. She was carrying a wicker basket and began to put some of the blackberries inside.

Anna sat forward, on the edge of her chair. Zosia was moving, smiling, waving to the camera – she was alive. She was eating a blackberry, brushing her hair from her forehead where the wind had blown it, smoothing down her dress. Then Janek ran up with a stick and began hitting her. Her smile turned to a scowl as she grabbed the stick off him and whacked him round the head with it.

Helena and Wanda, sitting watching the scene 30 years later, burst out laughing.

The next scene was indoors, in the sitting room. Right where they were now. A real fire was burning in the pink-tiled grate. Anna looked in amazement as she saw her great grandmother sitting on the sofa with three-year-old Janek on her lap. Barbara was wearing a green dress with black spots, her grey hair was tied up in a bun and she was trying to calm Janek as he wriggled and squirmed on her knee. Barbara looked up at the camera and suddenly smiled, her whole face lit up. Zosia was sitting next to her, their arms linked. The camera closed in on Zosia's face – her dark, plaited hair, her bright eyes and sweet face.

Anna looked at her Babcia and saw tears in her eyes. She reached over for the box of tissues and handed her one.

Back in the world of 1962, Pam and Wanda were laughing and giggling behind the sofa. Wanda made bunny ears over Zosia's head. The camera panned round and a young and beautiful Helena came into view carrying a tray of drinks. Everyone was talking but all was muted, no sound survived.

'Look how thin I was,' said Helena.

'You were a dish, Mum,' said Wanda. ' And you still are of course.'

'And there is Tadek, look in the corner,' Helena shouted.

'Ah, daddy,' said Wanda. 'That's so lovely.'

Anna looked at her mother and grandmother, reliving the old days, lost in the moment. She hugged a cushion to her chest while her mother rewound the tape and they watched it all over again.

Chapter 49

Derby, 2000

Her 50ᵗʰ birthday was approaching. Wanda picked up the post from the doormat. Along with the usual bills and junk mail were two letters with handwritten addresses. One was from Pawel. She stared at it for a while before opening the envelope. There was a card with a flower on it and inside it read (in Polish),

My darling wife

I want to be the first to wish you a very happy birthday and many happy returns. I have a proposal to make. I want to come and take you away for a holiday for your birthday. I can collect you in the car and bring you down to London where we will have dinner. I'm sorry I can't take you to see the Beatles, but I have two tickets to see the Rolling Stones at the Astoria Theatre. I have booked the night at a hotel. The next day we can have a walk in the park and choose somewhere to have lunch. I want to make it a very special time for you.

You are my one and only, forever

Please come
Pawel x

Wanda read the letter through a few times. She shook her head and smiled. She opened the other envelope. Inside was a card with a picture of the market in Camden Town on the front. Inside it read (in English).

Dear Wanda

You said you wanted to see Cats. It's closing soon so let's go. I can put up with Andrew Lloyd Webber as it's your special birthday. I've finally completed on the purchase of that flat in Hammersmith and I'm ridiculously proud of it. My favourite Italian restaurant is just around the corner so it's perfect. Come and have a look. Take the train down to London and I'll meet you at St Pancras

Love
Bronek

PS Never mind London, do you fancy Warsaw? The Beeb has offered me a post as correspondent there – initially for two years. What do you think? Want to come?

Wanda laughed. Two men, two invitations. She took the cards into the sitting room and sat at the table. Helena had been reading with the aid of a magnifying glass but had fallen asleep in her armchair. The sound of her soft breathing filled the room.

Wanda looked at the sunlight streaming in through the window, catching the dust particles as they danced and darted in the air. She gazed round the room, searching for an image of Zosia but her sister had vanished. She was lost in the sparkling motes of dust hovering in the air, she was transparent in the ray of morning sunshine, she had evaporated in the thin air.

Wanda looked at Anna's graduation photograph. Her daughter had been awarded a first class degree in English from Oxford. Wanda rested her chin in her hand, staring at the dancing ray of sunlight. Life was good.